THE NOTEBOOK OF GISMONDO CAVALLETTI

R. M. Lamming was born on the Isle of Man and was educated at St Anne's College, Oxford. She has written short stories which have been published in anthologies and magazines on both sides of the Atlantic. *The Notebook of Gismondo Cavalletti*, her first novel, won the David Higham First Novel Award in 1983.

ARENA

R. M. Lamming

THE NOTEBOOK OF GISMONDO CAVALLETTI

ARENA

An Arena Book
Published by Arrow Books Limited
17–21 Conway Street, London W1P 6JD

An imprint of the Hutchinson Publishing Group

London Melbourne Sydney Auckland
Johannesburg and agencies
throughout the world

First published by Jonathan Cape 1983
Arena edition 1985

Printed in Great Britain by
Guernsey Press Co. Ltd.,
Guernsey, C.I.

ISBN 0 09 941400 7

F

A

A M I C I S

I

L

I

Æ

I

FINE sport yesterday at our notary's house. After supper, we all went into the garden – the air was mild, so the ladies came with us – and there, by the light of torches, our host's sons baited a pig. Gabriello soon joined in. Round and round the creature rushed, while the young men flourished their brands before its eyes, or cracked their sticks across its spine; and as it squealed with fright, so the ladies squealed with pleasure, clapping their hands. A most noble entertainment! And when at last the pig lay heaving on its side, incapable of further antics, back we went to our cups, the victors with glowing faces. Then Gabriello turned to me, and observed, 'You look thoughtful, Gissy. What's the matter? Didn't we hit it hard enough?'

Which I could not fail to understand.

He has me penned in. Occasionally he baits me. It's only a matter of time before he begins his revels in earnest, yet I suffer it all. I make no attempt to escape.

Why?

Far into the night I lay awake examining the question, and finally perceived that it comes to this: I make no attempt for I see none to make. I am strangely blinded.

I fell asleep with no idea of remedy.

But today I stopped at a stationer's booth, and purchased these writing materials – I must have my own for the purpose – and now here I sit. The house is quiet. Gabriello is out. So I make a beginning.

My object is simple. To write down, as and when I can, all that's happened to me of real importance, and so to clear the mist and see plainly what to do. I must bring myself to a point of understanding. And first, I find, it is not my fears that have to be written. First I must set down this: an incident which many men might find trivial, but one which holds a special place in my memory. More vivid to me even than the burning of the Heretic.

In the year of Lorenzo de' Medici's death, a great snow fell on Florence. Ice formed on the Arno; the frozen bodies of sparrows lay in the streets; and – as they always will when things go harshly for a little longer than expected – many of the old and poor people perished.

I was fourteen.

Thinking about it now, I have the impression that all the snow fell at night, though almost certainly it didn't. That's just a trick of the mind. I can understand so much because I know, of course, that there were other winters, other snows – people mention them – and yet from my whole childhood, I remember only one snow, and that particularly in the mornings, when such a white, profound stillness lay on the city, that it was as if we had travelled while we slept, and woken in a place set closer to God. We had a new, unplanned Florence.

In piazzas, gardens and courtyards, the statues were transformed. Snow veiled their shoulders, their limbs were thickened and altered, the shields and spears they held were turned into shapes with mysterious meanings, and as for their faces, modified by the snow that clung where a lip curled or a nostril dilated, they no longer seemed serene nor familiar to us. We saw them as if for the first time.

It was the same with many things. Builders' scaffolds, for instance. Wherever these snow-swathed structures rose before one in the streets, they took on forms and designs no architect had dreamed of. And again, with much the same effect, the Cathedral dome glowed – I can still see it – like a giant, living pearl that watched men, and warned them not to boast that they had ever built it.

It was a new, unowned Florence, with the people muffled up, lumbering through the streets in so many cloaks and coats that they looked barely human – unless they stopped for a moment to blow on their fingers.

And silent. When I recall these people, they never speak. Each man's breath hangs before him in a vapour, and this is a sort of distilled silence.

Even the halls and kitchens are silent. Cats, dogs and geese make no sound, but huddle in corners half-frozen. The very church bells are still. Apparently I've chosen to forget the normal things: the hammering of smiths and builders, the shouts of boys and vendors, the curses of slaves shovelling snow from the doors of the rich, and the air so dense by noon with smoke from countless fires, that all the old men were set coughing.

I've forgotten something else, too. The snow must have been churned into muck-brown peaks and troughs by all the trafficking, all the endless carting back and forth of Florentine business, Florentine profit.

Normalities, forced out of mind by whiteness, strangeness, silence –

Then across it all comes Monna Margherita, her cheeks bloated like two bladders, her belly as round as a water melon, crying out for comfits, aniseed comfits.

In the way of most breeding women, she had inordinate appetites, and made a deal too much of them, although in her case there was reason. She was eight years married, still childless, and at last her prayers had been answered. So if she yammered at every whim, it was, I suppose, to be sure that no one in the household – no one down to the meanest slave – should be left in doubt that God had blessed her. Now she craved some white bread soaked in vinegar, and now a cake of marzipan. Today a fish baked with onions, yesterday roast chestnuts –

And on that morning, it was comfits. Why, she'd been dreaming of them all night. Nothing else – she'd faint – could satisfy her. And who could run so fast as Gismo? Who else knew exactly the kind she meant, and could be relied on not to dawdle?

So I set out.

I hurried – Monna Margherita had no great store of patience at any time – but the snow was deep; my feet sank into it up to the ankle, and I made slow progress. Exasperated I pictured her, pacing the hall, her face yellowing in a way it had when anything distressed her, and I could picture Piero Sassoli, anxious for her health – he never mentioned the child's, as if that was something indecent – refusing to leave the house until I'd returned, and all was as she wanted it.

So after that I concentrated, step by step; and the peop who trudged through the snow on either side or coming towards me were little more than shadows: I avoided them without looking up. The coin grew hot in my hand. I breathed hard. I did my best.

Knowing my character, I can write that. I did my best. It was honest effort, and it should have lasted. It should have carried me in the shortest time to the apothecary for Monna Margherita's comfits; and if the truth is otherwise, I have no explanation. Worse, I've given up asking myself for one.

For the truth is, in the Via Larga my concentration snapped. I looked up. Not along the street, but to my right at the Medici Palace, and there my glance, like an arrow that finds a mark despite small skill and less real purpose in the bowman, fell on light in darkness. In the massive wall the gate had been thrown open, and the archway was filled with brilliance – the reflected gleam of snow that lay in the courtyard.

And I forgot the comfits, and Monna Margherita's yellow face. I stopped.

But for *that* I can give reasons.

First, the wall itself stood in deep shadow, which made the light-filled archway fascinating.

Then, someone might be coming out or going in, and who could be indifferent to such possibilities? Lorenzo might be dead; his son might be no more than a worm in comparison, but even so the name Medici still drew cardinals and legates, bankers and adventurers, and all the foremost men of Florence.

Besides, gaping into the courtyards of the rich is a natural occupation among poor men, and a modest crowd had already gathered for this very purpose, edging as close as the guard would let them, all of them intent, craning their necks.

So I crossed the street. I became another fellow jostling for a view. I peered round elbows and through gaps, and what I saw retains, as I have said, a special place in my memory.

A white figure. It stood at the centre of the courtyard, with all around the snow – beneath a thin layer that had fallen overnight – ridged and pocked and in patches cleared away altogether, as though by some strange harvesting. A white figure. But that gives no impression. Better to say a sculpture, only the marble doesn't exist that could glow with such a startling whiteness.

A snow sculpture.

From the gate we saw this marvel in half profile. A Grecian warrior on a mound of snow that looked as permanent as rock. There he had taken his stand, and he was leaning – almost reeling – backwards, but with perfect balance and the confidence of youth, his body arched, the muscles of his calves and shoulders straining, the veins prominent on his neck, and his left hand flung forward to steady himself while in his right a spear of ice slanted upwards, high over the colonnade, over the Palace roof, an aim higher than is common or believable, the spear-head pointing beyond the flight of an eagle.

Why? The astonished onlooker had to ask. The question was shocked out of him. What menaced from the clouds? Where was the threat? But the warrior's frown was dispassionate, and somehow it said, 'Nowhere. There is none,' while the whiteness of his limbs conveyed an indestructible chastity, and that too seemed to say, 'None. No threat.' If the spear was raised, it was not in defence. And yet neither was it a boast, an act of youthful exuberance. Such certainty of purpose, and so much concentration were evident in the figure that no one could doubt this was a try in earnest, deliberately timed, at some specific mark not far short of heaven.

Well, we stared. A snow sculpture. A wonder. Something to compete, while it stood, with the painstaking collection of antiquities that filled the shadows of the colonnade: Psyches, fauns and the like. A statue to defy marble – and very close to blasphemous I thought it. To be honest, the beauty and energy of this creation, its whiteness and its bold aim, even its being there at all, facts as undeniable as a blow on the face, were also in their way just as deplorable. We stared, and we whispered.

Meanwhile, an individual who appeared to be no more than five years my senior walked thoughtfully round the warrior, surveying it with an air of ownership, stopping now and then with his arms akimbo to scrutinise from two paces back, or from close up, or from an angle. And now he would go up to the figure, take a brush or cloth – he carried both – and carefully remove a little loose snow that had gathered in a curve or on a shoulder, and now he would step back again to examine the result. But there wasn't much to be done. He must have been up before light, working on it.

A broadly built, handsome enough young man, at the time I paid no attention to him, which is odd, considering. For if his statue was so extraordinary, what must he himself have been? I should have felt some curiosity. But to my knowledge, I hardly looked at him. Yet now he struts in my mind continuously, happily aware of his audience, and even turns towards the gate with a smile, calling out to us, 'What do you think?'

Then after a pause, though whether this really happened I couldn't say, someone in our crowd shouts back, 'Not bad!'

I believe that was the only time they showed the statue. Afterwards, Piero de' Medici was content to let the rumours of it bring crowds to his gate, which he kept firmly shut; and thereby he enjoyed his private access to the figure, and his knowledge that half Florence shivered at his walls for a chance to glimpse it, as the one, ennobling experience.

As for myself, by the time I got back with the comfits, Monna Margherita had lost all interest in them, and was dining on roasted larks. But I was given some punishment all the same, and thought it well deserved. To be thought unreliable mortified me.

II

TWO questions.

What happened in the thaw? I've often wondered. I could even ask – knowing now, as I do, who the strutting fellow was. Did they patch the warrior up as best they could, for as long as they could? Stack blocks of ice about it, and protect it with an awning from the strengthening sun? I'm plagued by this vision: I see the Grecian's taut features slowly smoothing into shapeless lumps, the muscles of his strong limbs melting to a dribble of water, the spear-head breaking off.

Or at the first sign, did they pull it down? Quickly, before anyone could say it was less than perfect?

Because I hope so, I don't ask.

The second question is this:

Why, behind the Medici gate, and nowhere else? Snow lay at our feet across the whole of Florence, and there were other gifted artists, both in the city and the surrounding countryside: the snow would have cost them nothing. Yet I never heard of any other such figure, and no one I have ever asked has heard of any. There was only this one, in a rich man's courtyard.

III

PIERO Sassoli's son is a no-good and a boor. He has twice his father's ability but exercises none of it. He hunts, drinks, philanders, and fritters time. Every day is one long waste – doubly so, since his birth cost Monna Margherita her life.

And passionately he hates me. But that's a fact I've never found surprising; I saw from the start that he would. A character like his, which loves ease and the quickest path to gain, could find no other way to accommodate me, for I'm a peasant – so he implies – and a cuckoo in the nest.

In fact, as soon as he could prattle sense, he set to work discrediting me with lies, hints – how he'd heard Gismondo disapprove of this, or express contempt for that. And his father, though he never believed these tales, never saw any malice in them either. Instead he was fond of telling me, 'My dear Gismo, you mustn't look so black! Don't you see? The boy has his mother's playfulness. And you know, I think he secretly admires you. That's why you're at the centre of his little pranks!'

Could anything be more fatuous? But I said nothing. To criticise the golden boy would have smacked of jealousy. Besides, when Piero Sassoli was all aglow with parental pride – in those days the very thought of his son delighted him – how could I have answered back, 'Sir, your child is a monster'? I, of all people? No. I kept quiet. Or else I agreed that, yes, the boy had a fine, stylish knack for invention, and what an excellent joker he was!

So the monster thrived, and went unchecked.

He was cunning, too. For example, whenever he saw Piero Sassoli and myself together, he would always pay me some cloying tribute, some childish token of respect: perhaps he might ask, when *he* was a man, would he be as tall as I? And while he spoke, he'd raise such wide, mild eyes to mine as if he did, in truth, adore me.

So the years passed.

Then he took to baiting me, which he still does, whenever he can. This is most often when Piero Sassoli's absent at his farm, enjoying the beautiful slave he keeps there. Naturally I don't go with him on such visits, I stay at home, and so does Gabriello. He has his friends to supper. The wine flows. I'm ferreted out of my room and brought to the table.

'Good of you to join us, Gissy!' He grins across his cup: the candlelight hardens in his eyes. Down each side of the table, a row of heads – his perfumed, foul-breathed sycophants – turns towards me. Gabriello is most hospitable.

'Sit down, man. For God's sake, relax! Have something to drink! We want you to settle an argument for us!'

He waves to a chair, and I sit. I even smile. To squirm in the trap would be to give him exquisite pleasure. The nearest fool slops out wine, and pushes a cup towards me. I drink. There are two – no, three – brash-mouthed women in the company. I can smell the milky flesh of each of them.

'What is the argument?'

'Beauty!' says Gabriello. 'We've been haggling in the way of drunken sots, you know, but what we need is a real expert, a *sober* expert . . . and so we beg you, Gissy, settle it for us! Who would you say is the most beautiful man in Florence?'

Silence. Then everyone sniggers. The fools wait: their eyes are on my face. A woman leans across the table to whisper something behind her hand – she has stared at me the hardest. Oh, they take their baiting very seriously, if nothing else, and I know what they want: to see me redden, to hear me utter pompous sentiments . . .

Hoping to stave off worse things, I comply.

'It seems to me, Gabriello, that unless we define our terms, the question's meaningless. There can be any number of candidates . . . '

'Oh, to hell with terms!' He spits. Up comes his leg to dangle over the arm of his chair. 'What I mean is, when you pass a fellow in the street, and your gut jerks, and you say to yourself, "Now, if only I looked like *that* . . . "'

But here another woman interrupts him, flinging herself on her neighbour's neck with a spluttered laugh; and Gabriello grins.

I sip the wine: 'You may have such sensations, but I don't. Not at the sight of any man.'

'Really? How astonishing. You disappoint me, Gissy! I thought I could count on you for at least one admirer! But . . . well, women, then? There must be one? A single, perfect specimen?' On the word 'perfect' he rubs two smooth fingers together, as if he were feeling cloth. 'One flawless woman in all Florence? Surely any man with instincts must know *one*!'

And we stare at each other across the candles. His hatred is stretched like a thin blade down the length of the table, its point at my throat.

He would have me name her. He would have his toads spit poison and taint her in my presence. But I set down my wine and speak with the flat deliberation of a bookish monk: 'You know as well as I, you're talking nonsense . . . Nothing and no one is perfect. No earthly beauty is without some blemish . . . '

Excellent. Gabriello swings his cup so the wine splashes. He lolls back in his chair and shouts at the ceiling, 'Of course! Some blemish! Our Gissy's all for a blemish or two! Especially if by naming those he can save face!'

Such wit! Such a jest! He grins along his rows of guests in an ecstasy. The whole table howls with laughter. The women shriek. One comes flapping to my side, and smacks a kiss on my lips.

I have resolved the argument.

IV

SO, to set down the laughable, and be done with it. There's a growth, a kind of spreading wart, on my left cheek. It's as dark as a raisin. It began small and grew to the size of an acorn, then to a peachstone, and still it grows, sprouting hairs which I pluck out with a pair of tweezers.

It's a splendid joke in this age of Man – the glory of Man, the beauty of Adam – and even more so since apart from this I'd pass the test: I mean, I'd be more than commonly presentable. Even now – I'm thirty-seven – disregard the growth, and you couldn't fault me. When I turn to my image in the glass, I see clear, sharp eyes with brows that have a proud, natural arch to them, a strong chin, and a nose – if it weren't for the growth pressing against it – as straight and fine as any on a sculptor's 'David'. Then there's no flab on my bones, and my teeth are nothing like so discoloured as many younger men's.

I might have been remarkable, without the blemish.

Sometimes ladies study me. When they think I'm unaware of it, they stand to my right and view my profile. But I know that if I turned towards them, they would either look away with a grimace, or treat me to a long, cold stare. And I know, too, that between their admiration and disgust there comes another moment as swift as a lightning flash, when they could murder me. I fail them unforgivably by being hideous.

They'd prefer to see me crippled or a leper. At least that they could understand. I'd be part then of the world's evils – mildly distressing, like a pile of dung left beneath the window on a summer's day, or the buzz of horseflies. I'd in no way touch their ideals, unless it were to stir in them a sense of charity. I'd be a thing outside, with no share in this 'new age' and this vision we have of divinity in Man –

But I so nearly measure up. Who can blame them if they hate me, when I make their vision laughable?

Oh, it's a splendid joke. Living as I do among patrons, artists, discriminating people, I can hardly fail to be aware of it.

Still, my greatest aggravation must be this: I wasn't born with the blemish. That's the real cruelty. If I had been, how much simpler. How much pleasanter. I might have stayed on my father's farm, or apprenticed myself to some worthy craftsman. Before my twentieth year, I'd have married a plain girl from respectable stock; and long before my present age, I'd have had family, place, even friends. Also, a pleasing confidence in my abilities. I would have *known* I was superior. On winter evenings, seated by my fireside, I might have argued: 'Of course, if I'd been born in other circumstances, there are talents in me that could have found good use!' and in this knowledge, with the general agreement of all who knew me, why should I not have been content? What could a blotch on the cheek have signified then? I would never have been without it. And I've seen far worse disfigurements on shopkeepers, innkeepers and the like, who seem happy enough.

Simpler. Pleasanter. Think about it, and I end by feeling there's a privilege in knowing one's place from the start.

But nothing can be helped.

The truth is, as a child I was beautiful. I knew it, because the village crones took every opportunity of telling me, and my father, with a blunt distrust of good looks in his own son, punished me whenever he could, 'to be sure you don't grow up,' as he said, 'with fancy notions.' So I knew. I was beautiful. And that is why – though he'd deny it – Piero Sassoli noticed me, when he stopped one day to clear the dust from his throat.

While my mother ran to fetch wine, he watched me at some game with my sisters in the shadow of the dung-heap – we were piling pebbles as if they were counters – and because this great man with a soft, round face stared down at us from his horse, it occurred to me that I might charm him out of his soldi. I drew attention to myself. In a loud voice, I began to accuse my playmates of ignoring the rules – though none existed that I know of – and I yelled how, if so many pebbles were stacked in this pile, it stood to reason that a third as many must stand in the next, and four times as many in the pile over there . . .

Words devoid of meaning: I hadn't learned to count. But the good merchant was deeply impressed. A farmer's boy, who made up games out of numbers! Who could tell what genius might lie hidden in me? Immediately he proposed to my father that I went with him. 'To be educated . . . given a chance in life . . . as if he were my own son!'

And my father, who seems to have known all along that despite his beatings some terrible fate would overtake me, meekly agreed.

I was handed over.

It was not so extraordinary. It was a fashion of the time. Many of the middle rich aped the great Medici, and longed to play at patron. They scoured the countryside, prying among the poor for talents, gifts from heaven, for aptitudes that were lacking in their own blood, for brilliance in music, painting, sculpture . . . In short, for genius, flowing through peasant veins.

Genius! Piero Sassoli took me home with him because I was beautiful, and because he had no son. His wife was enchanted with me. I was ten years old and a sort of wild cherub. They clothed me; I was set to simple duties, running errands and so forth. A few weeks later, they began my education. I was put to sketch; they hired masters of the lute and viol; there were grave sessions with astronomers and philosophers. I was taught Latin and some Greek, and the rudiments of rhetoric – and everything they taught me I did competently, adequately, but not what anyone could call surpassingly well. Only at arithmetic I shone, and then – only to some extent.

Despite my lack of promise, for four years they loved me like a son. Until Monna Margherita conceived. Then I was lost in the rejoicing.

A child so late in a barren marriage could only come direct from God, like a messenger, an angel, and therefore, if it were a boy, why, they would call him Gabriello, and they would dote on him . . .

During the course of Monna Margherita's pregnancy, my domestic duties grew heavier. At the same time, I began to help with small chores at the warehouse.

And Gabriello, God's messenger – he came. The merchant was widowed. A wet nurse reigned supreme in the kitchen.

From then on, if he chanced to pass me while he was in the presence of some worthy visitor, Piero Sassoli would turn to his guest and explain, 'This is young Gismondo. A poor man's son whom I rescued, so to speak. A good lad. He has a certain tidiness of mind – but you can see that in his looks – and quite a gift for keeping records straight. Give him a batch of numbers, however muddled, and he'll sort it out in no time. Not much of a talent, I suppose, but useful . . . useful . . . '

And so I came to my life. And if I had no genius, at least I could combine usefulness with ornament . . . until I was seventeen.

Then, on my left cheek, there appeared a knob, a pimple . . . in a few weeks it would go away . . . It stayed. It grew.

I've thought many times of prising it off – like a snail off a barn door. I tell myself it would be a simple matter to take a clean, sharp knife and have a second blade at hand, kept red hot in a flame for the staunching. But I lack the courage.

Not that I fear pain; it's the risk, the teasing chance that before I could stem the flow of blood I'd faint, and if I did, I might bleed to death. Obviously a friend should be present.

But what if I have no friend? Gabriello's out of the question, and so are all his henchmen. Who then? I think of the men at the warehouse – secretive Rassuccio and that garrulous fool Rigogli. After that, I think of the household servants: in my mind I examine their time-serving faces, their pilfering hands, and the more I think, the clearer it is to me that I can trust no one.

For whoever were present at this surgery would see me in the most humiliating circumstances. I've always affected a vast indifference to this growth. I've borne myself with an air that says, 'Any man worth his salt is capable of admiring beauty without a craven lust for it, either in the possession of another, or in himself. This is the mark of a high mind, even if, in my case, it is also convenient.'

I've upheld the sentiment in every gesture, and – what? Shall I cast this defence aside? Scrape at my face like a mason, and as I faint, feebly beg some rascal with contempt in his eyes to 'staunch my wounds'? I can't do it.

As for entrusting the job to another – some bumbling friar or jovial barber – thank God I'm not so stupid! I know the tools they use. Fearful liquids that burn holes in the flesh, or rusty irons that have served for lancing plague spots. It would take an idiot to trust such means and hope to be made the fairer by them. No. Besides, I've been told by more than one physician that thc trouble rests in my blood, deep-rooted, and if I cut this growth, another will spring up overnight, or maybe even more than one . . . Then they shake their heads, these wise men, and sigh; and each of them assures me that my hope must lie in a certain costly draught known only to himself. But I suspect these draughts and their costliness. How could I tell whether any two physicians administered the same? These preparations are often colourless, odourless. And supposing that each draught *is* different, how can I know which to favour? I want no more random concoctions. That the trouble flows in my blood, I can believe, but as to a cure –

I tried one once.

I gave one Maestro Agnolo Berlinghieri three gold florins for it, which was all my pay for a month at the time; and it set me to such violent vomiting, accompanied by such pains and blinding lights, that I thought I must be dying. Piero Sassoli thought so too. He sent for a priest and spoke of dispatching a message to my father – but somehow I lived.

The growth also lived. The shame. To account for my illness, I was obliged to tell a tale about eating rotten cheese in a tavern; I took great care to conceal the phial with all that was left of the mixture, and even greater care not to hunt out the quack who had sold it me. I wanted to draw no more attention to the incident.

That was it. Shocked by a folly which had all but snatched away my life, and had at least exposed me to the risk of mockery, I determined for the future: draw no more attention to it. Concentrate on broader views. Be satisfied.

'I'm alive,' I argued, 'and that despite the Plague stalking all our shadows. Moreover, while scarcely two years pass without some army carving its path through the country, I have a position in a wealthy household, a family not so great that it falls with the great, nor yet so small that it dwindles to nothing in lean years. And I should also consider that if I must live with this thing on my face in an age of cultured men and exacting standards – what misery it would be to live on the rim! In a remote and drowsy spot where every thought or aspiration has to be brought from some other town. My mind cries out to be dignified against my appearance; how fortunate, then, that I live in the very hub of our times. In Florence. All this should count for something.'

And I still think so. It should. Without the taunts of Gabriello, it might even have been enough. No – not enough, but I could have been reconciled. Indeed, at times I've almost believed I was, or sought to believe it. Whereas in truth my situation is such that when Gabriello smiles, or murmurs his innuendoes, I tremble, and know I must look to the future. There's no more time for a partial blindness. I should scrutinise everything.

For instance – this blemish, which mars my life. Because it has no remedy, are there not remedies for other ills?

I must try not to write of the blemish again.

V

EXCEPT to say this –

Physicians, they're nearly all quacks, or fools at best. When Lorenzo de' Medici lay dying at Careggi, a Lombard physician went there–I forget his name–and in his endeavour to keep alive this first of men, this most valued citizen of Florence, what did he prescribe?

Why, pulverised pearls and precious stones!

He ground them up himself with a great deal of noise in the kitchen, which is how the story's known, for the servants watched him.

Pulverised pearls and precious stones. Why not? Don't the rich slip a few choice gems into the sauces that are served at their banquets? So why not gems for physic? Princely fare, to keep a princely frame from its dissolution?

The simpleton.

Any peasant could have told him. Draughts like that can profit no one, least of all the physician: they speedily send his patient beyond his reach for ever.

VI

FROM the household accounts:

35 florins to Agostino Gaddi, silversmith, for a basin in silver, decorated with a hunting scene. Round the outer rim, youths with spears and nets, and several sharp-eared dogs. The boar they chase runs inside at the centre.

20 florins to the same, for a candlestick also in silver, twisted like a vine, with leaves and clusters of pearls for grapes. A gift to the wife of Lodovico Romoli on the occasion of her fortieth birthday.

7 florins to a singer on the same occasion.

From the trade accounts:

60 florins to Giovanni Mannini in London for freight: 10 sacks of Cotswold wool.

30 florins to Francesco Delio in Pisa for Catalonian saffron.
98 florins to Piero degli Agli for 200 ounces of scarlet taffeta.

Immaculate numbers. My annotations kneel beside them – at a distance. In between I keep a reverential space, for this reason: words are corrupt. Full of imprecisions. Example, that silver basin. My description blurs even while revealing it. Does every youth on the rim carry both a spear and a net? Or the candlestick. Are the leaves also wrought of silver, as well as the vine? Or are they of some other, unspecified, metal?

Corrupt words. Humbly they kneel beside my numbers and acknowledge those for the certainties, adding or subtracting into certainties. 33 florins for this, 20 florins for that. No more, no less. I can count what remains in my purse, add the total from my columns – and there: a new number appears, which shows the amount I started with. So my methods are justified; I have no reason to doubt, and the affairs I manage go on. Or if the new number doesn't tally, then somewhere I know an error lurks; I can start at once to track it down; I'm confident that it exists – and of how many things can so much be said?

I thank God for numbers. On the columns they build I've stretched my life like a thin fabric that might otherwise drift into the filth of the gutter. And I thank God I work for a man who himself derives little joy from numbers but who gives me scope to work with them. Most Florentine merchants – those I've seen – watch like owls over their minions, ready to swoop at the smallest ink-blot, but Piero Sassoli is not one of those. He has faith in me. And with good cause. I've risked my life – I've been tried and proven. Let those who will whisper their hints and calumnies, well he might have faith in me!

He might have more.

All records of Sassoli trade in cloths and dyes are lodged at the warehouse, and there, almost every day I make the entries. But at evening, when the books are locked in their cabinet, Piero Sassoli hangs one key at his own belt, and not I, but complacent old Rigogli has the spare. Though I suppose it's only right. Rigogli may be tiresome, but he's worked for generations of the family, and he oversees the warehouse when the merchant's absent. As well as that, his son was sent to Milan on Sassoli business only to die of the Plague there, and his grandson – a great pimply youth full of a dog's loyalty – sleeps in the office every night on a trestle bed. So I can't deny that Rigogli deserves his key. But that I myself don't have one is an insulting piece of foolishness, especially since there's no one else who understands the ledgers. Rigogli might have understood them once, but now his eyes have grown too dim, and although he'll sometimes come to peer at the entries, it's plain that they mean nothing to him, for which I've heard him blame my script.

It's only sense that I should have a key. But as often as I mention it to Piero Sassoli, the reply is always the same: 'Yes, yes! Another key shall be made. I'll have it done!' Then he hurries away, and there the matter rests.

The household accounts, on the other hand, except for a vague perusal by the merchant every six or seven months, are mine entirely. A singular mark of trust. I've kept them for eleven years. I work on them at night, in the privacy of my room.

I look forward to it. The task soothes me. In my longing to make a start, on days when I sup with Piero Sassoli, I excuse myself early from the table, and with a smile he usually lets me go. If on occasion he won't, it's only because he has no love for taskmasters. But then I'm obliged to eat more than I want, and drink, and heave up laughs for his clumsy jokes, and thank God that such evenings happen rarely. Generally I sup alone – my own choice – and although at first Piero Sassoli objected, Gabriello, as I imagine, soon persuaded him: 'If the fellow wants to hide away, why shouldn't he?' I can hear him saying that. Of course, it irks our golden boy to see me treated as a relative. If he hadn't been born – or come to that, if he'd died in infancy – would I be sitting down to table cup in hand as the adopted son and heir of Piero Sassoli? When we all three sup together, the question blazes from his eyes. I see it, and I know its meaning. How could I not? The identical question probably burns in my own eyes.

So, whenever I can, I sup alone. Afterwards, I settle at my desk with lists, statements, inventories all before me, and the book in which I set down everything.

In winter I have two candles; they shed a golden light on the book, and on my hand moving over it. The shutters are closed. Rain beats against them; wind tugs at the hinges. From the hall comes the sound of a flute and the guests' loud, servile laughter. In the street, a dog yelps, someone shouts, a horse passes. And I hear these things from inside the candlelight as mere blurs, traces of the world's muddle, from which I'm set apart. I copy out amounts, totals, my hand golden, the page brilliant, and my shadow grows huge upon the wall, so that when I look up, I see the form of a giant bowed over his papers, and I feel I work on profound matters, mysteries, a harmony of laws the very least of which holds more truth and greater wisdom than any passion or pleasure known to man.

But in spring or summer the effect is different. Then I work by twilight; the shutters are open, and the soft, faintly golden evening flows into my room, bathing everything indiscriminately. The walls turn gold, and the floor, the desk, even the candlesticks, so that my book of numbers and my hand upon it are no longer singled out: we are merely part of a whole in which there are no points of brightness and no shadows, nor is there an encircling darkness to be kept at bay, and the sounds with it. Instead, all sounds mingle with the gold, flowing as it flows through my room: shrill-voiced urchins scrapping in the gutters, dogs barking, carts creaking, young bloods singing on their way to the taverns – even pigeons cooing on the roof – all sounds, and all stench: rotten fruit, slops thrown on to the street, dung and carcasses . . . They're all part of the gold, as I am. Nothing anywhere is left out. We are one. We are the life of the City. We flow together towards God.

Only autumn is difficult. Then the shutters still stand open, and there's still twilight, but by the hour I settle to these accounts, the air is thick with shadows, so I use a single candle which flickers in a breeze that's barely discernible, and the flame makes questions of its own light on the page. And in contradiction, there's a peculiar stillness; it's as if a smoky incense lay on Florence, with every sound that reaches me subdued – I can't explain it. Perhaps, after all, they're not subdued, only carried on a different note, but the effect's the same. They convey an idea that whatever binds our city together is giving way. In the cry of every man and beast there's a note of supplication – or, at least, of query.

On such evenings I round my numbers with unusual care, repeating to myself that in these, if nowhere else, there does lie certainty. That they're beyond the slow dissolvings of what men thought they had: faith, youth . . . A man can shelter beneath them.

But it's no use. Not in autumn. Every autumn brings evenings of doubt, which I set behind me at dawn; and this year resembles the others, except that at dawn I no longer forget, and this autumn stretches. I feel I shall have no end to it. Louder than at any other season, the great clock in the Piazza strikes, and a little courage falls from my soul. The familiar thoughts begin. I'm thirty-seven and nothing. I have no wealth. Scrupulous honesty keeps my purse very light. And if no wealth, and no gift that's exceptional, what then? I have no wife, and no children. I'm a nothing that will come to nothing. Piero Sassoli's words echo in the tones of the bell: '*A poor man's son . . . rescued, so to speak . . . a certain tidiness of mind. Not much of a talent, but useful . . . useful . . .*'

The clock strikes. I stare at my numbers until often, with that perversity of frightened men, I do the worst thing possible. I get up, go to my chest, and take out one of the two most valuable objects in my possession. A looking glass.

It's worth at least 30 florins, and it's as true as the day. The silvered glass is incredibly pure, there's scarcely a crinkle in it; and the back is made of warmly polished walnut, intricately carved with a tree, and a serpent.

A Christmas gift one year – from Gabriello.

VII

NOT just mirrors –
I loathe all crucifixes.

When I visit Fra Bernardino, for instance – that one.

Christ's veins appear to be outside, clinging passionately to the flesh, and His fingers curl round pain as if for once pain had substance, as if it were natural to hold, like fruit. He breathes from every part of Him. You can't help thinking about that – breath – for His ribs press fiercely against the skin, fighting to save Him, to stop for a solitary moment the thing that's happening. Once it's done, who knows what will happen next? His head is bowed; and so, to see the face – perhaps the artist never meant us to see it – one has to stand directly beneath and peer up at Him, which, I suppose, lacks reverence.

Of course, He's suffering. His eyes are shut with the horror of it, and on His brow the customary beads of blood and sweat have formed to drop off soon, and be collected by a thousand monks from a thousand abbeys, who wait at His feet with little phials. Oh yes, He's suffering. His cheeks are drawn tight. The lips are compressed.

These people have Him now. He's nailed out. Suffering *divinely* – never doubt it. No one could, because He's beautiful. Even racked like this, His limbs are perfect. The face, if it relaxed, would be perfect. Even writhing as He is, He's beautiful. And this could be love, not pain. His every twitch is a composition designed for the eye of a lover, and those thin lips – they curve – a terrible silence rests on them. They fascinate, and draw one's face up towards His. They wait to be kissed.

That's blasphemous.

And yet I'd do it, the invitation is so strong. If I could be sure that no one watched, I'd kiss Him. Then afterwards, lightning would flash, and the veil would be rent in the Temple, signs that I'd murdered God – bringing down His wrath upon me.

Men should be warned that somewhere there's a trick in this.

Yes, I loathe all crucifixes. Although that one – I believe the sculptor has a taste for boys – must be one of the worst.

I loathe confessors too, almost as much.

'Never forget,' pipes Fra Bernardino, his eyes bright from countless fasts and midnight penances, 'that the flesh is vile! Whatever artists say, it's not a thing to glory in. Martyr yourself. Mortify yourself . . . ' His long, spidery hands flicker from his sleeves; it's impossible not to see they're filthy. 'Besides,' he goes on with a flash of hope, 'it's not the outward blemish that counts. Not at all. Remember our Lord. He had time even for lepers. Find your comfort in that, my son, and pray!'

'For what, Father? To be cleansed as the lepers were?'

'No, no!' Fra Bernardino is horrified. His thin face turns pale. 'I meant for faith. To accept what the Lord sends!'

'In that case, you must quote me some other example. For it seems to me, Father, that Christ considered our "vile flesh" well worth holding together. Wherever He found it in poor repair, He took some pains to patch it up . . . '

At which point – for this conversation happens often – Fra Bernardino retreats into threats and commonplaces.

'You twist my meaning! It's a grave sin, Gismondo, to mock a priest! A grave sin!'

And I counter: 'But at least I'm here. What's a little mocking from a sinner? Do you expect me to come to Confession already saved?'

'Well . . . well . . . '

The old man sighs and shakes his head.

On the way out, he pats me on the back as one might pat a donkey, and repeats his wisdom: 'Keep your mind on higher things. Vanity is the Devil's snare. You'll lose the next life, that's for certain – and to what end? For you'll have no peace in this! I worry for you!'

Truly he does. I can see it in the lines round his simple mouth, and the moisture in his eyes. He worries for me. So, to cheer him, as we walk I comment on the new St John that's carved in a niche by the door.

Immediately his face lights up.

'Ah, yes!' he cries. 'Beautiful, isn't it?'

They're moon-mad, these priests.

And with regard to crucifixes – they're particularly proud of one in Santo Spirito: a wooden thing that hangs above the lunette of the high altar. Buonarroti made it. And why? As rental. Payment for the use of some rooms the good Prior lent him, to skin and study corpses in – those remnants of our flesh, which, while it lives, the priests would have us despise.

Moon-mad.

One final proof.

If flesh is 'vile', as they never tire of clamouring, why do they cherish carrion? A shrivelled hand, a mouldering skull? Why case them up in gold, or place them near the altar? Take the Baptist's festival. When his Thumb is borne through the streets in a jewelled casket, and the crowds gape to see it – is there no sin in that? In faith which stems from clinging to a scrap of flesh, is there no contradiction?

I put the question once to a Dominican scholar, a far abler man than Fra Bernardino, but he dodged the issue. Yet none too adroitly, either. For he might have said, 'Oh, relics are for peasants! Poor men need a show from time to time!' and I could only have agreed with him. I could even have acknowledged his compassion. But no. Staring hard at my face – particularly the left side – this scholar's eyes narrowed. Then he said, 'To be frank, I think you're inquiring in the wrong spirit. My advice to you is – leave off questions, and submit to Mother Church, while you still can.'

By which he meant, I take it, that my soul's in jeopardy. Trust the mad to know.

It's a theme on which I've no defence. My thoughts are full of forbidden questions, discords. It wasn't always the case, and I didn't choose it. If I could twist my mind back to an idiot simplicity, wouldn't I do it?

Maybe not.

It's fruitless to wish it, therefore I don't. For I've only to look in the glass, and if to despair damns us, then to Hell I'll go. Gabriello with his Christmas gift has seen to that.

And so I'll never be rid of him, since where else could a soul like *his* be vouchsafed eternity? And even there, I know he'll bait me, whispering through the flames, 'Look to your future, Gissy!' And when I reply, 'Here there is no future. Let me in peace!' he'll resort to a taunt that he knows can't fail: 'Wasn't there one? In all Florence? Any man with instincts could have named one!'

VIII

MADONNA –
Lucia da Fano.

She wears only black, mostly with pearls, sometimes with a cross of rubies. And though it shouldn't be said, her face is perfect. Seven years a wife, five a widow, and she's still perfect. The Holy Virgin Herself could be no lovelier. Her complexion is as pale as a nun's. Her throat has the most delicate curve that begs to be touched. The coils of her hair shine, as if in every strand were locked some dark fire; and her eyes, when they look at you, are filled with so much warmth that they surprise; they take your breath away.

But it's her smile that's the real trap; and that's hidden. It doesn't rest on her lips – those barely move unless she speaks – but it's there none the less, strange yet familiar, combining all the softness you'd expect in a spiritual woman with something just the opposite, and long before I could guess its meaning in Madonna, I'd read that smile on another face: on His, the Christ's, when I visit Fra Bernardino. The one inspires my loathing, and the other, love – but the message is the same: to kiss those lips would be a blasphemy.

I saw her first in Santa Croce. At Mass. I was thirteen, and she six or seven years younger, a mere child, a toy to pick up and dangle. But I noticed her. For when the Host was raised, she turned away from the altar and lifted her veil to stare – not at anyone in particular, but at everyone, baring the crowns of their heads in her direction. And I noticed that, because I, too, wasn't bowing. And ever after I noticed her.

A child's game. For a year or more she would raise her veil as the Host was raised, and if after that she learned discretion, there were still times when the veil moved: a cheek, a dark eye – I noted every detail.

Years of Masses. Years of winters shivering in the tomb-like cold of Santa Croce while the priest's mumbles turned to a fog above his head; years of summers sweltering in the rancid crowds of a saint's day Mass, just for a glimpse of her.

At fourteen she was betrothed to a merchant, one Giuliano da Fano, and two years later she married him.

Joylessly rich, tight-fisted da Fano. It's rumoured that he quibbled at the cost of his first wife's burial; and his servants, when they contrived a visit to the markets or the nearest tavern, spoke in whispers of the penance they paid for any imagined negligence or waste. These stories filtered into every household, and Piero Sassoli used to say that by all accounts Giuliano made an exacting husband. Then he'd laugh and wink, and wait for me to stretch a grin.

At the end of Mass, I took to waiting near the door, and when she passed, I'd bow low. By this I hoped she might understand, 'If ever you need help, remember I'll do anything!' But also: 'I bow so that you won't laugh at my face!' It was, of course, impertinence, this homage from a man in my position, and I knew it; but then, I argued, Piero Sassoli's business dealings with her husband would excuse me. And besides, I wasn't the only fool who waited there, ducking and bobbing at her.

Seven years of that. At the doors of Santa Croce, or when she passed in the street. Or on those days when she made a rare appearance at some public festival; and although she seldom turned her head, I always sensed she knew. She knew I watched her. She knew each of us who watched.

How to explain? There are people who see no more than where their eyes look, and who hear no more than what is said for their particular hearing; and there are others, who by an alertness, something cat-quick in their step, make it plain they perceive much more, that no matter where they look or to whom they incline their heads, there's not a shadow on the wall, not a feather touching the ground across the street, but they're aware of it. And Madonna Lucia, I'm convinced, has such a gift.

Seven years. Then da Fano sickened. Visibly he withered. The strong jaw-line sagged. Look closely, and there was something – I suppose it must have been pain, though it looked like maggots – crawling beneath his skin. A deep-seated terror stared from his eyes; his voice, like his hands, trembled. Soon his servants began to whisper of cries in the night from his bedroom, and of how Madonna Lucia would cradle him in her arms, as though he were an infant.

The best physicians were called. He spared no expense for once. But all the same he died. And just before he died, the physicians were dismissed, and two surgeons, thinking to remove the evil, opened him to find his entrails in such an advanced stage of putrefaction that one could almost have said the man was dead while still living.

Without doubt, he'd been poisoned.

A cook was arrested. In the previous months there had been an incident concerning some extravagance with spices and, as a result, the cook's pay had been halved, a cause of considerable hardship to his dependants – I believe there was a destitute sister somewhere, who had several children. So the case was clear. The wretch was duly tried and sent to the scaffold, loudly protesting his innocence, and I dare say there was abundant sympathy for him among da Fano's servants. Madonna Lucia was all compassion. From her own purse, she made allowance for the cook's dependants, even going so far as to send them to Rome, to work for her relatives there, where none need ever know of any smirch on their character.

Madonna –

With her property, her freedom and her friends, these past five years I've hardly dared to bow to her. I slink by. Her house is open: musicians, artists, architects, all are welcome, and most are mad with love for her. There's no need now for rescue. A dressed-up peasant, a kind of steward, dextrous in arithmetic but at the level of the market place – what has he to do with such a woman?

Even the sight of her door depresses me. I slink by.

And some day, it's inevitable, she'll marry again – though they say not. They say she's taken an oath. Strategy. All strategy. To curb her ambitious father, who must surely wish to marry her off as profitably a second time. Also she keeps her own house – da Fano's – and that's a great scandal, so she needs this rumour of an oath, to appear respectable. I place no trust in it. One day she'll remarry, and better for me that she does. Yet I dread it.

I'm filled with dread. There's a nightmare I have, only in autumn. I'm working late at my accounts; it's past midnight;

there are two candles; I have many columns to total – when suddenly the door opens, and in comes a servant with the sneering face of Gabriello. He announces a visitor. Then a woman enters. She's heavily veiled, but I know at once who it is, and I tremble with joy. She stands before my table. I jump up, and in my haste to offer her the chair, all my lists and inventories are scattered – but she ignores this confusion. Sitting down, she tells me in a voice so chaste that I can hardly bear to hear it: 'Gismondo Cavalletti, you're my only friend. You mustn't think I haven't noticed. And so I have to confide in you. I did it. I poisoned him.'

This gift falls from her lips. I almost dissolve with happiness. I kiss her feet in slavish gratitude. I'm overwhelmed. I could grovel before her for ever and be content – but there's a movement . . . She's raising her veil . . . I look up . . .

And – the horror! Her skin has turned a saffron yellow. It's pitted like a lemon rind. Red cracks have opened in her eyes. Her lips are like blue worms. There are overlapping folds on her neck. Her smile shows brown teeth.

The horror! I'd crawl away if I could and hide, but she holds me; her fingers chill my wrists.

'Take a good look!' she says.

I beg. 'Lower the veil!'

And suddenly she's veiled again, standing by the door.

Then I know I've been tricked. Beneath her veil, she's young, I'm certain of it, young and beautiful.

As she turns to go, she looks back once across her shoulder: 'Gismondo?' – and I understand the question, though when I wake its meaning vanishes. But whatever it means I reply, 'Yes. You poisoned him.'

These nightmares leave me weak with nausea. And they have this in common with the clock in autumn: they send me reaching for the mirror. There I stare at the face that could make such a dream, and my image in the glass stares with horror back at me, who made *it*.

Tricks. Legions of them.

IX

GABRIELLO wants her, that's no secret. He and his friends are for ever making lewd jokes. And often, when there are guests of the humbler sort to supper – agents and the like – if the conversation turns to women, our golden boy must make a display of his sentiments. 'Oh, she's a pretty morsel! One man down, she's just ripe. Ready for a Sassoli now. By God, I'll have her!' He bangs with his cup on the table. 'All these nit-wits that go mooning at her heels – they're too damned spiritual by half! They don't know what a woman wants. Especially these religious ones!'

And everybody laughs. If I catch his eye, Piero Sassoli winks. He likes to think that his son has wit, and the lout *must* marry.

– But that's a question to draw me out on a Sunday evening into the garden, where the merchant and I walk together between the flowerbeds. Around us insects buzz, the sun is warm on our backs; a scent of herbs sweetens the air. The merchant, as he's grown older and stouter, has taken to leaning heavily on my arm, especially when he has something unpleasant to say, whether he knows it or not.

'You admire her, eh? None better?' He wheezes, and his feet are unsteady, but his face watches mine steadfastly enough.

And I reply, 'Of course, it isn't for me to judge . . . But I can't help thinking as she's six, maybe seven years older . . . '

'Pah. What of it?' Piero Sassoli spits. The white froth settles on the gravel. 'A widow – that's exactly what he needs! She'll tame him. And not squeamish, like some slip of a thing. More to the point, she's wealthy, Gismo – where's your flair for calculations? Wealthy, and he needs *that*.'

'But her disposition and your son's . . . '

'Hang disposition! What's that got to do with it?' His fingers pinch me through my sleeve, a warning not to vex him, and his eyes glint. 'Sometimes, Gismo, I think you argue for the sake of it. Can't you see I'm worried? And by the way you talk,' he says, 'anyone might think you'd designs on the lady yourself!'

No. Never. Not I.

He makes this comment quite frequently in our discussions.

My gaze becomes fixed on the gravel, or on a lavender bush. My cheeks burn. It occurs to me that if he pursues the theme, I'll be provoked to strike him, and then my life will be over . . .

But the merchant, having dealt his blow, always desires to be genial, and so he smiles, and pats my wrist with a show of tenderness.

'Yes, yes,' he sighs. 'We must snare a mate for you, too! Maybe the Frizzoni girl . . . They say she has the sight of a gnat . . . How about it, Gismo? A good, solid family . . . you'd be doing well. Think it over . . . Think, but not till Doomsday! . . . And by the by . . . speaking of love, remember that cupid we saw in the spring? The one I wanted? Well, it's for sale again . . . '

X

THE instance serves for many.

A cupid done in terracotta, painted white and glazed to shine all over like a sugared pastry. The type's a fad in Florence. Piero Sassoli admires it. Myself, I call it rubbish. I wouldn't spend a soldo on it, and knowing I wouldn't, the merchant bristles with righteousness.

'So you don't like my cupid, eh? Well, you know, you needn't. What do I care? But let me tell you, it's a sound investment! This sort of thing's going up in value all the time. Why, I can sell this piece next year for twice what I've just paid for it!'

And out of long habit, when he speaks of trade, his eyes gleam, his voice grows brisk with enterprise – only, he won't sell. He knows it, I know it; so why say anything? The truth is that Piero Sassoli hoards. 'A collection for my heirs' I've heard him call it, but what he means is – confusion. Statues, pictures, worthless inventions and models of inventions left behind as sureties: he has rooms cram-full of them. Particularly inventions.

They are his pride and joy. Every day, when we come back from the warehouse, for an hour or so before his supper Piero Sassoli holds court. All the fools and charlatans in Tuscany have leave to come to his door with a new design for a water-sweetener, a new revolving lamp, or yet another model for a flying machine –

And willingly they come. In packs and droves they come.

And the merchant bubbles with ecstasy.

A device is set before him, which demonstrates how water can be pumped up from a greater depth than ever before. There are many impressive trimmings, but the main equipment is a tube of linen, waxed inside and out, and a wooden pipe that's placed in a bowl of water. Sassoli peers down into this; as the pipe begins to fill, he curses with excitement and, much encouraged, the inventor fusses round, pointing out the more unlikely features: anyone can see he's on to something, that the pump works, though the model, he admits, requires adjustments . . . And all he asks in return for a share in his genius is a little modest backing – which amounts to everything from timber to the construction of a village for the workmen near a flooded mine he's inherited . . . And his need is so great, this fool's, that he prattles on with costs and estimates, and entirely fails to see that Piero Sassoli now looks grave. He prattles on until the merchant starts to fidget, then to shake his head, and finally breaks in with, 'Yes, yes! I'd help you if I could, and no doubt end up the richer for it! But as it happens, so much of my capital's abroad at present . . . on the sea . . . I've two cargoes coming from Spain alone . . . that what with all the storms we've suffered lately, not to mention these damned pirates . . . regrettably . . . '

The inventor listens in astonishment. He stares. After such a propitious start, he can't believe that the fat old man is actually refusing him. An inventor never can believe it. But then, they're all possessed of an enviable skill in acting out the incredible, so without a word he gathers up his tubes, pipes and papers, and bows himself out politely. He'll be back. He knows that men less inspired than himself need hammering at.

Next, the marvels of a pair of bellows, worked by water-power! And on we go –

Frauds, lunatics and the out-of-date – they come in clusters, like counterfeit constellations. Sassoli, after all, is not a Medici. He's not even very rich.

But he's ever hopeful, with so constant a desire to be large in his own estimation that he's always willing to make the best – or more – of what he finds. This makes my task difficult. Someone has to restrain him when his judgment fails, and he depends on me. I know it, he knows it – another of those things we never mention. Yet if I protest when he offers to pay some vast price for a wind-powered mousetrap, I'm not always sure of thanks.

'An authority on these things, are you?' He turns and scowls. When he wants, he can stare and glare, so openly appraising me as his most costly investment, that my blood runs cold. 'My dear Gismo, and when, may I ask, did *you* ever invent anything? Anything whatever?'

It's a question that reduces me to silence – as he knows it must. At once I'm back in the shadow of the dung-heap, piling pebbles, and I can only shrug. The useless gadget is as good as bought. Helpless, I count out the fair gold florins. The inventor grabs them, and Piero Sassoli is reluctantly appeased. 'Well, well . . . what a fuss! Gismo, you know, you really shouldn't resent other men's talents! It's a flaw you have. A deplorable flaw in your character!'

And what is it, then, to resent the *lack* of talent in others? What's that? But I say nothing. I tie up his purse strings, note the expense, and there's an end to it. I never ask.

For here I'll make a confession. I've watched the flight of hornets, butterflies, and honeybees – spent hours on it. I've even examined a cockroach; I've made diagrams of its wings and tried to deduce from those the principles of flight, or how the design of windmills might be bettered by a study of the wing-case. I've placed a spider in a dish of water and carefully watched its movements, to see if it has anything to teach towards a system of paddles, whereby a single man might move a barge upstream. And I've experimented with shadows, projecting them on to the walls of my room, making theories for myself about their size and strange proportions. My chest is littered with these scraps and jottings, efforts I'd blush to set in anything called a 'book'. They can never merit that dignity.

They're pure pretence. All the time I study, or contrive studies – I know exactly where I am: in the farmyard dust. Still shamming. And worse. The most obvious trickster who comes to Piero Sassoli's door is better at that game than I am.

And no one resents this in myself more than I do.

Small wonder, then, that our sessions with the vagrant marvel-makers are a tribulation to me. The merchant will buy or rant, while I look sour; he thinks I'm dull and covetous; he looks to me to curb his will, yet he scoffs however he likes; and for years I've tamely accepted this, considered it a burden of necessity. Have I been wrong? His money will never be mine, but if Piero Sassoli threw gold to the fish in the Arno, would I not be concerned for him and his household? The man trusts me; so shall I add to his disappointment with the thing he buys – my own indifference? I've never been guilty of such a betrayal. I always protest, and – if he desires, he insults me.

But there are more painful encounters than these we have with rogues who come to the house. These evenings are nothing.

At the end of a session, Piero Sassoli's belly rumbles. He wants his supper. He has just acquired, perhaps, an over-elaborate set of scales, and has also lightened his purse of 40 florins to a splendid youth from Prato who dreams of building a catapult as tall as the Campanile. The merchant respects such fantasies. He has every kind of interest in a safer state. The youth had only to hint at his vision, and 40 florins were gone. Now Piero Sassoli sits back and yawns.

'Fine fellows, some of these young ones! No one can say they aren't, or that I don't do my bit to encourage them . . . But a new da Vinci, eh? Or a Buonarroti? Do you think I'll ever find one of those?'

His plump face grows wistful.

Da Vinci . . . Buonarroti . . . he has met them. He has even dined with da Vinci once, at some Guild fête or other, and taken a cup of wine with Buonarroti, though I suspect that both times he was lost in a crowd of merchants who gazed dumbly from afar.

Planets in our zenith, da Vinci, Buonarroti, with Dukes, Popes and Kings for patrons. Piero Sassoli uses a special voice when he speaks of them; and not just of the men themselves, but of any oaf who's sat at table next to them, or been honoured by them with more than the simplest civility.

It's degrading. To watch him bow and smile, and drink in every word of men whose larger purses buy them time in greater presences – it's degrading. Or to watch the pain and longing that mingle in his face when someone crows, 'I discussed precisely this with Michelangelo, and he was of my opinion . . . '

I, too, am degraded. When Piero Sassoli forgets his self-respect – and what else can I call it? – it is I who suffer.

Example. In search of Buonarroti, we go, on occasion, to Carrara. The warehouse is left to Rigogli; I myself am forced from my counting; the merchant orders a strong mule to be loaded with baskets of fruit, quail, cheeses and his best wine.

Then he and I make our pilgrimage.

It's a rough road to the quarries – if you can call it a road – and we go whenever the passion takes him, no matter how blistering the heat, or how numbing the cold. We arrive exhausted, our destination a chaos of carts, ropes and work-teams, and there we stand in everyone's way on some inconvenient spot, gaping at slabs of marble that have been carved from the hillside. They are wonderful, these slabs; they hint to the eye of the forms which are trapped in them, and not a single form in each but several, so that just as they lie, the slabs seem strangely worth preserving, each one as it is, for to shape them into any particular thing would be to lose a wealth of suggestions. They present a challenge, unworked stone against our need to define, and so in their way, the slabs are awesome.

But it's a long journey just for that. We try for a glimpse of Buonarroti. And when at last we succeed, Piero Sassoli offers up his mule like a sacrifice.

'Good day, sir! Everything going well, I trust? Well . . . well . . . We were coming out in this direction, so I thought to myself, "I wonder if Michelangelo . . . I wonder if they could use some fruit at the quarry . . . and some quail perhaps . . . some wine . . . " So, here, you see, we've brought along these trifles . . . If there's anything else . . . anything you lack?'

The noise in the quarry can be deafening, while the air is filled in places with a white powder so that Piero Sassoli and I, the stone-cutters and Buonarroti himself may all be coated in it. Grey pilgrims, the merchant and I stand before our grey idol, and Sassoli mouths his greetings. Then, as often as not, because he's sick of fools, or can't for his life remember who this Piero Sassoli is, our idol rewards us with a stare, an iced smile, and very few words. He excuses himself. There's work to be done. And that is all our thanks.

'The preoccupations of genius!' says Piero Sassoli ardently. 'Gifted people don't have to spell out their gratitude, Gismo. A noble spirit takes such things for granted.'

So he comes away quite jubilant.

'You see,' I remember him saying once, 'to men who truly admire greatness, no price is too high. Not in any real sense. Not if we can gain in return the goods we desire – a great man's friendship, a piece of his work . . . no, no . . . these things go far beyond the meaning of florins.'

And as he spoke, it seemed to me that there opened in his head a vast plateau, a kind of Eden, with flowers and sparkling streams, where anything was possible – anything except that Piero Sassoli should ever be asked a price that he couldn't pay.

But in reflective moments, his own extravagance alarms the merchant; that's why he depends on me. It's also why, whenever he goes to Rome, a city stuffed with 'greatness' if anywhere is, he always takes me with him, even though it would make more sense in other respects to leave me at the warehouse.

XI

ROME.

At the very mention of it, an itch developed on my left wrist – an excellent reason to lay down the pen, since my right hand had to do the scratching! And then I discovered my eyes were heavy. I went to bed. 'Tomorrow . . . ' I promised.

But this evening is no different. At the mention of Rome, my thoughts shrink. These familiar surroundings seem to close in. I'm aware that the bed is too large for the room, there's a crack in the footboard on this side of it, and that my chest, which Monna Margherita bought when I first came here, is vulnerable. It stands there open – I've taken these notes out – and I see that the lock is woefully inadequate, while the key which protrudes – any thief could snatch it. But that's nonsense. There's no one here but I, Gismondo. True, at times while I write, I feel there's someone else, a second Gismondo who stands by my shoulder, diligently reading. But I know that for what it is: the illusion of setting words down as if for another. I am alone. The key is safe. When I leave my room I take it with me. It hangs from my belt. My anxiety is mere distraction that serves to show a considerable wish in me not to write of Rome.

Detestable city. Whatever one hears may be believed. Infants are sold for a handful of coins in the streets; even the most contemptible rumours prove true.

A cardinal there, one highly regarded for piety and refinement, turns his back on a lady as she kneels to kiss his ring, and breaks wind in her face! The reason? A paltry jewel. A cup shaped like a lotus flower, studded with pearls. He was anxious to buy it from her, and she refused. But there are others who say the jewel His Eminence had in mind came closer to the lady's self.

Either way, it's a noble jest, and all who hear it laugh.

City of mercenaries. I myself have seen an artist hard at work on a devotional picture, a most delicate and beautiful fresco, scramble down his scaffold when a banker strolled into the chapel, and beg the honour of painting a portrait of this visitor's daughter. 'To commemorate her betrothal, sir! At your convenience. This poor stuff here . . . there are only the angels to do . . . I can break off here at any time!'

Well. It's claimed that our Holy Father has the powers of an alchemist, and I hope he has, for there's plenty of dross to be turned to gold in Rome. Yet I doubt if even the Pope can cleanse those streets. The city stinks. It teems with pests. Whereas in a gutter in Florence, you might see one rat in an evening, maybe two, in Rome you see whole litters, as plump and sleek as full-breasted pigeons – and as bold. The Plague City, I think of it. And judging from the way he behaves, Piero Sassoli thinks the same. He says little about it, but generally when we walk abroad in Rome, he holds a bunch of cloves to his nose, something he seldom troubles to do in Florence, and even when it involves a tedious detour, he always insists we avoid the filthiest alleys.

He hates it, I hate it, nevertheless we go.

We conduct our business. We visit our banker, then our agent's office. Nervous 'good Mario' fetches his books, and with every possible compliment, I glance down the columns. More than this token inspection Piero Sassoli has vetoed. It's typical of the whims he likes to indulge in. Mario is careless, the merchant knows it, and yet he insists, 'Gismo, if you check that poor man's books like a hen picking over a farmyard, I'll know where to lay the blame when he turns dishonest!' So. I merely glance. Then we listen to Mario's problems – he has too many aunts and nieces, too many cousins – we sympathise. We extol whatever we can in his business. And once this is done – it takes a day at the most – we're free for other, more important matters. We scratch for news of famous men. And introductions. We go visiting. We track down newcomers – sculptors, painters, youngsters homesick for their province, but hopeful, ever hopeful . . .

And finally, time and whims permitting, we consider those glories of Rome which any dolt may turn aside to contemplate, if he desires.

The Vatican. Buonarroti's ceiling.

Of all his works, the only one that fails me. How the mind that created the Grecian warrior could also have pictured this – I'm incapable of understanding. Oh, I pay most dutiful tribute.

Piero Sassoli and I have seen the ceiling often. There it all is: the Almighty's creation: the waters dividing, sun and moon, heathen seers, a havoc of serpents. And Jehovah, massive, powerful. The ceiling lours like a thundercloud. Jehovah's limbs are heavy with the might of earthquakes, while as for Adam, newly created, a being caught in the act of drawing his hand away from his Maker – I see no idyll in him. I see only a separation from God, encompassed by prophets and punishments.

It's a work that frowns. Of course, men marvel, they admire in whispers, but its grandeur is crushing. It lifts men up only to throw them back to the earth – or so I think. Something expected is missing, or else of something there's over-much. Piero Sassoli, of all men, has expressed it best.

One time we went there, he stood with his head thrown back on his fleshy neck, hand on hips, gazing up at Jehovah and Adam for such an age, that at last I feared he was in a cramp. I was wondering whether to speak, and so risk being thought insensitive, when he whirled round suddenly, and said, 'That's enough, and more than enough. Now let's find something manageable.'

So we called next on one Jacopo Marone, a skilled engraver of gemstones, a man who makes all kinds of exquisite cameos.

Which brings me – now I see my pen has led me by a crooked path – to events that have happened in Rome, which I'd prefer to forget. Blows that have stunned me, and how can a stunned man shape a future? I must write these things. Clear my mind.

And here's a nice distinction.

Despite the passage of years, the snow figure I summon to memory at will. I can picture it in immaculate detail, and all the people in the crowd. I draw comfort from it. But these Roman incidents, which took place much more recently, and which I never will myself to remember, rise of their own accord, only they do so in fragments: now a face, a hand – and yet each fragment has the strength of the whole, and repeats the blow.

Write them. Two vile episodes. And the first began, I suppose – no, it's not the beginning, but it centres on a cameo. For I bought a gemstone myself once, in Rome, not from Marone, but from another almost as good.

This is how it happened:

Piero Sassoli was in a mood to buy. He had already seized on a great cornelian set in gold, but there was also a turquoise – a pretty thing engraved with a coy Aphrodite – and in this lay his dilemma, for he could neither make up his mind to both nor decide which one to leave. So he hawed and puzzled, asked me for advice, which he brushed aside like a cobweb, then puzzled again. In the end, I knew what must be the outcome, and I lost patience. Abandoning him to the craftsman who hovered at his elbow full of soft persuasions, I took to roaming round the shop. I wandered into the back, and there, at a workbench, sat a ferret-faced boy washing stones in a basin, while on the bench beside him a row of gems lay drying – a topaz, two cameos in amber, a garnet, an opal . . .

Never had I seen such an opal. It was as smooth and pure as milk cut from the pail in January. It was as round as a newly minted coin. It made the other stones look like rejects. There was about it a quality which I can't describe, something – inevitable. Under the boy's hostile glare, I bent to examine it – and my breath stopped. I saw a woman's profile. Surely Madonna Lucia's! For a single, unreasoned moment I thought she must be there, in Rome, and had commissioned this work. But then I looked again, and I saw that the cheek was too full, the neck was too short, and the eye too slanting. I breathed deeply. It wasn't her. And yet so like her. Even the smile.

Well, I had to have it. The engraver's work in itself was excellent, delicate; the stone seemed barely touched. It was as if a thumb could have smudged that profile, and yet its features glowed: they looked warm with life. It was clearly the work of a great talent. But even if the engraving had been inferior stuff, I would still have had to buy it. I couldn't have permitted anyone else to own that opal.

The apprentice watched me closely. His red forearms rested on the rim of his basin, as if he were ready to spring to his feet and snatch the gemstone from me the instant I tried to pocket it – and that he thought I'd make the attempt was evident from his face.

Something had to be said.

'Your master's work?'

He nodded. 'Yes. His best, that is!'

And so I was given to understand that unmounted though it was, the opal wouldn't be parted with lightly.

I bought it. In secret: the merchant's eyes are sharp enough to know a likeness. As I counted out a pile of crowns from the Sassoli purse for the turquoise and cornelian, I managed to make an offer of my own, for the opal. The craftsman made some fuss. He grumbled beneath his breath that it went against the grain to let work go unfinished. Unfinished? I was full of fear. I protested at his modesty. I became urgent. But he muttered that any fool could see he'd not yet worked the shoulders, and if I'd come back the following evening . . .

My looks – and my gold – silenced him. Piero Sassoli, flustered by his purchases and anxious to be gone before he saw his money leave his purse, had strolled away to a silversmith's stall on the other side of the street, so I had my chance. Of my own coins, I emptied out all I had on to the craftsman's hand. To the last soldo. The opal was unfinished? Then I must salve his conscience –

Three times an honest price I paid for it.

Dismal folly. All the way back to Florence I was aware of that opal, burning like a coal in my purse. I had a hideous journey. We travelled in the company of a lawyer from Bologna and his clerk. The lawyer was polite and learned; we discussed a premiss out of Aristotle, the price of silk, the ruin of the Eastern Church, and God knows what else besides. Piero Sassoli can talk enough for two, and my own thoughts were fixed, for the most part, on the gem – and on the lawyer's fair-haired clerk who was beautiful, his countenance refined like those of angels in a sacred painting, but with a cold, unyielding hauteur to it, and sometimes I could feel this youth – who rode on my left – studying my face with knife-sharp interest; and then it seemed that my purse was about to burst into flames, the opal fall on to the road, and this cold seraph would point a mocking finger at it.

Not her, but like her.

For fear that while I'm out, someone breaks the lock and rummages through my chest, I should carry this opal on me always, day and night. But there are other risks. Who's to say I won't fall ill, or be attacked in the street? And should that happen, and someone came to tend me, loosening my tunic, perhaps they'd find the gem and steal it. Or do worse. They might hand it in with everything else to the Sassoli household!

But if no more than my keys were brought to the house, and the opal lay in the chest – where's the difference? It would come to light, just the same.

What a triumph for our golden boy, discovering I'd treasured this! How delightedly he'd squeal, 'The poor fool! He kept her likeness – or he thought he did. A cheap bauble bought in the market place!'

I'd swallow it sooner. As it is, I keep it on me sometimes, and sometimes in the chest. Once I sewed it into the lining of my coat, but worried until I took it out again, in case it fell through a tear in the cloth, and I'd be tormented not only by the loss of it, but by wondering where I'd lost it, and when.

The fact is, there's nowhere safe. Even here, alone in this room with the door fast shut, how dangerous it feels to take the opal out and set it where I can see it. I have it by my wrist. If I glance quickly when the candle flickers, I can deceive myself.

Lucia da Fano.

Brightness and loveliness incarnate. I desire her. Whatever there is in me of soul, she could save it. She has only to turn, smile a welcome – and I'd be saved.

Now the candle flares; the profile's made plain. A makeshift bought at enormous cost. A sop for a weakling.

Oh, there are things I could do with it. I could toss it into the Arno, or part with it to a beggar in some town far from Florence –

And so, all 36 florins I paid for it would be gone into mud – or Charity. Imagine: this face in the slime of the river-bed, along with the bones of criminals, offal and ashes. Or grubbed from hand to hand of wretches, breathed on and pored over.

I can tolerate neither.

Then there's the poor box. Cast it in, and turn my back. Let some priest dispose of it. But that seems cowardly. I'd have lost my florins and the opal, for certain, but with any gain of self-respect? The poor box is the way of a sneak.

As for taking it back to Rome, and trying to sell it again among the lesser tradesmen there, who neither know nor care about her –

That I've tried. And that was my mistake.

But to tell of it, I must tell of the women. The creatures I go to. A shame I hide in the Holy City – and where more appropriate?

XII

I confess, of course, to Fra Bernardino. I know he's listening for it. Through the ledger of my sins, I can feel his yellow finger running down the items, searching for it. And when I confess, his finger stops – there, on the account – and he peers at this item hard, eager for all the details. How many times? And where? The same house? The same woman?

Indeed, so zealously he inquires, that often I tell him, 'Twice, on this last visit, Father,' when the truth is – only once. Or I feel an urge to add a touch of make-believe and cry, 'Father, this time I must tell you one was a girl they'd taken from her family . . . She would be twelve or so!' When the truth is that they turn such girls from the door: there's no more room for them.

Oh, I do my best with details. Why am I there confessing if not to give them? And although he fails to grasp the fullness of my sin, Fra Bernardino absolves me.

Afterwards – admonishments. To prove he understands.

'My son,' he says, 'you think this sin of yours is baffling? I promise you it isn't! Who knows more about temptations? We in the holy life are plagued by them! Temptations fascinate. Oh yes. We stare one in the face to arm ourselves against it, and even while we stare, it lures us into evils that we never dreamed of. This is the work of Flesh, and Spiritual Pride. The Devil's agents.'

Words, as far as they go, that aim in the right direction.

But then – man to man – he smiles, a fatal token that he thinks this sin of mine is not so grave, and worse than that, those times I confess it, I'm rewarded: he pats my arm more affectionately. I've become more human to him.

It's as though, on account of this one sin, he'd allow me a niche in Purgatory, whereas otherwise I'm straight for Hell.

But these women –

First, they must be clean. Any odour, and I leave at once. I pay that they should be clean – and not to stare, despite the names they have for me: 'Peachstone', 'Plumstone' – names which I haven't troubled to suppress. I wish the women to see that I know what I am. I've no illusions.

We eat, and sip cheap wine. They talk among themselves. I take no part in their conversation, and they expect me to take none. I have them well instructed. They talk, I listen.

At times they discuss their clients, but that's a subject which soon bores them. They prefer to talk of holidays (for they observe the festivals of several saints) or else of gifts: perfume, trinkets, silks. They fondle the cat. They quarrel about the leaking roof, and who should fetch the bread. They joke about the self-styled prophet who comes shouting up at their windows in the night, exhorting the damned to rise and wash in hyssop. They sulk. One of them burps with the wine – and all of them giggle.

And being whores, they act as other women never would – unless, perhaps, in private. They hitch up their skirts to warm their thighs at the fire. They unlace to ease their breasts, and rub them absent-mindedly.

And I sit by, as it were unnoticed, risking the Plague and the French Sickness by drinking from tainted cups and eating the food they've had brought from ovens in just that sort of alley which Piero Sassoli and I so assiduously avoid.

All this for about an hour.

Then I get up, pay and leave.

The point is that I might not, but I always leave. I've done enough. I've run the risk. Every time, to the present, I've escaped without contagion – but it's no small hazard to sit for an hour, breast bared, so to speak, for God's retribution or malicious destiny to do its worst. Which is the essence of the thing: running the risk soothes me. Part of me craves and waits for these trials. Also there's pleasure, each time I leave without being mauled by the sluts – in knowing that they don't like that. They're jealous of their arts. However blighted I am, they've given themselves to more hideous men, and they'd entice me if they could. To prove their skill is the sap of life to them. I deny them survival by refusing. It's not enough that I pay. A man who needs their flesh – in him lies their hope for another year. If they're spared the Sickness.

But *I* fling their charms back in their teeth. In fact, I made it clear from the start that if any dared touch me, I would strike her.

From the start.

This then, in Rome, and only in Rome. Excursions once or twice at most, and often not even once.

They first hatched out of loneliness. Mario's house is packed with children and strident women, so Piero Sassoli will never lodge there. We pay for rooms instead. And when the merchant sups with someone well-to-do who doesn't care for 'hangers-on' (as I appear to many), the night can yawn like Cerberus. I sit in a borrowed cell, and my hands grow cold. Round me sprawls the city, but there's nothing for me to do except wait like a common hireling for Piero Sassoli's return, and that can be at dawn. He's brought back by some young sprigs, relatives of his host, wined and mellow; but no matter how mellow, he looks out sharply for me.

'What, Gismo,' he cries, 'are you sitting up? Worried because I'm late? *Such* a worrier, poor fellow! What would I do without you?'

His voice is rich with enjoyment. These, my little acts of devotion, are all part of the Sassoli hoard. We both know it. So I wait through the hours of darkness, and seldom even think of sleep.

But how to pass those nights?

I count the day's expenditure, then I sit. I stare into the fire; I watch the flames, and will them into shapes, fantasies. A twist of blue becomes a fabulous bird, rising out of the ashes. I see two figures, one in scarlet, the other in grey, who bow to each other with great solemnity, then fiercely embrace – like two brothers who meet in a crowded piazza, and feel a bond between them although they haven't met since childhood.

So I amuse myself.

And one evening, six or seven years ago, as I looked at the flames I thought: 'Will you do this for ever? When your hair's grey, and your knees are weak, will you still visit Rome, and spend your nights lurking in closets? In Florence you're known. There, with a face like yours, you can do nothing. But in a city as vast and ugly as this, you should sample life, before you lose it for good. No one can name you. And man is given his will to shape events for himself, experience. A man must make an effort.'

These ideas scorched me. It was as if the flames had leapt from the fire into my head.

I got up, and ran from the room. I hurried through the streets in any direction, until the night picked out one house from many. It seemed to be placed across my path. Above its door a lamp sputtered. Through its shutters I heard laughter – women's laughter. I banged hard on the door.

A smiling harridan came, who asked to see at least one coin. Then she led me in.

Suppose I set down here that my courage failed me? Or that I was disgusted? Or that, when they called me 'pretty' and 'a handsome fellow' their brazen lies revolted me? All this is true, and yet it amounts to nothing. I could have left.

In what appeared to be a general drinking room – a group of women. There were tables, cups and, sprawling in a corner, a drunken oaf who watched me blearily, while by his side crouched a girl soothing his brow, and holding his hand to her skirt. There was no one else. A slack evening. The women prowled round me. Animals I knew of only from a distance. Now unchained. The young ones thrust their faces up to mine. They smelt of sweat and intimacies. Some wore their clothes dishevelled, as if by chance; others were neat – yet they looked the more immodest for it. And all of them wore strange, predatory smiles – wide ones, of forced appetite.

Who would do? they asked. A room was free along the passage.

I vowed then, they would never have me.

One tried to squeeze my leg. I pushed her back. After that they stood, laughing – jokes were made – in a circle, with myself at the centre. I stood still. They fell silent.

We all waited.

I'd made my entry – I'd made an effort of sorts – and now, was I to run for the door?

I kept very still. For the space of time it might take a moth to fly once round a candle, not a thought rose in me. I was terrified. Then, in an instant, my terror turned to rage. Was I just another fool to be stretched out on the sacking? Their effrontery astonished me. I swelled with indignation. I glared round. Couldn't they see the kind of man I was?

I found, in truth, they saw.

Not just hideous, but different. Their smiles were growing more cautious. Their eyes no longer played on my face alone, but flickered to my purse, or the shoulders of my coat, and in their eyes lay something which – despite myself – I recognised. It was admiration.

True. I was admired. For the quality of the cloth I wore, and the good size of my purse. But still admired. As well as that, they were curious. They waited to know my pleasure. That, too, I noted, and it warmed me to have these creatures with their usual expectations shattered, uncertain what was required of them. I myself felt curious, and I discovered I was anxious not for a disentangling, but for something that would take me closer. Not too close. But for something that contained – a risk.

So I prescribed my pleasure.

And I'm not free of it yet.

The candles burn low. Great, cream-smooth candles, none but the best on Piero Sassoli's insistence. 'Now if it comes to working late, d'you hear me, Gismo? I won't have you squint through a damned smoke! Use as many as you like. Never let me find you struggling with some sickly taper! I won't have your eyes on my conscience, and I won't have you thinking it!'

But this isn't Sassoli work for which I burn his candles.

Well, I'll conserve tomorrow. To break off now would be unnatural. How all-of-a-piece it comes in the end, this tale of Rome! I perceive he was right, good Ser Bandini, who taught me the Latin I know. Short-tempered Bandini, with his glittering spectacles, and a trace of cinnamon when he coughed. Suffering from phlegm in the nose and throat, he was forever clutching a handkerchief, and because his affliction so troubled him, when he read aloud from some Latin text so that I might appreciate its elegance, his cheeks would turn purple, his voice would fade to a scratchy whisper – but he never broke off mid-sentence. And once, when I was translating a passage that seemed to fill the page without a break, and I foundered – he struck me across the cheek. 'Wretched boy!' he croaked. 'Faint-heart! How would you like it if bridges stopped in the middle of rivers? Or the staircase stopped half-way up the side of the house? This isn't how we do things, boy!'

So then, Rome. And having exposed my shame – these women – I return to the opal.

I did take it back, and try to sell it.

After a year or more of indecision, I made up my mind to salvage my florins, as many as I could. That, I thought, was right and healthful. In fact, over the months I'd convinced myself that to treasure a chance resemblance was more than just a foolishness, it was an insult – both to the beloved, and to me, who loved. For as the image was neither the true nor intended likeness of her, how could it give me honest comfort? Rather it humiliated, like something filched, or a secret thing spied through a chink in the door.

I resolved to be rid of it, and to Rome I took it.

There, my chance came one bright morning, when Piero Sassoli kept to his room consulting a tailor, a talkative man, who I knew would keep the merchant busy till noon. I acted quickly: I hurried off to a street of those less prestigious jewellers –

My plan was simple, but one that generally brings results. By showing the gem to several tradesmen before I'd settle with any, I meant to quote their prices against each other, and so to arrive at a fair bargain. In this way it seemed to me that I might hope for 12 or as many as 14 florins, in whatever coin they happened to have, I wasn't particular. Surely, I thought, no one could deny that the work was excellent, and the stone matchless.

But I had sadly miscalculated.

My eagerness to be rid of the opal had blinded me to a paradox. For in this age when every man is said to fight for himself – and the devil take his neighbours – there remains confederacy, a fellowship of rogues and thieves. And these lesser types of jewellers, tradesmen, so-called craftsmen, all have their understandings which hold their clans together, and are binding throughout the district. To such a conspiracy I fell victim. No one, no matter how keenly he eyed the gem, would bid above a third of its value. 4 florins here, 3 crowns there – this was the most they'd offer. And when I spoke of 8 florins as the very least I could consider, some of the villains laughed in my face. One had the gall to suggest that the stone didn't look like an opal in any case, but an unusually bland piece of quartz – which is monstrous. Others were just as dishonest, but sounded more plausible. One, for instance, a stocky, black-whiskered man with a smirk that no doubt I was meant to think kindly, said: 'Now, sir. I ask you. What would I do with it? Nobody likes to go adding shoulders to someone else's head, and I couldn't come up to the style of this. I know my limits. So why should I want it? I'd be taking it as a favour.'

And another, sighing all the while, told me: 'Take two crowns, sir. Here. That's generous . . . No? Then take it back where you got it from. But you've had it how long? A year you say? Then I wouldn't trouble.'

'Oh? Why not?' I asked.

The tradesman leered.

'Well, think about it,' he said. 'No disrespect to you, sir, but there's something peculiar here. This is commissioned work, by the look of it. But he let it go to you, unfinished. And a noble sum you must have paid! I'd say he had to sweat before he found another stone like this one. Then he'd have to do the engraving again . . . identical . . . and before his customer came, the one who'd commissioned it. Now, sir. Don't you think he'll find it awkward if this original piece turns up in his shop? Forget all about it. Take a crown. Take two, I'm generous.'

So they defeated me. To sell the stone was one decision, but to let it go for next to nothing – I found I'd made no pact with myself for that.

I came away, and, to ease the disgust I felt, I remember flinging the opal into my purse wrapped in its cloth as always, but without securing the cloth with a knot, as I usually did. A deliberate act of negligence. If the gem worked loose and rattled about among the coins and was scratched – why, so much the better! I hated it. I would have looked on the damage with delight. 36 florins. A fortune for someone in my position. All my savings. Slow gains rapidly lost.

I went back to Piero Sassoli in a savage mood.

The merchant was merry. His tailor had gone, and he was warm from a trying-on of coats, and parading about in lengths of velvet. In addition, he was greatly excited by some taffeta the tailor had shown him of a richness Piero Sassoli had never seen before, and which the tailor had bought from a merchant whose name was unknown to us. Now the great thing was to track this stranger down, and buy from him all the taffeta he'd spare as nothing like it was sold in Florence, and it hurt Piero Sassoli's pride to think his warehouse had none to offer. All this he told me with much bustle and urgency. He claimed he'd been waiting an age for me, and, in case I doubted him, waved at an empty bowl on the table: beside it stood a plate piled high with broken walnut shells, a sure sign that however long or short his wait, it had certainly been an impatient one.

So I closed my mood away. Taffeta and tailors, I was all attention. We hastened forth to make inquiries.

But as we went, with Piero Sassoli extolling every fibre of this cloth, there occurred one of those twisted moments by which we know that the heavens tease us.

'I tell you, Gismo,' he panted, 'this taffeta's so exceptional, our ladies will go on bended knees to their husbands for it. But the husbands, if they've any sense, will keep it all for themselves! I never saw such richness. I defy a saint to resist it. Particularly the scarlet. We'll tempt all the widows. We'll have them out of their black cloaks yet. Even Lucia da Fano!'

Her name – unexpected and terrible: after my wretched wrangling over the opal, it fell on me like a judgment. It was as though Piero Sassoli knew how I'd spent the morning; it was as though *she* knew, and through the merchant voiced her anger, either because I'd tried to sell the gem, failing to understand that she wished me to keep it, or else because I'd grown too mindful of florins, and hadn't carried through my purpose.

Confused by these ideas, I jerked my head; I stared at Piero Sassoli, who immediately burst out laughing.

'Come now!' he cried. 'Face the facts! She can't stay in black for ever!'

No indeed. And infinitely to be preferred if he thought I blanched at that than that he should sense any other reasons. After a pause, enough to settle my countenance, I hurried to give a show of interest: how much of this cloth could we hope to purchase? How best should we transport it? And if Piero Sassoli saw all this as a ruse to stop his talk of widows, he didn't care. He let the subject drop. It would do for another time. The matter now – was taffeta, to which we devoted the afternoon.

The opal lay in my purse, the dark mood lay in my mind, and neither caused me further trouble until the evening, when I found myself alone.

With the help of Mario's clerk, we'd traced our unknown merchant not to his office but to his house, an indiscreetly sumptuous affair graced by the newest kind of chimney. There we'd found him. A round-cheeked youngster nine or ten years my junior. He'd taken one look at me, then turned his undivided attention to Piero Sassoli, who had promptly explained our business. The fledgling declared himself gratified, but unfortunately we'd discovered him on the point of setting out to supper at the home of a friend and, although it would give him the greatest pleasure to take Piero Sassoli along as a fellow merchant, he feared it might look presumptuous to arrive at his friend's house not with one extra guest, but two . . .

So that evening, I supped alone.

I sat by the fire, and watched the flames, guessing at the purchase Piero Sassoli would have made in the sober morning, with me at his side; then I considered the price of his dealing alone, with his wits made slack by wine and easy fellowship. I calculated a heavy loss on this taffeta. After that, I studied the fireplace. I worked out its simple proportions. In short, I strove to keep my anger down, and my thoughts from straying to dishonest jewellers, lost florins of my own, from misery, and Lucia da Fano, laying aside her widow's clothes.

And when I failed, as I was bound to fail, I set out for the usual place.

Of those most often present, I know all their names: Domenica, Gianna, Dorotea, Angelica, Caterina, Tessa – and one they say was well-born, called Ginevra. Domenica's the oldest. There are flecks of grey in her hair, and her soft chin folds itself away in tiers. Her arms, as thick as a labourer's, are curiously mottled. The youngest is Ginevra. Well-born she might be, but she's rat-like. When she smiles, which she does often, her features sharpen. All her movements are sudden. And slight as she is, she eats voraciously.

The others are common whores, so that Dorotea replaced Maria, and Caterina came when Anna died – yet they remain the same.

Save one. Angelica. She's brown – the daughter of a slave from Africa – and she wears her hair cropped; not, I suppose, from modesty, but to display her throat and shoulders to their best advantage. There's something boyish in her looks, which may be the reason why the others took her in: they like to cater for all tastes. Angelica is quiet, unless, when there's nothing else to talk about, someone begs her to speak of Africa. Then, although she was born in Rome herself, the girl complies willingly. Not that she knows much. Only the foolish half-truths which her mother told her. Any merchant might know more. Yet here's a strange fact. Whether because she can't or she won't, she never elaborates her mother's tales. I've never heard her. She tells only what she's been told. Her wording scarcely varies. A few wonders, often repeated.

But it's worth the repetition just to watch her.

Far from losing heart at the reminder that she's lowest born even amongst these whores, when she's describing Africa, the girl brightens. Her voice grows strong. She tosses her head. Her hands move, conjuring images that make me forget it has all been told a score of times already. And she gives us the nonsense her mother taught her: lions and deserts. Kings who live in palaces built out of the skulls of their enemies. Drums and dancing. The future read in a scattering of bones. Black men's strength, and black girls' fertility – she, a whore, looks proud, and talks of fertility! Then, magic: how men can kill by smearing a trace of goat's blood –

But here her companions cry for silence. They cross themselves, and shudder piously.

'You heathen bitch!' they shout. 'Damned pagan! You'll burn in Hell, Angelica. Just like your mother!'

It's a ritual. She gazes at them in mock amazement, then lowers her eyes, crosses herself devoutly, and swears by all the saints in Heaven that she's as good a Christian as any of them. At this they laugh. Except once, when someone – perhaps it was Ginevra – answered that a slave should guard her tongue.

A slave. Who could deny it? Yet she has power, that's certain.

Her skin shines. Her legs are lean and smooth, the limbs of a swift-running animal that could surely find its freedom if it chose. Her hands are cunning in their movements. And when she laughs, as she does when she talks of Africa, the sound that comes from her throat catches in the blood.

She's dangerous. She embodies all the risk – and means to be more than risk. If she knew my fear – and I can feel her watching for it – if she knew I lived in dread of bringing away some sickness, I believe she'd make a mission of it. The most foully infected cup in Rome would be set on the table for me. And when time passed, and someone remarked how strange it was that Peachstone kept away – that would afford her marvellous satisfaction. My death would be a small thing to her, but to have winkled out my fear and served it up – oh, that would be glory! And to have dealt a blow, however slight, against the other women – for I pay them handsomely – that would give her most sweet pleasure.

All this I sense in her and, because of it, I desire her presence more than any of the others.

To this haven, then, I fled that night Piero Sassoli supped with the taffeta merchant. I took my black mood and my purse, and sought shelter.

Domenica opened the door.

She looked less enticing than ever, her hair matted, her skirts stained. A stench rose from her armpits, and I remember thinking, 'She must sponge herself before she sits in a room with me!' This thought came first. Only afterwards was I aware of the noise – young men's laughter, the girls shrieking. Someone was bawling for wine.

Domenica stood on the threshold, and barred my way. She'd answered my knock with a smile prepared for some other customer, and no sooner did she see who it was than her face changed. The smile vanished. She grimaced.

'Oh,' she said. 'So it's you, Peachstone.'

'As you see.'

She stood there, blockish. I waited for some warmer greeting, but none came. Instead, she assumed a stubborn, dull expression. Involuntarily, I thought of a jailer.

'Won't you let me pass?' I said.

'Can't you hear?' She nodded back at the room. 'Students. Rich ones, God be praised. The girls have more than enough tonight. Come back tomorrow, Peachstone.'

And she made to close the door.

I imagine, sometimes, that she closed it, and I walked away carrying my disappointment like a stolen goose, a faintly ridiculous thing muffled in my cloak. So easy to do. I should have done it. I can hardly credit the fact that I didn't –

Then I feel the wood. My hand's gone out to hold the door open.

'Wait!'

A delicious comedy! A show for mummers!

I was shocked. Wounded. That some night they'd have no time for me, that it was possible, I'd thought I understood, but the event, when it came, was unbearable. I was filled with horror. The prospect of slinking back to my lodging to brood on losses and Lucia da Fano –

'Wait!' I said.

Domenica stopped.

'Well, what is it?'

In the room behind her, a youth began a mawkish lovesong. Another responded by yelling obscenities. Cups clanked together. And these sounds robbed me of my remaining reason. I pined to be inside the building: life was worth nothing without it; to sit among the women, and undergo my orderly trial – I'd run mad without it. Howling through the streets. My mind was about to break like a fragile dish. I could say nothing.

I simply stood, holding the door ajar.

Domenica's eyes hardened.

'I'm busy,' she said. 'I've got to go.'

And then I begged her. I begged pity of a whore.

Had she no compassion? Was I not a well-paying customer? One who gave no trouble? How could she think to leave me desolate . . .

I whimpered. I heard myself with disbelief, and still I whimpered – until after a time, like the ageing of a piece of leather, the woman's face folded, and she smiled.

I almost choked on hope.

'All right,' she said. 'Listen, Peachstone. Just for you. I'll sit with you. And there's one girl. One's no use tonight; the way she is at the moment, they don't want her. We could sit cosy, just the three of us. Would you like that?'

And before I could reply, she'd called across her shoulder – for Angelica. Then she added, 'But you'll have to pay more tonight. You'll be keeping us to yourself while the others are serving many, and these students are very free with their crowns.'

'How much more?'

'Double.'

The girl appeared. Glistening. She came hurrying, but when she saw who stood outside, she stopped with her hands on her hips, and shrugged.

Double. I've always paid a high price for my visits, because, the women say, I occupy so many of them. And now – was I to squander twice the amount, when already racked with despair to think of what I'd thrown away on the opal?

Angelica was watching – and I knew I'd do it. There was conflict in my mind, but no indecision. Only I felt reluctant to speak. I wanted them to lead me in without a word.

The women misunderstood. When I kept silent, a low voice began to taunt: 'I don't believe he has that much! Shouldn't we see what's in his purse, before we agree to anything?'

And after she'd said it, Angelica laughed. Never before had I heard her laughter aimed at me. It tightened on my stomach. I felt weak.

Domenica's smile broadened.

'Wise girl!' she crowed. 'We should. Come closer, Peachstone. Show us you can pay!'

They watched me. The fat, jailer's face, and the brown one – white teeth, whites of eyes, the fine long neck.

And then, if not before, was the time to leave. To turn on my heel. Pride and discretion demanded it. But I told myself just the contrary: brazen it out, I thought, for dignity's sake.

So I stepped across the threshold. I came close enough to see the pits in Domenica's skin. And I opened my purse, contemptuously pouring out coins on to my hand, while I stared at the women with all I could imply of loathing; and even so, I was struggling to conceal how much I trembled in case they chose to refuse me. They peered down at my money. I could hear Domenica's breath as she leaned forwards. I could see the grime on her scalp. I could see that the brown girl glistened because there were snail-tracks of sweat all over her body –

'Well, well,' said Domenica, 'our Peachstone's bringing us trinkets now!'

Her hand stretched out. I glanced down.

The opal. There it lay, uppermost on my palm. Under the sickly whorehouse lamp – Madonna's face, gazing out of a bed of florins.

With finger and thumb, Domenica picked it up. I gave a shout. I grabbed, but she held it high to examine it in the light. Then Angelica came pressing forward.

'Let me see!' she cried.

'Pretty. Oh, very pretty!' smiled Domenica, giving it to her.

The brown girl held it delicately, and gazed.

'I'll kill you both . . . ' I was saying.

'You will? You want it?' Angelica's face shone. Slipping behind the older woman, she closed her fist on the opal, and held it out: 'Come and get it, Peachstone! I'll hide it in a part of me where you'll have to search! Long and hard! Can you do that, Peachstone? Long and hard!'

Domenica roared with laughter.

I pushed past. Coins scattered as I fumbled to return them to my purse, and have my hands free. I seized Angelica's wrist, and forced her fingers open. She was strong. She smiled all the while, even when my nails gouged into her. Then at last, she let go.

'Take your little egg,' she said.

I snatched it and ran. Their derision ringing after me.

The look in their eyes when they saw the engraving – pure contempt. No, not so pure neither. For there was anger in their faces, and desire. Above all, anger; which was caused, I suppose, by their understanding that I hadn't meant to offer the opal; also because it's beautiful, a thing beyond their lives.

But what victory for them! How I scampered like a frightened schoolboy – though it wasn't fear I felt. Desecration of all that's holy! That a whore should think to set this image – even the shadow of Madonna's – there. In the very crucible of her trade!

I returned to my room in a frenzy. The supper I'd thought well settled in my stomach rebelled – and I was sick into the water basin.

This is the first of the Roman incidents.

All night it's taken me. Not rats, but birds are scrabbling about in the nest above the window. My ears are schooled to the difference. And so I know that dawn is close.

XIII

AND so it's written.

When I laid down my pen this morning, I opened the window shutters, and looked out along the street. I thought it cleaner than I'd seen it for years. Also the air smelt fresher. And throughout the day I've felt no dullness for lack of sleep, only a nervousness, an impatience for evening to come, so that I might return to these notes. For now I see it. Less harm lies in the incident than in this fact:

I still go back.

A swineherd would have more respect for himself. Nevertheless I go.

And here's an irony. No one has ever again suggested that I pay double. Now they treat me with more restraint – which I explain as follows: the women saw that I had funds enough to pay all they demanded, and yet in the end I refused them. The reason is of no importance: I chose to leave. And so I set a limit to their play with me. I showed some power of discrimination – even if, at the time, I was close to losing it altogether.

Since then, I'm never teased. I suppose they fear I'd take my custom elsewhere – the abiding explanation of any decency in whores.

Still, I should shun the place. I go where I know I shouldn't. And this being so, is it strange that I see my future as a great darkness? How can I plan my actions when I know I act in ways that I myself can neither condone nor fully account for?

Why go back?

To speak of it as the Devil's work is mere avoidance.

Why should a man, who's resisted countless vices, be caught at last by one, as it were by accident? And once caught, why surrender – against his pride, and all he holds sacred? I find these questions terrify. The wretch who has no answers can never hope to trust himself. Or, if he argues: 'All the rest of the time I can be upright, but I must have these indulgences . . . ' then where shall he set his boundary? And if he tells his spirit: 'To this mark you may degrade yourself, but go no further' – how can he keep his mark from slipping, even as his spirit slips?

I've had nights of anguish. By visiting these women, do I vent some evil in my nature, or do I gather more?

Doubts. Tortures.

Am I better or worse than others? I mean – than other thinking men, with consciences? From the greater part of how I live, I draw a sustaining confidence that I'm better than most. At least, more honest and dependable. Disciplined.

But if I seek out harlots, am I not inferior?

To whom? Piero Sassoli? Never. For he scarcely thinks.

To Gabriello? If I am, justice has fled from the universe.

To old Rigogli, faithful forty years, drudging at the warehouse? But what do I know of the secrets hidden behind his mask of servility?

Better or worse? And where's the gauge?

Do all men behave in ways they could never explain?

The scrivener Rassuccio has a peculiar habit. At least, I've seen him do it twice, and such a pointless thing that to do it twice must merit the name of habit. Possibly he does it often.

All day at the warehouse this Rassuccio writes letters and copies of letters in an impeccable script. He rarely smiles. He speaks no more than he must but sits humped at his desk, and toils. His long, pale nose almost scrapes the papers. His brow unbends only as he takes his leave.

Then he walks home through the Old Market.

And twice I've seen him stop at a booth which sells the kind of pipe, simple and crudely fashioned, that children play. He carefully inspects them. With great deliberation he blows on three or four, and peeps down into them. At last he selects one, and pays his coin. Then he sets off with his prize gripped tightly.

On both occasions, I could have overtaken him, but the man so discourages conversation that I made no effort. I continued to walk behind. And so I saw – both times – when he left the market, the jerk of his elbow as he threw the pipe away.

Could he have given me a reason? If I'd run and asked, 'Rassuccio, why did you do that – '?

I believe not.

He might have said, 'What's it to you?' – or else devised some elaborate explanation, but the sense of his words would surely have amounted to: 'I don't know why.'

This I've considered. In the nature of ordinary men, there seem to be flaws which are meaningless, and it's because they're meaningless we are ordinary.

Whereas the great – oh, they have their weaknesses, women, dice, passions and so on – but with this difference: nothing they do is devoid of meaning, for from their very faults they benefit: they draw a spark – some advantageous understanding. Some perception. Even from those vices which they can't control they seem to farm a sustenance unknown to other men, and so they thrive. I learned this only recently. Once I thought that great men, though like any mortals they must be imperfect, had a constancy, and maintained fixed values – like my numbers. Child's thinking. They're inconstant like the rest, but they thrive, while we go into oblivion. Something of this I might have learned long ago from the Heretic, but I didn't. I learned it only last spring. In Rome.

That other episode.

XIV

A visit to the Holy City on which Piero Sassoli surpassed himself.

At first it was much as usual: promising youths, excellent craftsmen, talented painters – even a traveller who'd been to the east and collected exotic designs for water towers. We saw them all. But on this occasion, nothing charmed. The merchant remained unsatisfied. True, he smiled and nodded at all he saw, but for once his purse strings weren't untied, and in his smile I detected a blend of tolerance and impatience, as if at the slightest provocation he might suddenly shout, 'Yes, Yes! That's very fine! I see you do your best. Still . . . it doesn't amount to much!' Or some other remark, equally crushing.

This went on for three days, without apparent justification. But I knew the trouble. It was da Vinci.

Since our last visit, no less a person had come to Rome. The greatest rival to Buonarroti, and more than that: an intellect to turn all scholars into donkeys, and the greatest inventor of our age.

At the close of the previous year, Giuliano de' Medici had lent da Vinci the use of his summer palace; and from this eminent position the great man's presence blazed across all Rome, so that since Piero Sassoli and I had last been there, we found the atmosphere changed. It felt richer, even festive. And most of the men of substance we met seemed to give themselves airs, as if they thought it enhanced their personal standing to have da Vinci living amongst them.

I smiled at that. I found it odd, for when da Vinci lived in Florence, I was never aware of an atmosphere. I mean, an elation, merely because he lived amongst us. I don't think I'd have forgotten. He left seven years ago, at the most. But perhaps I failed to notice it: there were wars, troubles, many distractions. Besides, he worked on so many projects in those days, that he may have been too much occupied to come often before the public eye. Indeed, during the eight years he lived in Florence, I remember glimpsing him only on two occasions.

Once, when I was about twenty-four. He came hurrying out of the Sala del Papa, and Rigogli, who was with me, poked me in the ribs:

'That's da Vinci!' he whispered. 'That eagle nose over there!'

Then the second time, some eighteen months later, I saw him at a distance walking towards the Hospital of Santa Maria Nuova. At least I saw the same straight-backed individual with distinguished features, and hair of jet streaked with silver. But both times he was half-turned from me and hurrying, and both times there was a bevy of notables twittering round him, so that these glimpses served for next to nothing.

I made up my mind to that. To boast, 'On such and such a day I saw da Vinci . . . ' when I'd merely glimpsed him – that, I thought, would have been unworthy of him, and of my own intelligence. So I never spoke of it.

And I never looked for more. I thought him above seeking out and spying on. And he was proud by reputation, and said to have no liking for fuss, so he dwelt in the town without extraordinary fanfares – which is not to say that Florence was indifferent to him.

On the contrary: pride, awe, resentment – I remember hearing some expression of all of those. Pride, because he'd been born in the region. Awe, on account of his genius. And resentment, because he was one to come and go as he pleased, and would even number among his patrons men who had no love for Florence. But resent that as she may, his native city puts up with it. However it lacks convenience, there's a sentiment in Florence that da Vinci is exceptional, and can't be judged by normal concepts of what is fitting – or loyal. The result is this: his independence, which causes so much vexation, is also a source of the city's pride, for it's seen as the symptom of his genius. And the compensation for every grievance is that it remains, this genius, when all's been said, a Florentine product.

Naturally, other cities take a different view. Mention elsewhere that da Vinci comes from Florence, and it's an act of discourtesy. The men of Rome or Milan prefer to think of him as a benediction, an event from Heaven, the location of which, as it moves from state to state, bestows some sort of virtue on the inhabitants.

Odd. And significant. To be thought so God-like.

But I purchase my observations with hindsight, which they say is a treacherous coinage.

– To return to the visit.

It seemed to me that da Vinci's presence in Rome acted like a thorn in the flesh of Piero Sassoli, for none of the artists with whom we dealt could stand their ground before the Master, who now lived not at some vast distance, but a few poor streets away.

And as we went about for those three days, praising little and spending nothing, I came to the natural conclusion that Piero Sassoli was miserable. I see now that I had slight evidence. He drank more wine than usual and he seemed more restless, but these are not infallible signs of anything, and, as it turned out, depressed he was not. Only *suppressed*, though I'd no way of knowing at the time. I thought the merchant cowed. I thought I knew his ailment – well I might – the affliction of middleness, the discovery that one's self is neither high nor low, neither here nor there: I thought he caught sight for the first time in many years of the barren field which lies between himself and all the greatness that he woos like a lover. And curiously, I didn't find it amusing that Piero Sassoli should suffer this. Rather I pitied him. So I took pains to be cheerful and garrulous, full of interest for this or that, asking questions which might divert him. Once, by a small pretence at forgetfulness about some type of paint they use for frescoes, I even made him laugh. I did all I could – blindly, with a benighted understanding, since I took it for granted that Piero Sassoli sensed as I did, how great da Vinci had grown. Far too great to be troubled by simple merchants. And that he was, in any case, too grandly lodged.

But in this, as in so much else, the merchant's perception was otherwise.

The fourth day was our last in Rome. Piero Sassoli had risen early and dressed himself with particular care, as I knew the moment I saw him. He was wearing his most expensive belt, one that I think he'd never before risked on the journey; he had brushed the dust off his coat; his hair and beard were scrupulously combed. But what impressed me most were his gloves, for he wears them only for rare festivities, and there they were: he held them now in his right hand, now in his left, fidgeting as he told me: 'Well, Gismo, this is the day! We'll do it! I've thought it over, and see no reason why we shouldn't! I dined with him once, you know. And last October, that couple of days he spent in Florence, remember we saw him in the street? Remember he stared, then nodded? I've thought it over . . .'

Up and down he paced, chattering like this, and as he did so, slowly – for I felt most reluctant to be enlightened – I saw that, alas, there was no mistake. He meant to visit da Vinci. I recalled that day in October. We'd been walking home in the company of our Pisan agent, a grudging soul who always raises ten objections to any single project, and with whom I was arguing about a shipment of gall-nuts, when the merchant suddenly clutched my arm.

'Did you see?' he hissed. 'Going into that house? That was da Vinci! He gave us quite a stare! Then he spoke to the man he was with – and nodded . . . Well, of course, he must have remembered. I dined with him once!'

He talked of it for days, and was angry because, with my thoughts intent on business and the gloomy face of our agent, I'd missed the affair altogether. Again and again he demanded

– surely I'd seen? The stare? The nod? To all of which I had one reply. 'No. I saw nothing.'

Then, in time, the smiles of friends to whom he described the incident persuaded Piero Sassoli to treasure it in silence; and as for me – I tossed it out of mind.

But in Rome that morning, as he paced the room dressed like a princeling, and told me again how well acquainted they were, he and da Vinci, his October madness came back to me and, frankly, I was disappointed.

Why, I'd thought better of him. In my folly, I'd thought my efforts to cheer him had actually been of use, whereas now I saw I'd missed the mark entirely. And apart from that: visit da Vinci? Walk to the Belvedere gates without letters of introduction, and plead for admittance? To be turned back by some liveried underling?

Worse, far worse, than taking mules to Carrara!

I dared not trust myself to speak. I watched the hem of Piero Sassoli's coat – his plum-coloured velvet with the sable lining – and by this means avoided his eye. But in the end I must have looked up, for I recollect that he smiled, fiercely, his face very flushed, and ready to scowl if I uttered a word in protest. And his eyes, I thought, were unnaturally bright. They gave the impression that if I tried to reason with him, they'd reflect not the moods or frustrations of their owner, but two small images of myself, aping me.

So, we set out.

And the merchant carried his purse himself, a thing he dislikes to do in Rome, for he fears the city's thieves. But I suppose he meant to have all his dignity on him. He may also have hoped to buy some scrap of sketchwork – a half-finished horse's head, or any scribble the Master would part with – and as he carried his purse, he thought out his boast: 'You see this sketch by the hand of da Vinci? I had it of him. Oh, I insisted on paying. The man is far too generous! He'd have made a gift of it, but I set my purse on his desk and said, "You'll take a respectable sum, or I'll empty all I have on your papers!" '

A great, fat purse (since we'd made none of our usual Roman purchases), it hung at his belt with little discretion.

So we made our way.

The streets were already crowded, and perhaps because he had no mind to bawl above the vendors and the gossiping women – for the wider one opens one's mouth in Rome, the more of filth and flies cram in – Piero Sassoli now said little. Instead, he grew red with excitement. Soon, he began to pant. Then his eyes began to flitter. He flinched at every jostle. Every loafer we passed who gave so much as a glance towards us increased his terror, and caused him to tighten his clutch on my arm, so that, what with the risk of being stabbed for his purse, and the prospect of seeing the glorious da Vinci, by the time we reached the palace gates he was weak for want of breath, and leaned on me like an invalid.

The gates stood open, with a solitary drowsy guard before them.

There Piero Sassoli straightened himself. He released my arm. He surged forward and announced boldly, 'We've business with the Master.' Nothing more. As though a Medici guard could be put in his place like some rival merchant's errand boy! I thought it rash. Not all sluggards are docile.

But the fellow only yawned. Then he raised one leg and rubbed his heel on the ample calf of his other leg; then he moved his sleeve across his mouth – a long, luxurious process which might at last have led to speech, but we didn't wait so long. We bustled past, Piero Sassoli holding his head erect, and thrusting his thumbs into his belt.

Victory.

A few steps further, and the merchant leaned on my arm again, panting even harder, as though our small success was a burden to him, and I took this for a sign that now he'd played his part. It would be for me to bring him through any second challenge, such as I knew awaited us –

For the door, unlike the gates, was shut. And the guard who stood beside it was alert, watching us through crafty eyes. His lips twisted as we approached him, and his nose wrinkled. Here was no nap-snatcher. At the sight of him, I thought to myself with more than a little bitterness, 'How like the merchant to start – and leave me to finish.'

But yet again, I was wrong.

As soon as we reached the door, before I could open my mouth – indeed, before I'd thought what to say – a voice at my shoulder gasped, 'Piero Sassoli from Florence! And see you say from Florence!'

To which the guard, who looked so hostile, reacted like the tamest porter. He nodded, and rapped with his knuckles on the door.

By and by, a bolt went back, and the door opened. Not wide, but enough for a grey-haired servant to push out his head quickly, timidly, like a snail – a thin and harassed-looking servant of the kind that belongs to a place just as a wooden stool or a water pot might, something useful when the place is lived in, but shut up with the place when people leave it, as a thing of not sufficient value to be worth the carting. So, this snail peered inquiringly at the guard, who indicated the merchant, and the merchant said again, 'Piero Sassoli from Florence. And see you say from Florence!' – gabbling it off so vigorously that the words might have been a formula for universal acceptance which he'd found in some ancient book, and memorised.

The servant, however, showed no signs of being affected. The door closed with a bang, and we heard the bolt pushed home.

We waited.

I prepared myself for a proud walk back to the gates. Slowly, I thought, it must be slowly, as if to be turned away were a thing of little consequence. I'd not have the guards sniggering. But first, the inevitable interlude while behind the door our snail-friend counted a hundred, and then he'd bring us apologies, excuses –

Patiently we stood there. The early sun caused a prickling on my cheek. Piero Sassoli caught my eye, and winked. I looked away immediately: my face burned. And in my embarrassment – for such it was – I tried to distract myself.

'A capon,' I thought, 'and a raven. Piero Sassoli the capon, all in plum and sable, with that great bold medal on his chest, his belly round and comfortable, and his coat, though new last year, cut in the style of sixteen years ago. Then his belt, his gloves – such plumage! While I, towering head and shoulders above him – I'm the raven. Lean, and dressed in browns and indigo, a superior fashion, but dull, dull. What's to be made of us? My sense of style is excellent. Strangers are confused by it, they don't know where to place me. In fact, I make a striking appearance – or might have done – far surpassing Piero Sassoli's. For whatever he wears, he looks homely. But he possesses belligerence, and that saves him from being the sport of many. Oh, they may laugh to his face – he'll laugh with them – and he cares not a fig what jokes men make behind his back; but a sneer he'll take from no one. He rages, he bellows and curses, a splendid performance. Whereas I – my rage turns inwards. Anger makes me silent, and I'm sober still. Yet I'm mocked all the more for it.' Then I asked myself, 'Could I have managed these guards as well as Piero Sassoli has done?' No, I decided. But then, I was less in love with our mission – or so I thought, although the closer we came to being admitted, the faster my heart was beating, and surely it mattered: to stand face to face with da Vinci . . . if it were possible, what a bonus! Having come this far, I couldn't deny to myself that I was eager for it; but I hoped that no one could read this eagerness in my behaviour. I glanced at Piero Sassoli, and was thankful to find him much preoccupied with his gloves, twisting and pulling at the fingers. And mercifully, the presence of a guard did away with any need for small talk.

A cat strolled round our feet. She pressed against the merchant's ankles, but he said nothing. The guard looked his fill at my blemish, and at Piero Sassoli's bulging purse. The sweat on my neck itched. Our cat abandoned us. And then an unwelcome new thought came: what if unsuitable callers were left at the door like this, without aid or hindrance, until at last they came to their senses, and crept away? Such perfect contempt!

This idea grew to a certainty in me. Again I turned to the merchant:

'We may have come at the wrong time. Perhaps we should leave . . . '

'No, no!' he hissed. Then he shook his head. 'We wait!' he whispered.

And so we did.

Not, in the end, such a long wait. To my amazement, the door was suddenly opened, and a smiling green-eyed youth invited us to enter.

Why?

As we passed the guard and crossed the threshold, I remember that I speculated – had da Vinci formed a policy to receive any fool who came from Florence? He might have, I thought, not because he was overfond of his native city, but because it was also the home of his host, and so he received all Florentines as a compliment to his patron. It would also reduce the risk of turning away some oaf who enjoyed Medici favour.

'Yes,' I thought. 'That's it. That brings us as far as the hall, and there we'll find a steward waiting to see what kind of men we are, and to tell us the Master's indisposed – '

This, then, was my mind, as we stepped from the sunlight.

We were admitted.

But as soon as we were, the fact seemed less extraordinary, for if we were in, so was half the world besides. In the hall – magnificent, of course, but one hardly noticed – in the passages and on the staircase stood whole congresses of fops, down-at-heel students, scholarly clerics, and rich, paunchy merchants just like Sassoli. In fact, men of every sort, chattering or whispering, and some of them holding a portentous silence. A king's court could be no more crowded.

Piero Sassoli wasn't pleased. I think he'd expected more of a shrine-like atmosphere; and jabbing our boy in the back, he panted, 'Who *are* all these people? What are they doing here?'

To which the servant, who was nimbly guiding us up the stairs, round a scholar's elbow here and over a monk's foot there, replied with a grin across his shoulder, 'Waiting to see the Master, sir! What else?'

Indeed. What else? Scroungers and worshippers alike. All waiting. So why not us? But the question, I saw, hadn't entered Piero Sassoli's head. He only grunted, and pushed aside whoever stood in his way. In his zeal he took our miraculous progress for granted, and so we proceeded, up the stairs . . .

Stairs with dust in the corners, and spittle stains, and on one, a pile of dog's excrement: despite so many people packed together, I noticed that. And although there's nothing strange in a little filth – palaces, by all accounts, are full of it – I noticed it with emotion. For the Medici, I thought, like other men, might have their share of dirt in the house, but not da Vinci.

No. That's untrue.

It wasn't so much the filth as the neglect it spoke of. It took on significance. It seemed a sign of lesser perfections being laid aside while the search went on for greater ones. Comic, to be awed by dung, but so I was.

– Though I barely had time to think of it, before Piero Sassoli, stopping just ahead of me to catch his breath, took a deep sniff and cried, 'Good God, boy, what's that stink? Have you sickness here? Not Plague, is it?'

And at that moment I smelt it too. A sickly, sweet odour, like the one that comes from a carcass left to rot in the sun. And considering that this was Rome, the original den of pestilence, I too felt panic.

But our guide was all serenity.

'Oh no, sir!' Inside his serenity, he was even proud. 'It's from the Master's experiments.'

'Aaaaah.'

Wonderful!

Piero Sassoli was immensely gratified. He turned to me with an absurd smile, as much as to say, 'You hear that?' and we hurried on, without much dignity, up the stairs . . .

To the Master's door.

The great da Vinci.

Our guide didn't knock, which surprised me, but opened the door at once and, as it opened, the stench struck with full force. It wasn't mere decay. Ordure, sweat, sulphurous powders and rancid smelling glues had all contributed. It was enough to make one heave. And another shock: a seemingly inexplicable squawking, scratching and gibbering met us . . . But then we saw, ranged down one side of the room, cages, and cages piled on top of cages, each containing a monkey, or rats, lizards, squirrels and so on. In fact, as we entered, a shadow in one of these cages gave me a start by opening wings and hopping from its perch to a second one further from the bars. I think this bird was an owl, though I can't be sure: there was too much else to look at.

Down the length of the room – which was a generous size by any standard – stood trestle tables, each one loaded with such a clutter of phials, mirrors, basins, wooden cubes and frames, so many charts and scaled-down constructions that the whole jumble both held and alarmed the eye. Held, by profusion: an incredible variety of shapes, colours and combinations, where the strangest objects stood side by side with the most ordinary:

and alarmed by apparent chaos, for the eye searched in vain for order, and the mind shrank from the evidence of an energy that could bring such things together – such a random-seeming collection – and spend itself on a study of them.

My reaction was this: I didn't look for da Vinci. It didn't even occur to me that he was not in the room. I saw him there. And – it seemed to me – he was mad.

But Piero Sassoli reacted differently. He saw at once that the Master was absent, and all the joy and reverence promptly slipped from his face. He gasped out, 'But he isn't here!'

'If you'll follow me.'

The boy moved forwards. Behind us, as by some enchantment, the door shut with a gentle click, a sound so eloquent against the jabbering of the animals, that I heard it. I glanced back, and there, one either side of the door, stood two broad-shouldered young fellows who had an air about them that didn't suggest apprenticeship: they both stood and looked like guards. But what was their task? To keep the caged things – and all manner of secrets – in? Or to keep the sycophants out? I brushed against a table wondering, and a wooden model that was poised on the very edge, wobbled. I saw it. I put out my hand to steady it. I heard Sassoli squeal with horror. The thing teetered and fell with a crunch at my feet. The whole contraption wasn't much larger than a man's arm from wrist to elbow, and not much harm was done, just one shaft snapped and a strap come loose. But what now? Would the heavens collapse? Had I ruined da Vinci's latest marvel? I stood locked in agony. As for the merchant, his eyes burned. 'Jesu Maria!' he gasped. 'You great oaf! You knob-faced idiot!' – his only explicit insult of the kind. It served as a countershock: I rallied. I found I could move . . . but the servant was there before me, deftly scooping the model up and setting it back on the table, all of which he did with such apparent nonchalance, as if the deed were nothing, that I was astonished. And I was the more astonished when he turned to me – this boy, this da Vinci acolyte – and smiled.

'It's happened before,' he said. 'He probably won't even notice.'

Then he propped up the broken shaft so ingeniously that I

myself couldn't have sworn it was damaged.

Piero Sassoli shuddered. A deep, distraught sigh came from him. Then we continued –

Down the room to the end, to an opening, an archway to the left, and into a smaller chamber that was filled with clear northern light. In the very heart of the stench.

The great da Vinci.

And all at once I wanted to laugh. I wanted to stamp, and shout: 'Look at this bowed old man with his stained coat and tangled hair! What in the world's in that? And what, in God's name, are these?' For around him – but at a distance, because the smell was overwhelming – stood the rich few in all their silken finery, their hose smattered with the scum that greased the floor, and each politely wide-eyed, holding to his nose a handkerchief or scented orange while he watched. And at da Vinci's side, on a table not so great as the disc of the average sundial, stood an impossible creature: a lizard, but not a lizard, an insect, but not an insect.

A living, piecemeal creation, and it stank.

It had wings, three pairs attached along its back, transparent and glittering; it had a fleshy horn above its brow that had come from God knows what part of what thing's anatomy; and there were feathers along its tail, and eyes – fish-eyes – shining along its flanks. A monster of borrowings and glue. In the rays of the morning sun, it responded sluggishly to prods from da Vinci's finger, while a voice as cold and firm as a shaft of iron told us: 'I patch these playmates together, thereby to learn why Nature's never made them.'

Appreciative murmurs rose from behind the oranges.

Our guide was nudging Piero Sassoli forward – but I hung back.

Da Vinci.

Now I looked at him again, and found him terrible. His face showed all the power of a pagan god: he was vain – and the poor friar calls *me* vain – his beauty ruined. Since I'd last glimpsed him, or now that I truly saw him, I found his features narrowed by so much scorn and a look so irritable that I could only ask mutely: 'Who *is* this? Can this lunatic be the man who made that drawing of Our Lady with St Anne and Christ, the treasure of the Servite Friars? The loveliest work of devotion in all

Tuscany? And those other works, so warm with compassion? Never. I can't believe it. I never will.'

I longed to turn and run.

Meanwhile, the merchant had gone close enough to be noticed.

'Piero Sassoli from Florence?' Da Vinci's tone was one of quest and expectation, as if something mislaid might at any moment come to hand again. He gazed at this visitor, an eagle over a capon. 'When I heard your name,' he said, 'I desired very much to meet you . . . '

Words beyond belief! Puce with delight, Piero Sassoli grinned, and bobbed his head, and prattled a hundred compliments. He'd ventured up to the table, and was aware, I think, that nobler men than he stood in the outer circle, which made him blink a deal – unless that was an effect of the stench.

Da Vinci let him prattle. He heard the merchant out, stood still and watched him, waiting as one might wait for an ache to pass, while the lizard-thing enjoyed its reprieve, and basked in a sunbeam. At last, when Piero Sassoli had run out of breath, the great man said, 'But are you alone? I think I've heard you seldom travel alone. You have an able companion . . . '

Then he turned his head, and his eyes drank me.

For an instant the merchant was taken aback. There was a silence. But suddenly, almost convulsed with his longing to please, he shrieked out, 'Yes! Gismondo Cavalletti! He's here!'

And I knew. I knew why we'd been admitted. I knew why da Vinci had stared that day in October – if indeed he had stared. It was not at the merchant who'd dined with him, but at me. And afterwards he'd made inquiries: Who was that man with the fine stance and the huge wart? And he'd remembered.

Now da Vinci asked me a question, but I made no sense of it. His eyes still drank me. He came striding across, and the eyes of the rich men turned. They all turned, and feasted. The hand that had lately prodded a freak of a reptile was raised to my face, while a voice that shattered all my powers of resistance asked: 'Permit me?'

His stinking fingers touched my chin, tilted it. He reeked of glue and animals. I thought I'd vomit. Instead, I submitted. My left cheek was raised to the light. I froze internally. I submitted. 'So be it!' I thought. 'Let them look! Let them treat me like an object. What are any of them to me? What am I to them? What's anyone – or anything – to anyone? So be it. So be it.'

I froze into hatred.

And yet – it's disgusting, but da Vinci had a skill of touch one might have dreamed about, with a strength that soothed, and a gentleness –

Somehow my eyes closed. Possibly I swayed. I felt my face being drawn towards his.

When we left, we were honoured by his presence to the door; and in a fit of conscience Piero Sassoli gabbled forth a tale about the model. He even pointed at it and, as he did so, the blood drained from his face. But da Vinci only laughed. Not, I think, to reassure us. Rather it was the laugh of a man who's outwitted Fate by keeping one step ahead.

'It's nothing,' he said. 'I've a better version. One that works!' Then, as though the thought had brightened him: 'It's a machine for sharpening needles. Think of it, Ser Sassoli! Four hundred perfect needles a hundred times an hour. That's forty thousand in the hour, or four hundred and eighty thousand every twelve hours. Think of it. The profit. I've worked it out, and the very least is sixty thousand ducats a year!'

'Sixty thousand ducats!'

All from needles. Piero Sassoli gaped. He was still recovering when we were wished good day, and the Master's door clicked shut.

Needles. Paltry household things. A refinement of needles, and all for profit. And the same mind to peer into my face!

To be scrutinised. My blemish pointed out before those elegant gentlemen. To be viewed so openly –

As a punishment I could understand it, but unprovoked, as a whim –

And then, when he took his hand away and, opening my eyes, I found in his own a kind of triumph as if he'd sucked out knowledge of me through my skin. That was horrible.

But even so, if he'd made some comment, if he'd said,

'Remarkable! A fine countenance, but for the blemish!' or 'Interesting!' or 'Unfortunate!' – or anything, I might have forgiven him. The whole room waited for such a word, Piero Sassoli with his lips apart to swallow it for easy carrying. Everyone waited. And I had the impression that if da Vinci chose to say, 'Here's a face that combines integrity with great misfortune!' or, 'Here's the most devilish mask I ever saw!' – either way, the heads would have wagged, and saint or devil I'd have been.

But he only grunted.

He took from me what he would, and grunted. Afterwards he nodded, first at no one, but a second time specifically at Piero Sassoli, as though to thank him for this display of his chattels. Then he returned to the lizard. He picked it up without ceremony and placed it in a lidless wooden box. This done, he moved to a desk strewn with books and papers, and sitting down, he smiled at one of the gentlemen:

'You were asking just now about the powers of vision. Whether an object such as the sun, which we view from a distance, is seen with the same rapidity . . .'

I didn't listen. I heard just the opening phrases, and saw da Vinci begin to scribble diagrams. His pupils crowded to their lesson. Piero Sassoli stood at the back and looked blank. I believe he saw nothing. This merchant, who empties his purse for gimcracks and baubles – was already replete. Overwhelmed. He stood like a gatepost.

– While I kept away altogether. I turned my back and peered through the window. Next, I gazed at the wall. I pushed with my toe at some pomegranate skin on the floor. I studied the stains on the ceiling. I discharged some spittle. By every method I knew I showed that the Master's talk meant nothing to me, and none of this brilliant assembly was to my taste. I despised them all.

And still da Vinci talked of heavenly bodies and waves of light. And still Piero Sassoli stood uncomprehending, staring at him. To me, da Vinci was no longer visible – his listeners had mobbed him – but his voice droned on . . .

I strolled to the circular table. I looked down at the lizard in its box: a rank, trapped thing. The fit was tight – no doubt by design. An experiment. For the box was long but had no breadth, so the creature could move, if it wished, either forward or back, but turn round – never.

Not that this seemed important: it showed no desire to move at all.

It crouched there motionless. Smelling foully. Revolting in the way that some things are which nevertheless compel one to touch them. I stroked its head, just behind its horn, and then rubbed its back as far as the first pair of wings. Cold. Rigid. I drew back quickly, and found a smirch of paint on my hand. Green. Even its colour was borrowed.

And never a movement – though the skin round its eye, I thought, strained to crease.

Paint and glue had sealed this monster in.

I touched it again – on its throat – and squeezed. Then wandered back to the window, leaving da Vinci's 'playmate' much as I'd found it. Stiffening. In its box.

I squinted out at Rome, and counted rooftops – until, finally, a miracle: while the gentlemen passed round diagrams, or pored over sketches which da Vinci had laid on his desk, the Master approached Sassoli, and offered to walk with him to the door!

Of course, we were out of place. Also it gave him a chance to view my blotch again. Some such reasons. But the merchant was overcome by so much attention, and saw no hint of dismissal, only the honour. So we went, Piero Sassoli and I, back through the rooms with da Vinci. And we might have walked all three together, but to keep those eyes from consuming me, I took up position behind, from where I saw da Vinci raise his hand, as if to set it on the merchant, and hurry him along. But he lowered it again almost at once. I observed a piece of vermilion thread in the great man's hair, and that his coat hung from his shoulders not in the manner of cloth, but like a slack skin. I flung my hatred at his back.

Still, I'd tried to settle the score: I'd dispatched his lizard. So – if only there'd been no talk of needles! Models and needles! I might have forgiven him. Not then, but later. All the clutter of objects we passed, the worthless and priceless heaped together – remembering those when I was calmer, I might have been able to say, 'Da Vinci? Yes, I met him. But only when he was in his dotage.'

And I'd have forgiven.

I believe I still hoped to. Despite my anger, as we walked to the door, I watched for a sign. For in honouring one who's acknowledged to be great by the finest men and mightiest kings – there lies some comfort, and I was loathe to lose it. I hardly knew if I could afford the loss. Before we reached the door, I believe I longed to hear him speak some noble sentiment that might redeem him. But Piero Sassoli destroyed that hope, blabbing about the model I'd damaged – which set da Vinci counting in thousands of needles.

Needles and ducats. Calculations for gain. Thoughts no loftier than the talk of thc warehouse. And this man dared to scrutinise *me*.

I'll never soften.

Not towards da Vinci. Nor towards those ogling, long-faced worshippers, those would-be connoisseurs, so ready with their nods and agreements, whatever the judgment. Even towards Piero Sassoli I felt such hatred that morning that for the rest of the day I could barely bring myself to speak to him, which he failed to notice: he was much too excited. And sometimes, still, when I remember, I hate the merchant. I hate everyone.

Save one. And sometimes, I think, even her. For what does Lucia da Fano give me but pain? Isn't she just another who stares, and turns away with no comment?

Madonna.

All this evil from one visit.

Two nights this account has taken me and now it's done I feel no better. If anything, I'm worse. The candle flickers. My breath comes and goes like a whipped cur's, and I feel sick.

It comes to this. Where it's least looked for lies the greatest cruelty. Gabriello, for all his spite these many years, has harmed me no more than da Vinci did in the space of an hour.

XV

BOUNTY at this cold season:

Worth 8 florins, 30 soldi: 10 braccia of pale blue cloth for the slave called Oronetta, who lives on Piero Sassoli's farm.

Worth 4 florins, 2 soldi: 2 sheepskin linings; one for Sandra at the farm, and one for Bartola, our cook in Florence.

Worth 1 florin: a jerkin for the man Tommaso, who works the farm.

Worth 15 soldi: a pair of spectacles for the same, so he may learn to read his instructions.

Worth 2 florins: scarlet hose for Bruno our stablehand, who asked for them, and for the new man Filippo, who will tend the garden here, and help on the farm in certain months.

Worth 50 soldi: a cap for our potboy.

Worth 1 florin, 6 soldi: 5 braccia of unbleached woollen cloth, which Anna the maid requested, to do with as she will.

Worth 3 florins, 40 soldi: a grey hood for Gismondo Cavalletti.

Worth 5 florins: gloves made of kid for the same.

And so Christ, when He's born again, shall find us warm enough in the Sassoli household.

Oh, Piero Sassoli's most considerate. Magnanimous. This list he gave me today – as I read it, he beamed, and said, 'Yes, Gismo, hood *and* gloves. I insist you accept them both!' – by which I see I'm valued at ten soldi more than Oronetta, his slave.

I'm surely cherished.

And not solely for my usefulness. Oronetta for her beauty, and I – since Rome last spring – perhaps for having none.

For after our visit to da Vinci, I recall the merchant said, 'To think, Gismo, he remembered you! Not as well as myself, of course, but all the same! Even a wart has its merits!'

And I saw that my blotch had become a Sassoli asset. I don't doubt that it gives him pleasure, when he sups with friends, to cry out over the wine:

'I was never more surprised in my life! You know my Gismo, who keeps the accounts? That big knob on his face? Well, da Vinci was fascinated by it! He has an eye for peculiarities, and though I say it myself, there was never a face like Gismo's!'

Which is gross exaggeration.

My blotch is not unique. Everywhere there are worse, especially in Rome. So why should I have provoked such interest? Does da Vinci collect us? Are we to have a treatise on growths?

Or for one of his works of art, was he in search of a countenance? An apostle, perhaps?

A thief?

Judas?

How Gabriello would relish that! To make me Judas! Precisely his own endeavour, by taunts and threats. And I, half stupefied by them –

XVI

ONE morning as we walked from Mass – it was November in the year the Spaniards ravaged Prato, and Piero Sassoli's brother-in-law had come, his house in ruins, half his property gone, to recover his nerves with us – as we walked from Mass, this brother-in-law and Piero Sassoli took the lead, while Gabriello and I followed together. An almost unheard-of arrangement. Gabriello's being with us at all was rare and wonderful. He detests 'a family promenade' as he calls it, but greatly respects his uncle – or so he claims – and in this visitor's honour had agreed to keep us company.

But instead of smirking and dancing about at his uncle's elbow, as I'd expected, he'd placed himself at my side, and – more extraordinary still – he drew me back, actually laying a hand on my arm. Thus he delayed me, while the older men walked on.

Then his voice rose, gently, like a suitor's.

'You've been avoiding me, Gissy. What's the matter? Ever since our uncle Jacopo came – '

How beautifully he used that phrase: 'our uncle'!

I said, 'No more than usual.'

'Oh, really, Gissy, I think so.' He favoured me with his smile. 'Are you troubled?' he asked. 'Something you've heard our uncle say?'

'What do you mean?'

I stared at the brooch on his hat: a costly piece in gold, with liquid-seeming pearls that hung and swayed as he moved, like drops of venom.

'What do you mean?' I said.

'Oh, come!' More smiles. His voice sank to a whisper. 'You must have heard his comment on the changed appearance of – his brother-in-law!'

Not even for this teasing whim of fraternity could Gabriello share his father with me, and so it was 'uncle Jacopo's brother-in-law', which made his words vague. No matter. I was in any case all bewilderment.

'I know nothing of these comments.'

Gabriello sighed.

'Gissy . . . of course you have no liking for me, and this conversation isn't welcome – but can you deny it? Our uncle, who hasn't seen him for five months or more, is pained and concerned by the change. I've heard him say it. Whereas we, who see him every day, have been blind. But now my eyes are open. I admit, I'm worried. I can see he's aged. He's lost agility. And I've no mind to receive my inheritance yet . . . Whatever *you* may think, I'm as loving a son as any . . . '

These were his words, or very like.

So. It was certain. He spoke of Piero Sassoli – and of mortality.

In my shock, I could think of nothing to say. We crossed the street. We entered the Via dei Servi, where the good Jacopo looked back with an indulgent nod for his nephew, and Gabriello called out that he should note the recent improvements to some gate or other. All this, before I could think of an answer.

For it was true, and I hadn't been blind. In a year of wars, with alarms and havoc in Tuscany, governments falling and unrest in Florence, Piero Sassoli had lost much of his vigour. He'd grown more paunchy and more winded. His lips already displayed at times that shade of violet which now rests on them permanently. He had, in short, aged. But I'd explained all this to my satisfaction by considering the increase in his anxieties, and I'd assured myself that with quieter times, he'd soon recover. He was only tired.

But Gabriello was hinting at some deeper illness. And indeed, he was ready to do more than that. For when at last I said, 'He has changed, certainly,' – this fond son whispered, 'Well, there you are! Even you can see it! He won't live till the Second Coming.'

And with this reflection, he nodded briskly at his father's back.

I quickened my pace. I tried to set a gap between us. A bleakness fell on me.

True. Piero Sassoli wouldn't live till the Second Coming – but for how long? It was a question that I always shrank from, and Gabriello had discovered it. He smiled as he walked, taking pleasure in my silence and his own performance. A fine, sensitive face he had, as one who's shared a sad but beautiful confidence. And as we walked, from inside a courtyard somewhere there came the yapping of a dog – by the sound of it, one of those pampered lapdogs that live on dainties, and draw fleas from the women's skirts.

I paid great attention to this yapping, and wished Gabriello an early grave.

Then, as we passed the Chigi gates, he broke in on my reverie, softly, casually, as though what he said followed with obvious logic on all that had gone before, or as though I'd missed several links in the conversation:

'But this needn't trouble you much. I suppose your future's secure . . . Your purse must have a noble lining by now . . . '

'What?' Oh, I'd heard. I stopped; he smiled at me sweetly.

'You can't think . . .' I began, but he had no intention of hearing me. With a shake of his head, as much as to say, 'Don't waste your breath!' he was gone, shouting out to uncle Jacopo.

Oh, it was expertly done. He'd sown a seed of evil in my mind, and he sprinted off before any more talk could rake it out again.

The seed lay. It germinated. And produced – thorns.

Was he, being a scoundrel, judging me by a scoundrel's standards? Did he truly take me for a thief? And what could he mean to do about it?

I suffered. Sleep deserted me. Anger, disbelief and apprehension pierced through every argument by which I tried to calm myself. I looked at all hours for my accuser, but Gabriello eluded me for days. It was almost a week before I found him, and then it was by accident as he was coming from the stables.

I seized my opportunity. I stood in his path, and said boldly, 'It's imperative I speak with you!' – which he couldn't choose to ignore, because the stablehand was with him, and before the servants he takes some pains to maintain a show of civility.

But my greeting was far from his liking, I saw that. He gave me a look of surprise, dismissed Bruno, and said, 'Well?'

'When we spoke, about your father's health . . .'

At that, a false merriment broke out in him, and he started to walk again.

'Oh, that!' he said. 'What about it? I hope you haven't been wittering? If you tell a man how sick he looks – it doesn't help. That's bad physic. I'd leave well alone if I were you . . . Now I must go. There's Andreuccio waiting!'

And sure enough, one of his smiling, idiot friends had appeared, and was coming towards us from the house.

This encounter incensed me; but it was nothing to the one which followed.

Later that same day I saw him in the street, and perceiving he was alone, I ran to catch up with him. I snatched hold of his sleeve:

'Gabriello, listen! That conversation on our way from Mass . . .'

He was the very image of astonishment. He jerked his sleeve free.

'Gissy!' he cried. 'What's wrong with you? You can't go

around – jumping on people! Well, what about it? What is it now?'

'On our way from Mass, you made certain allegations . . . '

'I did?' His eyebrows rose. 'My dear Gissy,' he said, 'you're supposed to be such a clever fellow. Can't a man have a joke?'

But I wasn't to be fooled so easily. I hurried along beside him, and spoke in his ear, quickly, clearly, for now he looked straight ahead with a set smile.

'Do you deny you implied I'm a thief? And that after your father dies, you think I'll make off with Sassoli funds? That I've been . . . hoarding? I suppose you'll use this as a sop to your conscience. You'll say I'm dishonest, and cast me off without so much as a . . . '

'Cast you off?' He savoured the phrase. He stopped, and twisted round with a shout of laughter. 'I'm hurt!' he declared. 'What an opinion you have of me! Cast you off? Aren't you my brother? I'm sure I'll find you some niche – if you want it! As for lining your purse . . . Really, you're the most pompous ass! Either you've looked out for yourself, or you haven't. And one way you're a rogue, and by rights I should see you hang for it, and the other way you're a fool, who can't be worth employing! Now I'll be late if you start a sermon . . . Try not to be so tedious!'

I let him go. I saw how it flourished, this evil; I could never hope to root it out by blustering in the street.

Nothing has rooted it out. A small joke here, a comment there – he tends it well.

So, what to do?

Shall I stay honest? To be cunningly shown in the end for a thief, and cast off destitute? Or shall I let myself be provoked to a scoundrel's standards – and start thieving?

Which course, if I took it, would give him greater pleasure?

What's to happen?

It'll be late to start again as errand boy to another merchant.

I've always supposed that Piero Sassoli will make some provision for me. It's natural to think so. But he never hints at anything. And how simply he could, if he wished!

'By the by . . . about your future, Gismo. You can sleep with an easy mind at night. I've seen to that!'

But – nothing. Ever. And he's wilfully blind to Gabriello's malice. He may leave me not funds, but some appointment. He may name me as agent for Avignon, or some other far-flung office, which his son will find reason to close within a year.

Or – most fearful of all: may he not simply commend me 'to Gabriello's love'?

I should speak with him.

Up, smartly, Gismondo, and crow to the merchant, 'Sir, when you come to die, I beg you to leave me better off than you found me . . . '

Oh, first rate! This is most in keeping with my character!

But to filch, to cheat –

I pity genteel thieves. All those men of education who're dishonest. I pity them, though I know they make a strong majority. A man who has enough – and more than enough – in the way of skills or charm or scholarship, and yet he feels his fingers itch for some trifle of his neighbour's – he's a contemptible wretch. He's turned inside out, and has less substance than his shadow. Everything he says, regardless of the sentiment, which might be wise or amiable – is nothing. Cicero's words in the mouth of such a man are so much stale air. For he's a hypocrite. And this can be readily put to the test by taking some of his own possessions from him – and seeing how he likes it.

And I pity those who're not genteel, but able. The quick-witted and fit. Those still young enough to learn and apply themselves to a decent trade, but who choose instead the lives of tricksters. Who throw away their assets from a mistaken fancy that they'll stay young and sharper than their fellows for ever. I pity them their delusions.

Only the truly destitute, all those poor who can boast of nothing that passes for skill, and of little understanding – wretches crazed with the fear of starving, who pluck a loaf from the market place – only those I've never pitied. I see no need, for they at least are honestly what they are, and that's their substance; they are what they are from necessity. And if, in the end, such people hang, or have an arm lopped off – I see no tragedy in it. Such thieves are little more than beggars, an inevitable ill in the world, a pest, and every day they live is a bonus to them. Besides, in as much as these thieves break no man's trust – for who would trust them? – I think they spend less time in Hell.

Now, where in this survey of villains would I stand?

Am I not educated? Skilled? Noble in sentiment?

Despite the farmyard – a gentleman?

And I care nothing how widespread the practice is, nor how politely it's done, a gentleman who steals – haven't I said of all men he's the most abject? He loses all his worth.

And this, I think, Gabriello wishes for me.

Well, but surely it's laughable!

How could I waver and lose myself in his strategy, or even fear it? Considerable trials have proved me honest; actions that go beyond any common dutifulness. And shall I think them insignificant? Ordeals, by which the merchant's trust in me is more than justified.

XVII

THE first – I was not yet seventeen – when the French king came to Florence. No blood was shed, but none the less he came as conqueror, we all knew that. Pisa had fallen, and here he was, a scourge for our sins – just as the holy men had promised us.

He entered through the Porta San Freliano, magnificent in cloth of gold, mounted on a giant, brutish warhorse, and bearing a lance so we should know that cheer as loud as we might, and smile at him till our jaws ached, still he came as victor. Charles of France. Reaching over the Alps to snatch at Naples, and we, because we lay in his path, were forfeit.

His army choked our streets. Thousands of Swiss and Gascon infantry, Breton archers and thickset men from the North came marching into the heart of the city. They had wary, unloving faces, even those who grinned, and they were all sharp-eyed, watching – so it seemed to us – for some pre-arranged signal on which they'd break from their lines and rip our throats. Women locked themselves in their rooms. From their windows, citizens stared at these surly, well-armed travellers, and quaked for their books and vases. Old men on the balconies cried, 'Viva Francia!' while tears streamed down their cheeks.

Florence had fallen.

No one forgets such a day; but in my memory, the night before can rival it.

Piero Sassoli panicked. He'd already sent vast sums of money out of the city with old Rigogli's son, but there still remained his personal treasures; and these, or the most valuable, I thought he'd hidden in the garden. How I came to think this I forget – perhaps the merchant made some comment: I thought he'd buried certain precious objects deep among the lilac beds, but if he had, he couldn't trust himself – I mean, not to tell where they were if his life was threatened – and they must have been dug up again. He took a sweat for these treasures. Not for his models and inventions – he simply locked all those in the cellar – but for his jewels: rings and brooches, gold medallions, and a belt with flowers of pearls and emeralds that had belonged to Monna Margherita. These, together with some forks in which he takes a monstrous pride, he gathered back from their hiding places, if, in fact, he'd hidden them, and laid in a small iron chest. Then he scribbled out an inventory, and the chest was locked.

All this he did in the depths of the night.

Before dawn, he was standing over my bed, whispering, 'Get up, Gismo. Quickly!'

He held a candle barely a nose-length from my face, and bent low to peer at me, so that when I awoke and heard him say these words, all I could see was the flame which quivered as he breathed, and in the broken shadows beyond it, his great cheeks hanging in flaps from his skull, and his eyes bulging, the whites showing yellow; a sight so sinister and unexpected that I lay motionless with my mouth open.

He began to shake me by the shoulder.

'Quick!' he whispered. 'Get up and come to my room! Be as quiet as you can!'

Then he hurried out, taking the candle with him.

I dressed in the dark, stumbling over a shoe, groping for my jerkin. I remember I hit my hand on the bedpost, and as the pain flowed round my wrist, a sudden joy flared up in me. Piero Sassoli had taken such scant note of my existence for so many months, that this visit in the night, singling me out for something secret and urgent, felt like a wonderful compliment.

I made all haste to his room. There I found him seated on a stool he used to keep by the window for his infant son to clamber on and peep out at the roofs. He sat with a paper in his hand at which he frowned and muttered, and by his feet stood the candle, and an iron chest which I couldn't recall having seen before. It was two hands deep, but scarcely the length of a forearm, and it looked strong enough to withstand the cruellest axe. It was secured with a truly formidable lock. Not a chest to hold linen, or velvet coats, but one that spoke with silent emphasis of momentous contents.

I stood uncertain in the doorway, and Piero Sassoli, when he looked up at last and saw me eyeing the chest, flapped his paper.

'I have it all here!' he said. 'You want to know what's in it? Read! Read!' – and the paper stirred in the draught from the open shutters as he passed it to me. I held it close to the candle and read with care, committing what I could to memory – a wisdom I'd already learned since the merchant often loses papers – and while I read, Piero Sassoli explained: 'Heirlooms, Gismo. Household treasures. We can't let the French just take their pick. We must all look after our own!'

'I suppose not, sir. Yes. I see.'

'Certainly not!' He squirmed on his stool in agitation – then suddenly grew still, and I was pleased to find him studying me with lively interest. 'What you have to do . . . ' he said, ' . . . there's not a moment to lose . . . ' He twisted to the window, and glared out at the sky, which was as yet untroubled, I thought, by any trace of daylight. But the merchant evidently thought otherwise. He got up abruptly, lifted the chest without more ado, and thrust it into my arms.

'Off you go!' he panted. 'Go somewhere and bury this! Don't tell me where . . . See that no one's watching, and mark the spot. Do it quickly!'

Then he snatched back the inventory which despite the chest I still held crumpled in my fist, and led the way downstairs.

He unbolted the door and the courtyard gate himself.

I was pushed out into the night with Piero Sassoli's treasures.

That chest weighed heavily; and soon I found I held it at an uncomfortable angle, but I didn't dare set it down and re-arrange matters: once outside, I could sense the approach of dawn. So I scurried along, keeping – wherever possible – to the humbler, silent streets, and to the middle of those streets, for fear of robbers lurking in doorways, and I made for a place behind the Piazza Santa Maria Novella.

My good fortune, that I knew of a place at all.

For five days or more – ever since it was certain that the French would come to Florence – I'd been thinking of possible hiding places. Not to hide things of my own, but in the hope – a faint one – that if Piero Sassoli happened to say, 'Now, where could a man conceal valuables?' I might dazzle him with my ingenuity.

But he hadn't asked.

Nevertheless, I was carrying his jewels to my chosen hiding place.

It was a burnt-out house. A property destroyed in a blaze the previous summer. And I knew, because it was common knowledge, that the owner had gone to Rome, where he hoped to earn all the more quickly the sum he needed for rebuilding.

The house he'd left behind I thought an excellent place. So fierce had been the fire that nothing remained except blackened stones and a few charred fragments, long since raked over by the inquisitive and needy; and as this rubble afforded no shelter from the sky, it was no longer of interest to anyone.

So there I hid the chest. My fingers in the slime and weeds, I cleared away stones, piling them till I'd made a pit. In the pit I laid the chest. Then I piled the stones back again. My hands bled and my heart pounded. Every shadow seemed to creep, a man with a knife. It was desperate, dangerous work – but I gloried in it. That the merchant should show this trust in me! Heirlooms, he'd said. He'd stressed 'heirlooms'. 'We must all look to our own,' he'd said – as much as to say they concerned me too, these things of his family. Why, I thought, he'd as good as called me his son.

And while I broke the skin on my knuckles and strained my back piling stones, I forgave Piero Sassoli all his recent neglect of me.

I hid his precious objects.

Afterwards, as I ran back eager to tell him the chest was safe, morning dawned; a grey light stole along beside me, returning features to the houses; and then I enjoyed a most inappropriate sensation, considering a conqueror stood at the gates: happiness. I felt that this city, to which I'd come in the clothes of a farmboy and clutching the back of a stranger's coat, had finally accepted me. All the people who rose in Florence that morning, I felt they belonged to a single family, and I with them. Together we'd face the French, or whatever came! We were one. And every stone in the buildings I passed seemed familiar to me. I knew them all. I ran exulting through the streets, and the city held me with a kind of tenderness, as a child might hold an insect on her hand.

The French stayed twelve days. Then they marched south.

When they'd gone, I went by night to retrieve the chest. I carried it back to Piero Sassoli in an ecstasy of relief – for those days had tortured me. The more I'd seen of the sly, experienced mercenaries who roamed the streets, the less faith I'd had in my hiding place, until gradually I'd put together a picture of returning for the chest only to find the pit empty – a picture so horrible, that on the evening of the eleventh day, I'd begged the merchant to let me go at once, and fetch his treasure. But the idea had shocked him. While the French remained in Florence, he wouldn't hear of such folly. Then he'd laughed, and patted my arm, saying he had 'complete and perfect confidence' in the place I'd chosen. And it's true that throughout the time the enemy held the city, he behaved as if no fear for his valuables ever darkened his thoughts. In contrast to other men, he wore a placid countenance – a fact which I believed with trembling was entirely due to his trust in me.

But now, I sometimes think otherwise.

I remember his face that morning when I came back and said the chest was hidden.

'*Well* hidden?' he asked.

'I think so. Yes.'

'You think so?'

'Well hidden. Yes. It is.'

'And no one saw you?'

'No.'

'You're sure of that?'

'Yes.'

His face relaxed, or rather, it opened into a bland smile that was curiously unpleasing. As though his treasures no longer concerned him. They had become the charge of another. And if they were lost – why, then he'd do what he must, and punish me for a gross deceiver. What more could be asked of an honest man?

Convenient thoughts, in which he'd taken refuge.

I suppose I saw little of that at the time. I only observed a something too easy in his smile, and thought him light-headed because he'd been up all night.

But twelve days later, when I returned the chest and discovered I needn't have hoped for thanks – I remember that grieved me bitterly. The merchant's eyes glowed to see his treasures again. He asked where they'd been. I told him, and he rubbed his hands. He laughed. He remarked that I could be shrewd enough when I wanted – but that was all. I stood before him waiting for greater tribute. My faithfulness, my courage – since the risks had been real – I thought they deserved some richer praise. 'Well done, Gismo. Bravely done. Loyally done!' The words rang in my head, so fervently I longed to hear them – but already he'd fitted the key to the lock and was pushing back the lid. There was no more time for compliments. It was, 'Leave me . . . Off you go! I want to renew acquaintance . . . Look, the lid's all scratched! . . . Now, let's see . . . '

I left him rummaging.

I heard no more about it.

No reward. Not so much as a florin.

And I nursed a grudge for the rest of the day.

– But how we work to convince ourselves that virtue is rewarded! By the next afternoon, I'd made up my mind that all was as it should be. For if he'd seen nothing remarkable in my services, didn't that prove Piero Sassoli thought of me as a son?

I arranged with myself to think so.

I strangled my resentment, and seven years passed before the merchant set me such a test again.

When he did, it was a greater test, as I discovered, because my resentment was all the greater.

That was when Cesare Borgia brought his men into Tuscany. Bastard upstart. He came with a mind to seize whatever he could, even the wealth of Florence, and tales of his greed came running before him like beasts before a forest fire.

I was sent with gold to Venice.

It was a hazardous enterprise.

Quite apart from the Borgia rabble, every other lawless man was out, encouraged by the example, and either robbed as he liked on his own, or joined with others in a band; and these lesser villains terrorised the countryside. In fact, how to ride from one town to another without loss of goods or life had become a puzzling business, for which reason, I was to carry the gold in two great flasks topped with wine; and if anyone eyed these conspicuous objects, then begged me to favour him with a drink, I was to ignore him, and ride on. But if he persisted, I was to show my knife. These were my instructions. And Piero Sassoli made it plain that he saw no reason why I should scruple to draw blood on the slightest suspicion.

'Take no nonsense!' he told me. 'Not from anyone!'

It was, as I say, a hazardous enterprise.

A boy from the warehouse was to have kept me company, but he fell strangely sick on the day. This, Piero Sassoli saw as a hint from Providence that solitary travellers draw less attention to themselves – and so I made my own best speed to Venice.

A six days' journey I made in five.

I avoided people as much as I could. At the inns where I stopped, I pretended to have a speech defect which discouraged conversation, and in the presence of anyone I drank only the tainted wine from the flasks. And I stayed at no inn at night, but instead I rode, except for the darkest hours when I'd perch in a tree or crouch in a ditch with my knife in my hand, and watch, and listen. Four long, evil nights. And during the day, while I travelled, I scanned every bush for a cut-throat lurking behind it, every farm for a band of thieves hidden behind a wall, so that day or night, riding or not, I was in such a frenzy of vigilance that I should have had no time for thoughts.

And yet thoughts came.

It wasn't that I said to myself: 'Now Gabriello's almost grown, and a fine time I'll have of it once he reaches manhood! But here's my chance to escape with a fortune . . . '

That temptation never crossed my mind. But questions came, which I'd have willingly done without:

'If I'm attacked and killed, will Piero Sassoli weep for me?'

and:

'If I don't return and his money's lost, will he know it's because I'm dead? Stabbed, or cudgelled, lying by the road? Or will he think I've made off with his gold, and curse me?'

and:

'Why does he risk my life for a heap of coins we might just as well have buried in the garden? Can this metal mean more to him than I do?'

These were the issues. They came at me from the shadows, and from all those small events well-known to the traveller: two peasants walking towards me, a cockerel crowing in a farmyard, the bark of a dog in the undergrowth. At each of these details, my spirit shrank. The questions in me soared, even as my terror soared – and couldn't be suppressed.

The road to Venice is one I've hated ever since.

On the way back, to keep my resentment curbed, I sang for much of the time. Every song I knew, then the ones I half knew, and when I'd finished I started all over, until, on the fifth day, fortune decided to pity me and I overtook a priest. He was a thin, very nervous man on a slow, fat mule, who was making his way to Prato. Twisting his head round, he watched my approach with horror. Then the moment I reached him, he squealed, 'If it's money you want, I haven't any!'

I'd meant to ride past, but at this cry I spoke to assure him he had nothing to fear from me and, in his despair, he instantly believed it. He begged me to ride with him. He said there was a cruel-looking rascal who'd somehow contrived to pass him twice, both times coming from the other direction, and who even now was probably following, or else waiting on the road ahead . . .

So I agreed to keep to the poor man's side. No longer encumbered with gold, I was glad of any distraction – even a priest – and I asked him to shorten our miles with a few good precepts. He readily obliged. Out came a series of sermons which he must have had by heart, so rapidly he delivered them, and without a falter. They weren't entirely ridiculous. They held passages of sense which kept me from my own thoughts – and so I came back safely.

I gave Piero Sassoli the banker's receipt for his gold, and took particular pains not to expect any thanks. But this time,-perversely, thanks there were.

He seized my hand, and breathed a flavour of mint in my face:

'What a load off my mind!' he gasped. 'I thank you, Gismo. Truly, I thank you!'

There was even reward of sorts. Within a month he'd given me charge of the household accounts.

And so I passed that second test.

Then, two years ago, when the Spaniards came, ransacking towns as close as Prato – wasn't that a third test? Again, the belts, the forks, the medallions – who dug a hole one night in a corner of the stables, and buried them?

Not Gabriello, but I.

There they lay till the scare had passed, deep in Sassoli soil – though the merchant thought them safely out of his keeping: I suppose I deceived him in that. 'Do as you did that other time!' he'd said – but another dangerous escapade to save some trifles didn't appeal: at the thought, a wall rose in my mind. I could see neither round it nor over it, so I remained on the inner side, and there I took what measures I could. Burying the things in the stables.

'Do as you did that other time' was not, after all, specific.

Therefore I credit myself – I passed this test, too.

Always honest. And not proved so by these tests alone, but by my everyday practice, despite numerous slights and provocations –

I covet nothing of any man's.

And shall Gabriello – 'our fun-loving Gabby' as the merchant calls him – take that from me? Without it, could I live?

Oh, like the Serpent, our 'Gabby's' insights are far superior to his character! Make me a thief, and he knows that although I stole half his inheritance, and nothing could ever be proved – he would still have destroyed me!

But haven't I said it's laughable?

Then why do I fear it?

XVIII

THE birth of Christ.

At Mass, Madonna, wearing her cross of rubies. She stopped to speak with Piero Sassoli, thanking him for a gift of oranges. Her voice is unlike other women's. It's stronger, in some way cleaner, and yet it's quiet.

While she talked, I busied myself with my gloves – these kid-leather frivolities which the merchant insisted on my acquiring – and I took such care as I drew them on that no one could say I'd gaped at her – nor that she had ignored me. But before she turned to leave, I had to look, for courtesy's sake, and I bowed. In terror. Hating myself. How childish, to think my greeting a thing of so much consequence! The moment I straightened up, I'd find her gone –

She was still there, watching.

She even acknowledged me. A nod. And then I saw her lips move, as if she meant to burst out laughing. She didn't. She walked away, and I praised God for it. I suffered enough. She'd noticed me.

Gabriello went hurrying after her. He said he'd forgotten to give her a message from someone or other – but I think it was jealousy. He desired me to know my place. He walked with her to the door, then vanished, and neither Piero Sassoli nor I saw him again until he came this evening to Ser Romoli's house.

There we supped, father, son and I – all three of us guests together.

A simpleton, a glutton, Lodovico Romoli must rank as one of the best-liked men in Florence. He's tender towards his mindless, gossip wife. He beams with indulgent love on his freckled daughters. His servants are plump and cheery. In fact, nothing could be more extraordinary than to hear him with these servants. He makes very free with his jokes, and even the lowest of his maids will answer him back with a quip or a smart innuendo. I've no doubt they filch from him monstrously, but it's easy to see that they're fond of him. Their master is their boast. They smile at his guests as much as to say, 'Isn't he unusual?' and steal from him though they might, I believe they'd die to save him from the world besides. This jars with my notions on trust, but Ser Romoli evidently prospers, great fool that he is.

We had handsome fare. The roast pike stuffed with raisins and a pudding of rice and almonds were exceptionally good.

I sat with the tutor they have for the girls. A foolish, melancholic man much given to quoting in Latin, and suddenly laughing aloud at thoughts which he doesn't trouble to share. He told me he was homesick for Siena; and twice he drank out of my cup by mistake.

Thus we paid our dues to Christ's Nativity.

Piero Sassoli's pleased, I think, with my gift of a curio – a giant bird's egg from Africa. He says he intends to have it mounted, and that he'll design the base himself. Tonight, when we came home, he called me into his room, and pressed on me a book – the first he's ever given me. It's written by one Bartolomeo Sacchi, and entitled: *On Honest Recreation*.

From Gabriello, dice. Weighted dice. He rolled them on to my dish in front of all the Romoli family.

'May they improve your luck for you, Gissy!'

I politely thanked him. 'But', I said, 'I never gamble.'

At that he sniggered. He appeared to take it for a joke.

He pretends not to notice the fact that this year I've given him nothing.

Madonna –

A buffoon, does she think me? This morning when I bowed to her – was she about to laugh? Or is it possible, she might have smiled? And did Gabriello think so?

But this isn't a subject for speculation. Laugh or smile – neither occurred, because she behaved as she wished. She walked away.

As for the dice, I'll give them to our potboy. Then, when Gabriello next teases him into risking his soldi on a throw – '*His* soldi against *my* florin, Gissy! I ask you, isn't that fair?' – it will be. Just for once.

XIX

GABRIELLO –

'Pompous' he calls me, and 'tedious' – jibes not worth their space on the air – but he isn't alone in this. Piero Sassoli thinks the same. He often implies that I lack merriment.

I can hardly deny it to either of them since they both make jokes at my expense – and who would laugh while a blade twists in his side?

There's also Rigogli –

When he starts on one of his tales stuffed with cheap suggestions, he tells it with so many pauses and senile simperings that it pains me to listen. Then sometimes I shout in his face, 'Excuse me! You must tell me later!' and I leave him with his mouth wide open, his whiskers trembling. He can't comprehend it. He takes great pride in his nonsense – stories Piero Sassoli loves to hear, so why not I? Even the errand boys grin. Only Rassuccio fails to smile – he copies his letters – and I, to whom the nods and winks in these tales act as an irritant. But how could I explain? Am I to tell him, 'Rigogli, I mean no offence, but these bedroom tales of yours disgust me'?

Surely I do him a kindness by simply hurrying away.

So there's another who considers me deficient.

And even Fra Bernardino –

I remember once we were walking in the cloister garden. I forget our discussion, but I know it concerned myself, and was a matter of some importance. I'd asked for advice, and was listening intently to the old man's reply. While we walked, he spoke gravely, apparently weighing each word before he delivered it – but then all at once, gaping across the gravel paths and flowerbeds, Fra Bernardino broke out giggling. He squeezed my arm. 'Look!' he whispered. 'Over there! Look at Fra Giuseppe! What a mess he's made!' So I looked, and saw, on the other side of the garden, a young friar who was tending the plants. And in his eagerness to trim a misshapen bush into the size and likeness of its fellows, he'd reduced it almost to nothing. A wreckage of foliage lay at his feet, and now he stood over the stump of the bush with an air of helpless despondency.

Well, I smiled. I thought the sight had some slight bearing on our discussion, whatever that was, and because of the relevance, it was worth a smile . . .

But Fra Bernardino appeared to have lost our talk altogether. Instead of continuing it, as I'd expected, he began to prattle, 'The young pup's learned a lesson! So confident! Boasting he knew all about gardens! "Just wait till you see how I make things grow!" He said nothing of snipping our trees to pieces . . . Well, now he'll have to start on the others, to hide his mistake . . .'

And more of the like. None of which had any significance.

So I grew angry.

Was I at fault? To stop short, to make jokes and relish this trivial amusement while I was consulting him on a serious issue

– where lies the virtue in that? I found nothing but insult. But thinking I'd be uncouth to say so, I made my feelings plain only by the look on my face, so that when the old man glanced at me to be sure I enjoyed his facetiousness, he saw I did not. And the giggling stopped. He looked offended. Then he clicked his tongue, and assumed a most pitying expression.

'My son!' he cried. 'This is more of your vanity! Are we never to smile again, because you have your cross to bear?'

Which was, I think, an unjust thing to say.

It's not true I lack mirth. When the time is right, if I'm not the victim, I can laugh as well as another. But almost always I choose to laugh in silence, either because I see a joke where no one else has seen it, or often because, when everyone round me bellows with laughter, they look such a sorry sight with their watering eyes and sagging chins, that I've no wish to add to their number. In this I know I'm fastidious – and glad of it. It's easy enough to laugh with the crowd, and then repent at leisure.

That birthday supper Piero Sassoli held some three or four years ago – there's my example.

The meal was finished, but still we sat round the table. Compliments flew. The wine, the lamb, the pie of dates and chickens – all had been 'food for the gods'. As for the fish: 'The Pope's own cook couldn't have surpassed it.' This and other fulsome praise fluttered about over the cups, and from where he sat, Piero Sassoli would snatch at it as it passed, netting it in smiles.

An unusually successful occasion.

Gabriello was civil to everyone. I myself was in excellent spirits. I sat by a youth so scarred with smallpox that I knew at a glance he was even less beautiful than I am, and this lent me encouragement.

The evening progressed pleasantly.

From the head of the table, Piero Sassoli shone down on everyone. From the staircase, a group of hired musicians piped away without offence. And once the main business of eating had ended, there were two wide trays stacked with sweetmeats from every part of Tuscany – which caused the sort of excitement Piero Sassoli loves.

But our greatest treat was to be the last – a feast not for the palate, but the mind. The merchant's heart was set on it. Indeed, all through the meal, from time to time he'd eyed the wine flasks and his guests with some anxiety, and when he'd caught sight of anyone draining his cup too fast, he'd cried down the table, 'Drink as much as you like! Feel free! But – remember! I've something rare for the end!' – a plea which made him blush like a child. Nevertheless, he'd often repeated it.

But now at last his moment came. The sweetmeats lay scattered on our dishes, and Piero Sassoli rose to his feet.

He clapped for silence.

'My friends,' he began, 'now we reach the crown of the evening. I've discovered a singer. Oh, not just any! This is a man who's delighted the greatest families of Venice – he was offered prodigious sums to stay there . . . but, no! He turned his thoughts to Florence. He's barely arrived. He came, you might say, a stranger to my gates. Today of all days he makes his appearance quite unexpectedly, and shows me a letter from an old acquaintance of mine – someone who knows I'm not indifferent to talent, wherever I find it. Enough! I asked him to sing. And you shall hear for yourselves. Oh, I can't presume to keep him. He's destined to perch on some loftier bench than mine . . . but he's here for tonight, which I take as an omen of great good fortune for all of us. Gentlemen, you must judge for yourselves, whether you've heard such a singer!'

Around the table, smiles. Everyone guessed, of course. Piero Sassoli had instructed his agent in Venice to seek out some fashionable musician, and bribe him to come. Only a fool wouldn't have known it. But the merchant never suspects his guests of any understanding, which saves them from embarrassment. So they all looked pleased and surprised. A polite suspense was achieved. The piping musicians were hustled away, and in came our Venetian.

He made a good appearance. A tall, strong-featured man of thirty years or so, dressed in black and green. He bore himself with dignity, and looked very like a Spaniard – but without a Spaniard's stiffness, for he walked not in the style of so many performers, as if he preened himself on being the main attraction, or loved to feel the eyes of his audience on him, but rather like one who listens. That was my impression. He was a man who extracts from every sound – each cough, or scrape of a cup on the table – some knowledge concerning those who wait for him to sing. And somehow I knew that here was an artist who cared nothing for facile applause. His own assessment of his performance – that alone could matter to him.

Such was the person who entered the room.

Without a word, he walked towards us. And he gave no bow – a fact which startled the guests into silence – until he'd come within arm's length of Piero Sassoli's chair. Then, swiftly, he did bow – although I hardly remember it because, as he straightened, his fingers touched his lute, and he began to sing.

It was a courtly lovesong. Soft and plaintive. Several guests, when they recognised it, sighed. One dumbly mouthed the opening lines and shut his eyes. Another sat rigid, staring into his cup, as if he'd been stabbed in the back. The Venetian sang of fading youth and lasting fidelity. A sadness welled up round the table. Hands lay idle and smiles slackened. Piero Sassoli forgot to look proud, and looked dazed. Gabriello, as I judged from his face, was lost in perfect vacuity. But after that, I took little notice of anyone, except the Venetian.

As he sang, he drew back into the shadows until soon we could see only his hands, his face –

And now his voice soothed us; and now it grew bold, and sent a tingling through the blood. And now it was gentle, and filled me with such a yearning that I felt close to tears. I half closed my eyes. People became shapes. The guests who sat opposite, some of them twisted about on their seats towards the singer, others bolt upright – they all blurred. The candle flames blurred. I blinked to clear the mist –

The Venetian came striding back into the light, his voice shivering across the plates, and he sang a triumphant avowal of love. Let the woman be made immortal, his passion could last for ever. Let grey hairs come, and his eyes grow dim, he would still remain constant . . .

His voice distressed us like too beautiful a gift – or a rare thing that's found by accident. A bewildering miracle to discover in flesh and blood, it carried us with it to hopeless love, hopeless heights –

Twang!

I saw it go. Or else I imagine I did. The catgut, flashing from his hand across his fingers. I saw him wince. His voice broke, and his head jerked down. From the bowl of the lute, the snapped string hung like a rat's tail. The singer could only stare at it. He made no attempt to continue. He wore an expression of profound astonishment.

All this, I suppose, for a single moment.

And if we at the table had given him grace, he would surely have recovered, finishing his song unaccompanied, then quietly fetching a second lute.

But he looked so cheated – and the song was cut off at so ardent a point – that mouths began to twitch, eyes to flicker . . . and in the space of a breath there broke out round the table an explosion of laughter.

Men clutched at each other's arms and wheezed with merriment. Their sides heaved. Sweat poured off their foreheads. Even Piero Sassoli, after a short, pained silence, guffawed loudly. My own neighbour roared at the joke, and I – I, too, could feel mirth rising.

Then the singer looked up. He surveyed all these boisterous gentlemen, and smiled. Not in a servile way, nor was it awkwardness, but – the thought occurred to me, and my laughter died in my throat – as if he observed in his audience a joke of his own.

I followed his gaze. I saw the guests as he must have seen them: the spittle flying, the moisture seeping from their eyes, their wine-red noses. I took fine note of this exhibition; then I returned the Venetian's smile.

But he kept his eyes from mine.

He bowed deeply to us all, and left.

The guests laughed, then they waited. When he didn't come back, Piero Sassoli went hurrying after him. Too late. The singer had gone from the house.

Occasions I've found for laughter.

Simone Noseda, the notary. His liking for German hats. Being uncommonly short – he barely reaches Piero Sassoli's shoulder – perhaps he thinks they lend him height. The truth is just the contrary, and whenever I see him decked in his hat I think of a mushroom walking.

Two nuns last summer, on the road to Fiesole. Small-jawed,

tight-lipped women, seated on donkeys that wouldn't budge. As I came by, an ancient servant armed with a stick was running from one to the other of these beasts, whacking them on the rump; and the donkeys brayed with indignation while the ladies sat in religious silence. The servant swore and ranted. A basket of geese he'd set by the roadside gave a derisive chorus, their necks stretched out through the wicker of their cage.

A customer at the warehouse. A man who likes to blow his nose before he parts with money. One day he blew too hard, and his nose began to bleed.

Luigi Rigogli, telling a story with his usual zeal, only to find when he reached the middle that he couldn't remember the end of it.

These instances come to mind so readily, that I know there must be others. It's not true I lack mirth.

But I begin to see how it is. Men are quick to impose that condition on anyone they think hideous.

Our Gabby, because he shines like an angel, all golden-haired and divinely favoured – it's taken for granted that *he* has an amiable nature, whereas the pox-scarred youth who sat beside me that night at Piero Sassoli's birthday supper, he had the sweeter nature by far, but did anyone notice except myself?

How ill looks shackle a man!

Any half-witted oaf may presume to bow to Madonna, and his action would be allowed. But if I bow – why, I must risk a laugh!

It's no sort of bargain. A hideous man is to have no liking for humour, and is always to be ridiculous. It's supposed he lives in his body like a wretch in a dungeon, decently aware of his misery, and there he squats and glowers, while free men pass by outside and laugh till his dungeon walls ring with the sound.

Trapped. Helpless. So they have us.

But not all of us.

I can think of exceptions. Men I've seen – Charles of France, and the Heretic – whose ugliness in no way impaired their standing. In fact, they drew authority from it. And there's our Pope, our own good Leo.

The Holy Father must be the size of an ox. His face is purple.

His eyes are so small they'd do well in a hog. And when he walks, his belly goes out before him like a herald, while his head rests deep on his shoulders with the consummate grace of a cannonball. Then, as if that weren't enough, it's rumoured he suffers from an abscess, which is why wherever he goes the air smells corrupt. (But others say he merely suffers from wind.) In any case he's gross, and neither pomp nor gorgeous robes can conceal it.

Yet he's still magnificent. Strange, but it's undeniable. There's an energy in his ugliness which fascinates, just as beauty does in other men. I myself have felt it. And when he rides out in procession, lolling beneath his canopy all affability and brazen fatness, his fingers are covered with women's kisses.

And with the Heretic it was similar, although his looks were different. He was small and sickly complexioned, possessing a great beak of a nose, and thick, slack lips, but his looks were never a prison. No one studied his face, and mocked it for its want of proportion. Rather he made us feel that it came from a different mould to other men's as a mark of his special destiny.

As for Charles of France – he derived much advantage from his looks. I saw it. He thrived on the terror they inspired. He was a kind of homunculus. He walked as if he were pulled along on strings. His hands twitched convulsively; his mouth hung open. His eyes squinted. He was, in truth, a botched thing, an abortion, and he hopped along with a slouch – but none of this was a handicap. His ugliness was his greatest weapon.

The day he entered Florence at the head of his army: when he rode to the Cathedral for a thanksgiving Mass, I was there, in the Piazza. So I know. As he dismounted, the whole crowd gasped. Our dutiful cheers fell into the dust at our feet. We saw how doll-like he was, and hideous. He grimaced. He hopped a couple of paces, and looked round on the people of Florence with his mouth askew. We couldn't believe it. Was this our conqueror? We'd heard rumours of his cruelty and lack of beauty; nevertheless we'd expected our 'scourge of God' to have at least a dignified bearing. But here was a frenzied fiend. The shock could have been no greater if Satan himself had taken the city.

The Piazza filled with our silence. Charles of France hopped and grinned, twisting his head this way and that. I believe he wanted us all to see him. And when at last he was satisfied that we had, he showed us his power. Stretching his hand out – a huge, gloved hand that fitted to his arm like a shovel to a twig – slowly he raised it in greeting; and as he did so, our cheer went up again.

Ugliness, a species of power.

But this is only for the few. For those who either by birth or merit can claim to be extraordinary. It has little to do with the rest of us.

XX

TODAY, I came home to the spectacle of Gabriello dressed in all his finery, about to leave for a supper somewhere. He was wearing red velvet. The brooch on his cloak was one which I'd never seen before, and I was assessing its value as I passed – for he shamelessly squanders every florin he's given – when he put out a hand to stop me.

'I'm glad to see you, Gissy. I've a favour to ask of you.'

'Oh?'

I stepped aside. The perfume he uses is more appropriate to a woman. It's a taunt of some kind, though I fail to understand.

'Those gloves of yours,' he said, 'the kid ones. Will you lend them to me? I long to know what they feel like.'

'You've gloves of your own . . . '

'Yes, but none like yours. Mine are commonplace gloves. I can pull them on in no time. But yours, I've noticed, give you so much pleasure that you draw them on as slowly as possible. They must be exquisite. I fully expect a new sensation for every finger . . . Lend them to me, Gissy!'

I pushed past while he laughed.

He was referring, of course, to the other morning. Mass, and Madonna –

Our golden boy must have his joke.

Nursery games. They're not worth anger.

As to the thoughts I wrote down yesterday, concerning ugliness: in my sleep last night I pictured a Christ devoid of harmony, one covered by honest scabs and wounds, with his limbs in a foul disorder. Instead of a perfect face, one that's pocked, or disfigured by protruding teeth, or a hare-lip. And on waking I thought, here might be the crucifix that's acceptable to me.

I might even pay some artist to carve it, if any is willing. I'd like to see such a Christ. Would He be merely disgusting? Or could He be made, so that even while He repelled, He drew men to Him?

Teasing questions. Meaningless in the end, for it's only a test of the artist – not of God.

But ideas like these – I watch them stem from each other, and I ask myself should I afford them ink and paper? Are they to my purpose? I must guard against the folly of writing to entertain myself, so where should I prune this growth?

I mustn't run out of time.

Only this evening Piero Sassoli complained of pains in his side and went to bed early, declining an invitation to supper.

I mustn't forget what I'm about. To know my mind – how I should act in the future.

XXI

A new whim of the merchant's.

This morning he declared his pain 'a thing of the past'. He said he was feeling much refreshed, and he did, in fact, look rather less swollen round his eyes than at any time since Christmas. Buoyed up by this recovery, he went visiting, and afterwards, at noon, he came to the warehouse. There he dictated letters, and his mood was jovial. He had a nod and a smile for everyone. Our day passed smoothly.

But when we left to come home together, a thing without precedent happened. He moved a short way from the door, then stopped and said, 'Gismo, I've a mind to see the river! Will you come with me? Take the air?'

He has always hated the cold. In my surprise, I not only said I would go, I said I would be delighted. So we turned towards the Arno.

Already it was twilight and the air was sharp with frost, but Piero Sassoli seemed determined not to mind such details. As we went, instead of hunching in his coat, he stretched his neck out, sniffed like a hound, and more than once he told me, 'Breathe in, Gismo! Chase away the cobwebs!'

Such an altered attitude defied belief, but he offered no explanation.

At first our talk was cinnamon. He has just received a gift of it. Where, he wanted to know, did I think the finest came from? And did I have any faith in its healing powers? He himself had noticed that if he sucked on a stick at night . . . This, until we reached the river. I paid little attention. I considered his talk a prelude to some new debate on Gabriello's marriage prospects – or else on mine – since the only occasions on which he invites me 'to take the air' are when he means to discuss those topics – although never before in the cold by the Arno: he has always preferred a fragrant evening, and the privacy of his garden.

But I needn't have feared. Not one word did he speak about marriages. His chief concern was, indeed, to walk. For on reaching the riverbank, he cried, 'Now then! Briskly!' and stepped out ahead of me, his arms swinging, his plump legs working, while I stood astonished.

I soon caught up. Side by side we proceeded. The icy breeze was nothing to us. We thrust our faces into it as if we found it as tepid as milk straight from the cow, and keeping the river on our left, we marched. It couldn't last long, however. Piero Sassoli was forced to halt to catch his breath. This he did, staring first at the water, then across at the hills, until all at once he panted, 'Hemmed in! That's the trouble! Men weren't made to live in towns. All this . . . ' he waved at the nearest buildings. 'It's rubbish!'

Rubbish. Florence, which he loves. I could think of no safe comment. Luckily, he appeared to require none. He began to march again, head up, face set, eyes weeping with the cold, and so vigorously we went that I was beginning to warm by the time he said, 'Enough!' and turned aside down an alley, back into the town.

After that he grew reflective. We still had a distance to walk before we reached the house, and yet the 'airing' he'd wished for was apparently over. He sank further into his coat. His pace slowed, and nothing was said until, as we entered the Piazza Madonna, he suddenly looked round at me.

'Well now, Gismo, what do you think?'

It felt like an ambush. The truth is, I'd been wondering whether this evening march was to become a pattern. I was puzzled to know how he'd come by this love of air, which he certainly didn't have yesterday. But I thought it best not to ask. So, thinking to entertain him –

'Stars,' I replied. 'That bright one we saw, over the river. The forms that painters give them are really only tokens. Stars aren't star-shaped at all . . . '

But I might have spared myself the trouble. Piero Sassoli frowned.

'No, no!' he said. 'I meant about the cinnamon. You haven't told me yet. Which country grows the best, would you say?'

XXII

YET more whims. The merchant feels so 'hemmed in' that these past two nights he has slept at the farm; and so the house is filled with revels. Gabriello entertains. Tonight he exceeds all boundaries. He has fourteen guests, and two groups of minstrels which at first he set playing against each other, but now – *Deo gratias* – they play together.

How the music distracts me. My fingers are trembling.

In company I don't think of it, but when I'm alone, the sound of a lute will often have so much influence that my fingers search for the skill they've almost forgotten. I believe I played well for the tutoring I had. I might have become more than competent.

But at eighteen, I heard a sermon.

Fra Domenico da Pescia gave it, and it left me persuaded that the lute is a dangerous frivolity, much favoured by the Devil. So I threw mine away. For the glory of God and my own salvation, from this same room I flung it out of the window. I watched it roll down the roof, heard it smash in the street. And I felt faint with relief.

Some days afterwards, Piero Sassoli asked me to play for one of his guests, and when he discovered my loss – I told him I'd dropped it by accident – my carelessness so angered him that he vowed I should have 'a lengthy wait' before he bought me another lute. A promise which he kept, for he never did replace it. Gabriello was already learning to play, and one minstrel in the household seemed sufficient to the merchant.

Still, tonight – it's an illusion, but granted the blessing of an instrument, my fingers feel as if they'd remember, and without my sanction could produce melodies to astound me.

And at times like this, I contemplate a purchase. There's nothing to hinder it. Any day I could buy a lute, and bring it back, sit on the edge of my bed, and pick out the notes –

But the thought never fails to depress me, and I don't do it.

There. Such merriment. Someone's told a prize joke! I can make out Andreuccio when he laughs, and now his brother, needle-witted Francesco. The one barks like a dog; the other makes the sound of a door, creaking on its hinges.

Gabriello has two laughs. One that's musical, and one that's hard and bright like quartz, which he's using tonight.

And feeble, long-nosed Agnolo – his is the sound of a sick mule.

Strange, how I can distinguish particulars of men I consider beneath contempt. I've never studied to know them, and yet I must pay them too much attention.

Well, let them revel. Provided they keep from banging on my door, what are they to me?

I have these notes to write. I could read my book. My *Honest Recreation*. I could place the opal just where it best deceives me, on the very border of the candlelight. Or I could drink four times my customary cup of wine.

I too can be reckless –

XXIII

TRUE.

Not last night when I boasted it. Then I achieved nothing more adventurous than these miserable sketches on the page: dishes and candlesticks!

But today – an escapade. And I've come cleanly off with a prize, a small fact concerning myself, which keeps me wakeful.

Or is it Madonna who keeps me wakeful?

No matter –

Piero Sassoli sleeps in the house again. These long rides out to his farm each evening and back in the morning seem to have cured him of craving for hills and open spaces. Or even for the arms of his slave, Oronetta. His mood has changed and, to mark it, today he acquired a clock. A thing of no beauty. The seller is bankrupt. He came to the warehouse, begging the merchant to buy this clock, and Piero Sassoli immediately left his papers to go and see it. It was brought on a cart to the door this evening. Now there it stands, a graceless object, crowding the hall. A token to signify the merchant is home, and that he relishes Florence with all her devices, whatever he might say.

So Gabriello's friends are discreetly absent. Peace dwells with us. It's an alteration I thought I'd welcome, but this evening, once I'd finished my work, I discovered that the quietness palled. The room seemed to stifle me. I took out this notebook, and the prospect of scratching down thoughts – as I did last night and may do tomorrow night – filled me with panic. Suddenly I longed for air, movement . . . I snatched up my coat and hat – and fled.

At the foot of the stairs – who but Gabriello? He was listlessly gazing at the clock, but the sight of me proved far more interesting, and he called in a tone of surprise, 'An assignation, Gissy?'

I pretended not to hear.

A cloudless, crystal night. There's a quarter moon with a murderous aspect to it, thin and sharp like a Turk's blade. The very stars look compassionless. But the air is pure: all the stench from the river and gutters is stopped up in ice. And as though the lulling of one sense can sharpen another, the noises that come through the air sound wonderfully close and significant. Thus, the rasping of my breath, a shutter slammed several houses away, a baby yowling, footsteps somewhere along the street – they all seemed intimate and urgent, like personal messages. Such a night should have a meaning.

But I could think of none; and for want of any particular direction, I set off towards the Corso, walking slowly while I considered, 'There must be somewhere I can go. Some point to aim at. How ugly, just to walk . . . '

One street as good as another.

An assignation, Gissy?

None. Unless with Fra Bernardino, in his mildewed cell. Where else?

Then gently it came, an idea that warmed me like a shaft of sunlight glowing through the ice.

Her house. Madonna's.

Oh, I knew I'd slink, I'd creep. The thought of being seen, sniffing like a dog at her gates, has always been a source of terror. And yet, to be near her –

I changed direction.

A torch blazed in the bracket, an orange flare staining the wall.

And above the gate, despite the cold, a shutter stood open, with a meagre gleam showing through the wax of the window, so that I knew a single candle burned in the room beyond. And from this window flowed music. Someone was playing on a flute. Intricate music of the mind – a melody linked together like a series of coins, with contradictions and witty variations. No doubt a suitor had composed this piece to show off his skills to Madonna, and now he was doing his best, performing his tricks like a juggler, while she sat in the shadows and indulged him. I felt convinced she was there, listening, since the music was played not idly in the way one plays for one's own pleasure, nor was it tentative, but it was played to impress, with an edge of effort. A performancc for Madonna. And just one candle.

I stopped. I stood directly beneath the window, and listened. How cunningly wrought this music was! I could sense that the mind which had fashioned it gloried in complications, cynicisms and paradoxes, was a mind that knew itself to be elegant – and cared for little besides displaying the fact.

Hear me, said the music. I pour out my talents for you, Madonna – do you know my match? Don't I excel? And all this you may have . . .

I was helpless with jealousy. I remained there gaping up, my face in the torchlight, until, with a last ingenious flourish, the music ended. Then before I could hear too much – either her voice, or amorous words spoken by anyone – I walked away.

Walked.

For once, no slinking. Nor was there any of that struggle to keep my legs from scuttling along that has happened in the past. I walked away like a gentleman.

It might have been otherwise. If she'd appeared at the window – why, then I'd have blustered and bowed, grinned like a great baboon, or else, tugging at my hat, I'd have scampered off down the street like a thief. And in either case, I believe she'd have known who it was, and why I'd been standing there. A terrible risk. It horrifies me now.

But God be praised, none of that happened, and I walked away – with this discovery.

There's a shift, a something new in me. Oh, nothing vast. Indeed, it's so delicate that in the end it may come to nothing.

Nevertheless, why deny it? As I stood outside Madonna's house, I found a thing I hadn't expected.

At first there was only jealousy. Then had come the usual temptation to let my pride shrink, until it became like a worm that's fallen out of some peasant's basket, and lies ridiculous, stranded in a great Piazza . . . But even while I felt this urge to despise myself, while the candle burned in the window, and the fluteplayer dazzled with his brilliance – I remembered these pages. These scribblings. And – how to describe it? 'There!' I thought. 'There, at least, I belong. And no one can shut me out.' I set it down with a smile, for haven't I written in the past that my ledgers – my columns of sums and totals – *those* are my refuge? Whereas words, I said, are corrupt. But tonight I thought of these notes, and my spirit rallied. They walled me round with protection as family and friendship have never done. No, nor the prayers of holy men neither.

Yet what are they, these notes?

The more I study them, the less I understand. Often the words on the page are simple, but the thought that runs through them like a hidden current seems to me the work of a stranger. And some of the things I write feel true at the time, but later feel dishonest. And often, while I labour to describe an event or set down a thought – it seems that I labour all the more to conceal it. And at times, I fear that these notes will offer me a prospect which the person who wrote them would never choose to see.

So how can that person be myself?

And how can such a mystery be a shelter?

As with every discovery, it seems I know less than I did before.

But the fact remains. I walked away from Madonna's with something very like dignity. I resembled a man who's stumbled across a single precious possession, which he sets against the world of all that's denied to him.

XXIV

FIRECRACKERS –
The air sputters.

Today we heard rumours of harsh taxation to fall on us in the spring, and the house is dark with gloom. But somewhere along the Via Bufalini there are people who care not a fig for taxes – or else they've decided they'll mourn tomorrow. Tonight, they mean to celebrate. There's an energetic frolicking. Piero Sassoli has supped at home, alone, in silence, and so I suppose this festive occasion means nothing to us. Betrothal, birthday, or wedding feast, it doesn't concern us: the family is unknown. Still, these people, whoever they are, wish us to know they rejoice. They light up the sky with their happiness, and all the space in the streets feels crammed with enjoyment. It's as if they would have us breathe in the air and inquire, 'Who *are* these happy ones? And why am I not of their party?'

They tease us with firecrackers.

A scent of smoke and powder, and a magical glow above the roofs – these are signals designed to inform the world that some people share a joke, while others do not – the value of which is obvious, for any pleasure is twice the pleasure if we know it's denied our fellows, and that they know it also.

A rocket. Blue with emerald, soaring past the window! It puts me in mind of Leo's election – our Medici Pope. What celebrations then. What wild thanksgiving. For four days the bells rang out. What a booming of cannon. We had crackers and bonfires. Magnificent! And bands of youths roamed the streets brandishing torches, with their faces concealed behind fantastical masks, and as they went they howled out, 'Palle! Palle!' Piero Sassoli was all in favour. He frequently repeated, 'Miraculous! The Pope has become a Florentine!' And then he'd roar with mirth. Or sometimes he'd vary the jest for propriety's sake: 'That a Florentine should become the Pope! Miraculous!' – which struck him as no less amusing, and so again, the mirth.

There! A second rocket! Green flowers in the pit of night, shaming the stars. Unnatural, they dominate the sky, these flowers, as if they were made to last for ever.

I could climb to her window. As she slept, I could soothe my hands on her limbs.

And when she awoke?

I could write to her:

'Madonna. I beg to bring myself to your attention. Look not among your closest acquaintance. Seek among those beyond it – for one who's divided: part of his person may be repellent, but viewed correctly, he can equal any of those who hope to win your favour. Allow me to serve you. Approach you. Let me prove that your suitors feel nothing. They offer wit and poetics to magnify mere flickerings of their senses. But only permit me to kneel before you – and you shall know the nature of a true desire. You shall feel it lapping about your knees like flames, as I burn towards you.'

To make a copy of this, and write her name upon it – what could be simpler?

Now they come spilling out, the younger guests, into the streets. Perhaps they have no more firecrackers, and so at last they invite us to share their pleasure. They want us to open our shutters wide, and smile down on them. With pipes and clappers they go, with shouts and laughter. A joke – a crude one – as they pass beneath the window. I'll not look out. It's all a tease. 'Join us!' shrill the pipes. 'Complement our merry-making!' But why accept a late invitation? Here I sit and write my notes. In the hall below sits the merchant, fretting about his taxes. Outside in the night, a few of the youth of Florence cavort through the streets – friends who intend to stay friends for life, well wined and feasted. As for the rest of the world, there's betrothal for some, and not for others. What's that to me?

'Come join us!' shrill the pipes, as if they truly meant it. How far their voice can carry!

XXV

SOUNDS –

In the warehouse, often I don't even notice Rigogli's chatter, because the sound is incessant. He'll gossip to couriers, visiting merchants, our own errand boys – to anyone who's willing to listen, and if there's no one, he'll converse with himself. He titters and mutters; whistling noises come from between his teeth, and he's rarely silent – to all of which I've grown accustomed. His chatter disturbs me no more than does the creak of my stool, or the rustling of papers; and unless I decide to raise my head and look about, sometimes I couldn't say for certain whether he was in the room.

But with Rassuccio, the case is different. He speaks so seldom that on any occasion he does speak – though it's only to bid a boy fetch coals for the pot on which he warms his hands – I always listen. I take involuntary note of his words, no matter how hard I might be working, and I rarely fail to hear what he says, despite the fact that he never speaks above a whisper.

How nicely the ear discriminates.

– And yet it frequently cheats us. I've observed, for example, that the sweetest music comes from an unknown source. The tunes of a bridal procession sound happier by far before the procession comes into sight, especially before I can see the players. And with singing, I think I'd make it a rule – except for one, the Venetian, but even he kept in the shadows for the most part – that the sight of the singer limits the power of the song; whereas a voice that apparently comes from nowhere can be so astonishingly beautiful, it seems to surpass all human bounds.

I found such a voice last summer, in an alley behind the Porta Rossa.

In the blaze of an afternoon, when the air was so fiery it might have issued straight from Hell, and all who could remained indoors, there were documents for the notary. And for some politic reason or other, Piero Sassoli declared that none but I could deliver them. So there I was, hurrying along, perspiring unpleasantly – and the heat was such that I lost my wits. Burying my face in my handkerchief, I rushed without thinking into the shade of an alley. A wretched place. I regretted my action at once, for the alley stank. 'But even so,' I thought, 'if I turn back now, I shall only be adding to my labours. Best to go on . . . ' So I walked as fast as I could down this pestilential crack in the city, dodging the heaps of filth, my handkerchief tight to my nose –

And then, from an upper window somewhere, a song began. A single, untrained voice, tuneful but lacking any pretensions, it came flowing towards me, sweet and cool –

I laugh to think of it now.

It was only the voice of a child. And the song was only one of those country rhymes that children repeat without understanding.

But I was stunned by its loveliness. I almost stopped walking. I lowered my handkerchief and, squinting up at the foul walls that enclosed me, I saw at one of the windows, his elbows raw on the ledge, a ragged boy with great ears, a long mouth and narrow shoulders. And while he sang, he gazed at me, his greenish features wearing such an insolent expression that I sensed with a shock – he was wondering how far he could spit.

Well.

The instance tells the tale. Once I behold the singer, the song is inevitably tainted.

Even that fop who played for Madonna – the magician of the flute – if I'd been able to see him, with his shoulders heaving and his cheeks puffed out – would I have thought his music so elegant?

'*Madonna, I beg to bring myself to your attention . . .*'

What amazing lunacy! Scribbling away like a half-wit! And now – vanished.

I remember my actions. I copied out the note; I folded it and wrote upon it, 'Lucia da Fano' – as one copies out a charm, meaning to burn the thing in the candle flame, and hoping to find my thoughts the easier for it. But somehow the Fiend obstructed me. I was loath to destroy my work, so I thought to postpone the ritual until this evening. I gathered my notes together; I placed them in the chest; and this morning when I rose, I hurried to the warehouse, taking with me several papers concerning Piero Sassoli's recent expenses.

They lie on my desk. The note must lie on my desk, in the warehouse!

XXVI

RIGOGLI claims he hasn't touched my papers, although I know that after I've left in the evening, he often goes prying and spying. He pulled his longest face when I asked.

'Papers?' he squealed. 'Why should I touch them? Is anything missing?' – and when I replied that I only thought I'd left my work more neatly arranged: 'Mice!' he exclaimed. 'Haven't you noticed? They're everywhere! But what have you lost? Have you asked our troop of Mercuries?' – by which he referred to the errand boys.

I said it was nothing important. 'Only the text of a Moorish poem. A friend of the family collects such things, and sets them to music. If you should find it, be good enough to return it to me . . .'

'Of course! Of course!' And away he scampers, sniggering.

And all day long, the errand boys were quiet and unobtrusive – unusually so.

And every page I've turned in the ledgers, and twice through the notebook; and I've emptied the chest.

XXVII

TODAY – not a smirk. Not a whisper. Whereas, if they'd found it, surely I'd know by my persecution, their remarks and guffaws.

Yet what if they've not only read the note, but also delivered it?

My name – at least that's written nowhere: but a boy in Sassoli livery carrying my folly to her gates, handing it in to her steward –

It doesn't bear thinking of!

Better believe – as I do – that Rigogli has it, and pores over each line with an eyeglass, licking his lips as he spells the words out.

If it should reach her –

God grant anonymity! Grant me to know by instinct the streets she treads, that I may avoid them! Never to see her.

I've examined the chest. The lock I believe to be sound. I can find no scratches nor other signs of tampering. And this is well, since to entertain fears in that direction would be intolerable.

As it is, I can scarcely bear it. Am I to cringe and blush at a word from anyone? Everywhere, I'm alert for papers. The edge of a letter clutched by Rigogli, and round goes my head at an angle, to peep at the writing. A scrap of an inventory drifting across the merchant's desk – and I'm all trepidation.

I must put this note from me.

This is the kind of sneering sport life makes of a momentary weakness.

And the best defence? I can think of none but an outright lie: it never happened.

XXVIII

PEACE.

A great relief smiles on the household.

The past four days I've been denied my freedom to come here in the evening, and spend time on my own thoughts. Piero Sassoli and I have been working together after supper, estimating and worrying how to avoid these taxes – or, at any rate, too cruel a blow. How to disguise some modest pockets of income.

Equipped with paper and pens, we sat in the upper hall, side by side at the table, and agonised. And every evening, the merchant consumed a dishful of marzipan sweetmeats, which stood by his elbow, scooping them up and pushing them into his mouth whenever we disagreed – which was sadly often.

Thank God it's done with.

Few kinds of work can be more vexatious. The very notion of taxes so enrages Piero Sassoli that all proposals, no matter how delicate or advantageous, are met with suspicion and objections. Every evening as the hours wore on, as the stock of marzipan dwindled in the dish, and ash began to settle in the fireplace, my role grew more impossible. I was always to have some new suggestion, I was always to know of some cunning trick – yet none could ever be good enough; and by degrees, Piero Sassoli would slip into a state of mind so morose that nothing could rouse him. Then he'd start to harangue. Florence, he'd say, has consistently chosen to murder those sons who love her best. It hardly pays to be honest. If enterprise is never to have its reward . . . On and on. A formula I've heard so often in the markets, that I could have recited it for him.

And at this point, I knew each evening was lost. I'd begin to shuffle the papers.

'Perhaps,' I'd say, 'if we sleep on the problem . . . '

'Sleep?' – his face bright red with indignation – 'Yes!' he'd cry. 'Sleep if you can. If you have no worries. It's all very well for some!'

'But I share your concern . . . '

'Hah! How could you?'

Then angrily he'd rise, and throwing a last, disgusted glance at the table, shamble away to his bed, muttering all the while – behaviour that was surely an act, at least in part. For Piero Sassoli is not so bewildered by figures and totals as he'd have me suppose. His confusion is sometimes a method of testing. He watches to catch me off-guard – and fails. He's devious. And in much the same fashion, in all his talk of 'biased procedures' and 'stabs in the back', or how 'Some men won't be pleased until they see me a bankrupt' – I detect a sort of mummery.

Last night, for example: just before he rose to leave, I was collecting the papers together, when suddenly he said, 'Gismo, if they mean to take every last soldo – I don't see why I shouldn't spend them myself! I think I'll build a monument. They couldn't snatch that very easily!'

'A monument?'

'A tomb.' He glared. 'Why not? If they won't let me live . . . '

Of course, I laughed. He looked surprised, but I laughed all the more, until after a moment or so he began to smile, though grudgingly.

I saw his purpose. He wished to imply that heavy taxation can justify any extravagance – and extravagance of all kinds he loves.

It's frequently so with Piero Sassoli. He schemes to indulge himself, even on the most unlikely occasion.

Still, I disliked this talk of tombs, whatever he meant by it. *Absit omen*.

And today the gloom has lifted.

These rumours which had us totalling our assets are proved to be ghosts and chimeras. No such taxes are contemplated, and the air moves freely through Florence again. How Piero Sassoli came by the news, I haven't discovered, but a message – or else some sort of token – must have been brought to the warehouse; for when he arrived there this morning, the merchant's temper was far from sweet, but by noon he was smiling. Yet I myself saw nothing extraordinary. A single courier came with a note, which was passed to me. And two gentlemen came, both of them known to me, to place their orders. But somehow Piero

Sassoli received his news; and calling me to him, he assured me in a barely audible undertone that our worries were over. He had information, he said, 'from a certain official whose business it is to know these things' – but he wouldn't say from whom, and indeed the matter was not yet public: our lips must be sealed . . . He dearly loves a conspiracy. So we kept our relief to ourselves, and the afternoon went by in silence. Yet by now it seems that the whole world knows. When I left the warehouse this evening, I found such a joyous crowd in the streets, such a smiling and nodding, that clearly the news is everywhere. Angels have been abroad in Florence, and the cloth trade is saved.

Our gratitude flows in amicable gestures, and wine. Piero Sassoli, despite his fatigue – he looks pale and sickly from the week's anxiety and a poor digestion – has gone forth to rejoice. He must feast and be thankful. A long night's sleep might have served him better, but when I ventured to hint as much – he looked aghast.

'Oh, certainly!' he scoffed. 'I expect you're right. But confound it, man, I've just been saved! Reprieved! And you want me to lie down and snore! I'll look to my health tomorrow. Goodnight, good Gismo!' and he hurried off, laughing.

Dressed like a monstrous cockerel in russet and brown, with a jewel in his hat, he's gone to sup and be glad with Ser Romoli.

And Gabriello – he's also out.

But before he went, waiting until his father left – he came banging on my door.

I shouted to know who it was, and he trilled back, 'Good news, isn't it, Gissy? The Sassoli coffers aren't to be emptied after all! I suppose you're pleased?'

'Of course I am,' I said to the door. 'Aren't you?'

'Oh yes.'

I heard him running down the stairs.

One more jibe. One more attempt to nourish the lie that my fist dips deep into Sassoli coin, whenever I can manage it. Then away to follies and frivolities.

Amen to that.

Our golden boy's a fool. I refuse to be roused. I remain honest. And if he cares to think of that with contempt, if he calls me an idiot because I refuse to act like a squirrel and snatch what I can for the future – let him answer this:

What provision has Gabriello made?

One evening, while we were puzzling together over the accounts, Piero Sassoli looked up from a list of figures and sighed, 'Really, you know, Gabby should be here. All these insurance charges . . . freight . . . debts . . . He has no idea. He must take an interest sooner or later. He'll have to learn one day!'

One day.

Why, the little lad is barely three and twenty. Let him breathe. Youth is precious.

Quant' è bella giovinezza!

And who am I to feel concern? As the merchant has so graciously expressed it: How *could* I share his concern?

Time drags on the weights of that brute clock in the hall. A new, but old-fashioned contraption with a loud click. Why Piero Sassoli chose to buy it baffles me. On quiet nights such as this, if I open the door and concentrate, I can hear the clicking as one by one the teeth on the weight-driven wheel are released, and when I hear it, I tremble. Click . . . click . . . The wheel turns, and the future rolls on to the present.

XXIX

'THAT paper you lost,' asks Rigogli, 'did you find it? Your Moorish poem?'

'No. In fact, I'd forgotten about it.'

'Indeed? Well, you were angry enough at the time! As if I'd go rummaging through your things at night!'

'I meant no offence.'

'Oh, and none taken . . . I was merely wondering whether you found your poem.'

I'm sure he has it. I can sense the hope he has for signs of alarm and discomfort; but I'll brazen it out. Politely. For if I offend him, how might this lecherous fool not punish me?

He might yet send the note.

XXX

A ridiculous occurrence. And – eels.

This morning Piero Sassoli announced that he planned not to go to the warehouse – and that neither should I go. 'We must let Rigogli have his times of power,' he said. 'He has to be kept in trim. While you and I . . . ' – here he broke off, yawning, and I waited in apprehension. I expected one of our simpering visits to Buonarroti. But no. It was, ' . . . while you and I see to a piece of domestic business. You know I've a mind to buy more land? Particularly since this last scare! (He meant the taxes.) Well, there's just the place for sale – so you and I must pay the man a visit.'

And after he'd made this announcement, Piero Sassoli smiled vigorously, a thing he does when he wishes to know I'm pleased.

But I felt far from pleased. I've never pretended to any knowledge of land, nor to those things which guarantee a purchase of it. True, I might tell a lump of rock from a handful of soil, but on every finer point I'm ignorant.

Bluntly I said as much. I said I'd be no use to him. I'd be better employed writing to the fool in Minorca who under-insures our cargoes . . . Besides, I said, Gabriello, who loves to ride, would surely be delighted to go . . .

All these protests were brushed aside. The merchant clicked his tongue and flapping his hand as though my words were so much smoke, he interrupted –

'Tch! About the land you needn't worry! I already know it's excellent. But I want you with me. Gabby would be a distraction, and someone I must have. The man I'm going to see is worthy – really estimable – but, Gismo, he talks too much!'

Then he paused, as if this explained everything.

'He does?'

'So I shall depend on you to remind me – once we've concluded the business – that I've another engagement. Otherwise I'll be there for ever. And I want to be home this afternoon. That fellow's coming – the one who makes pedal chairs. He's bringing me a model.'

Ah. The pedal chairs. An inventor came to us some days ago armed with designs for a kind of stool on wheels, the whole to be propelled along by means of pedals worked by the feet. I'd forgotten his promised return, but the man I remembered: bright-eyed, young, and how he'd watched the merchant while explaining his drawings, this catch, that lever . . . Yes, he'd mentioned a model. He hadn't been able to show it at the time – someone else was examining it; and the first of his full-size creations, although it was nearing completion, was not yet perfected . . . I hadn't taken him seriously.

But now I remembered the sum of money he'd mentioned as necessary to his advancement, and I made up my mind.

So be it. I'd go with Piero Sassoli to see this land. And every time he came close to agreeing the price with its owner, I'd think up some new complication. I'd keep the merchant there till late in the afternoon, when by all the laws of courtesy he must be asked to stay to supper. Then, with luck, we'd come home too late for any interest in pedal chairs. And by tomorrow, the inventor might well be knocking on another door.

This was how I reasoned it, and I said I'd have the horses fetched.

Piero Sassoli showed not the least surprise at my compliance, but answered quickly, 'No need for that. We'll walk. It isn't far.'

'Aren't we to view the land?'

'I tell you, I've seen it. All we have to do today is visit a man in the Ognissanti. The owner keeps a house there . . . '

A bright, blue-skied morning. The kind which is common in early February, whorishly tempting us to believe that spring has come, that only a fool would anticipate further frosts, and that we'll wake up the next day – or the next – to find ourselves in May, with flowers tied round the door-latches. As if a year could contract, by a whim of compassion, and cast out half its bitterness.

Piero Sassoli was greatly pleased by the weather. He beamed up at the sky, and declared it a perfect day for anything to do with 'land'. In fact, he seemed exceedingly pleased with everything. There were compliments for a butcher we passed on the size of a sheep he had hanging by his stall, there were kind words for a peasant woman whose basket brushed against the merchant, and who thought it prudent to make her apologies. There were smiles for everyone.

'Is he excited', I wondered, 'about the land he hopes to purchase – or more about the pedal chair?'

His joviality filled me with unease – and I probed for clues.

'This gentleman who owns the land,' I asked, 'do you think he has need of money? Or would you call him rich?'

'Oh, no! But – worthy! Worthy!' said Piero Sassoli, avoiding the question. 'A very sound person . . . Can you smell those bread ovens, Gismo? What a morning! Doesn't the smell of bread tease your stomach?'

And nothing more could I draw from him until we came to our destination.

A smaller house than I'd expected. Less than twelve years old, I'd say, and built of good-quality brick, with the interior walls well plastered and tempered, everything clean, and fresh reed matting – but not a great man's place. To be truthful, it was obvious from a glance that every room must have mean proportions, while the walls were barren, and the furnishings so plain as to leave no doubt that whoever lived there had no particular standing in Florence – and little share in the city's refinements.

Which was contrary to all I'd been led to look for by Piero Sassoli's praise. 'But then,' I thought, 'I've known him to enthuse for the strangest reasons – '

An ogling lad, not unlike our own simple potboy, had opened the door and received us without much ceremony. The merchant had just contrived to say, 'Is your master at home? I'm Piero Sassoli, come to discuss . . . ' when the boy cried out, 'Oh, yes! Please enter!' and turned his back to lead us in.

We were left to stand before a fire in the hall, while the master was summoned. There, to fill the silence, the merchant smiled at me, brightly, hopefully – and yet this was scarcely done before with bustlings and cries of joy, as swiftly as if he'd watched us from some inner chamber and could barely wait the instant required by decency, a thrush of a personage came towards us, all ruffled and chirruping, 'Welcome! Welcome!'

He and Piero Sassoli embraced – with a sort of servile tenderness, I thought, on the thrush's part, and with a hearty excessiveness on Piero Sassoli's. Then both men turned to me.

'Ser Frizzoni,' said the merchant, in a voice full of feeling, 'may I present Gismondo Cavalletti, who gives me staunch and faithful help in my concerns?'

Frizzoni.

I recalled the name. At once my suspicions swarmed in their thousands. Still, they were only suspicions, and I told myself I might be mistaken. I worked to look calm. I bowed. And when I raised my head again, there was Frizzoni amiably nodding, with a smile, bemused as though to say, 'Well, well! He's not as bad as I feared!' – while his eyes said just the opposite, dwelling with hopeless fascination on the left side of my face.

Piero Sassoli cleared his throat.

'My dear sir,' he began, 'I've come – I know you're busy, so I'll not waste time – because I've heard you might be willing to sell that vineyard near Grignano. An excellent place I've always thought it, and if these reports are true . . . '

The thrush puffed out his chest in amazement.

'Sell it? Where did you hear such a story?'

'Oh . . . In the Guild, about the markets . . . ' Piero Sassoli was unperturbed. 'You know how one hears these things . . . '

'Quite so. Oh yes, I know . . . '

And the two men smiled at each other. Then Frizzoni, with a little start, set up a-piping: 'But please forgive me! What am I doing? Be seated! Allow me to offer refreshment . . . Chestnuts . . . Will you taste some chestnuts? Only the best . . . Here, sit by the fire! I'll have Bianca fetch some . . . '

And before Piero Sassoli chose to control or oppose these events, our flustered host had hurried away, clapping his hands, and shouting into the back of the house.

The merchant and I sat awkwardly. There was only a bench: elbow to elbow we sat.

'It appears', I said, 'you've been cheated by a rumour.'

'Oh, one can't tell yet. Of course he'll deny it at first!' said Piero Sassoli with a sideways glance at me. At my right side.

Already Frizzoni was hurrying back.

'Now, about the vineyard!' he cried. 'I fear you've come on a fruitless errand. Yet I can't regret it. I'm much too pleased to see you here . . . But as to the vineyard, you must understand it's the dowry I plan for my eldest daughter . . . '

'Then you don't mean to sell it?'

'Unfortunately not.' Frizzoni looked sorrowful. He stood with his hands spread out. 'How could I?' he protested. 'Of course, if ever I thought of selling – but a father's duties . . . Ah, here's Bianca. Come forward, child. Bring them here!'

The chestnuts. Surely roasted and waiting before we'd reached the street. They were brought to us on a white glass dish, and the girl who brought them was a big-boned creature of some fifteen years with mouse-brown hair and a ruddy complexion made all the darker by her embarrassment. I saw how her neck burned. Her shoulders were rounded; she walked with her head down, and as she thrust out the dish towards Piero Sassoli, I noted that it trembled. I suppose the heat of the chestnuts burned her through the glass. An impractical dish, used only for special occasions.

'Ser Sassoli,' fluttered our host, 'Ser Cavalletti – this is my eldest. Bianca. Well, look up, child. Look at the gentlemen!'

Dully she obeyed him. A broad and stupid face with green eyes, gummed at the corners.

'Charming! Charming!'

Piero Sassoli half rose. He patted her arm, took a fistful of chestnuts, then collapsed on the bench again.

I myself had risen. I bowed. And straightening up, I took, since I must, a chestnut. She lowered her gaze immediately. I sat, and busied myself with a most meticulous peeling of the blackened skin, while her father watched me. Then all at once seizing the dish, he shooed her from us. 'Go now! Off you go!'

And she scuttled out of sight.

Ser Frizzoni sighed.

'There. You see,' he said. 'You see how nervous she is? She's not short of modesty. She has no idea she's a fine-looking girl. Her mother and I have done our best. She's skilled with her needle. Makes excellent jellies and vinegar. She's trained in every womanly duty. But quiet. So quiet. So very – restrained. You see, she deserves that vineyard . . . '

'Certainly she does!' said Piero Sassoli quickly. 'I'm disappointed, I don't mind saying it. Land near Grignano – that was just what I wanted. But a girl like her deserves the best. Being a parent myself, I can understand. Why, she'd be a blessing to any household. Don't you think so, Gismo? Eh?'

I confined my response to a smile, and this apparently troubled our host, for he turned pale. A moment of silence followed, which he broke at last by smiting his brow and exclaiming, 'But forgive me! Wine! I've forgotten to offer you wine! May I have Bianca fetch some . . . ?'

No. No more Bianca. At the very name a panic gripped me. I sprang to my feet – and did it so promptly that Frizzoni stepped backwards. He actually flinched as though he considered it possible I might strike him. Astounding behaviour. I took great pains not to appear as if I'd observed it, and addressed myself to the merchant.

'Sir,' I said, with all the calmness I could muster; 'you asked me to remind you of your other engagement. If this vineyard isn't for sale, I'm sure that Ser Frizzoni will understand. The other matter won't wait long.'

'Ah.'

Piero Sassoli looked tired. He gazed up at me wearily, rubbed the palm of a hand on the edge of the bench – in the other he clutched several chestnut skins – and I realised he had no stronger desire than to sit there all morning, sipping wine. I feared he'd betray me. He allowed me the time to think it. At last, slowly, he got to his feet.

Then our host began to plead. How sad this was! Surely we needn't leave so soon? Just one small cup . . .

But his pleading was feeble. He seemed uncertain whether or not he presumed by pressing us to stay; and as if to put his mind at rest, Piero Sassoli signalled vaguely, a princely gesture implying, 'Peace! You've done all that we require!'

Then to soothe the offence, if any he'd given – 'Magnificent chestnuts!' he grunted, carefully laying the skins he held on the bench. 'Splendid start to the morning! My compliments to your daughter, Frizzoni. She knows how to see they're roasted without being burned to cinders. Charming girl. Well, Gismo, you see, will have me trot. A restless fellow. He's very industrious. If you change your mind about that land . . . '

'I won't . . . But call and inquire whenever you like!' panted Frizzoni, bustling us forth to the door, and now his face wore an expression which any uncharitable man would have taken for one of relief. 'Always an honour. You – and Ser Cavalletti!'

Indeed we would call. Indeed we would inquire. The merchant promised.

After that, the street lay before us.

Splendid chestnuts. An ideal first food in the day. Why, Piero Sassoli had known a man who lived to be ninety-five and had sworn by chestnuts. Every day from his fortieth year he'd taken a handful in the morning, and then fasted till supper . . .

The merchant talked loudly and quickly all the way to the warehouse – and all the talk was chestnuts. Not until we entered the building could I find a chance to say, 'It must grieve you to lose that vineyard. If I hear of another – '

At that he laughed. He glanced up, and his eyes sparkled. Then, shaking his head, he pushed past me to go to his desk.

Never have I seen him disguise his anger so well.

This afternoon he left early, hastening home to redeem his day by viewing the model pedal chair. My own walk home was therefore solitary.

And feeling the merchant's displeasure on me, I took my time about it, so that I need neither creep to my room past the various rogues in the hall, nor offend the merchant further by speaking up, as I ought, against the follies he was buying.

So I strolled as far as the Porta al Prato, then back by way of Santa Maria Novella; and in the Piazza, for the good of my soul, I gave a quattrino to a beggar. I've noticed this: the days I'm most loath to come home are the days I give to the poor.

But all too soon I approached the Via de' Gori, and finding

myself reluctant to proceed, I turned away again, towards the Cathedral. Thus eventually I came to within a street of where I'd started, which felt foolish. There, at one of the booths I bought a mess of boiled eels, and ate them where I stood without a thought for who might see me. For I considered it wiser to spend my defiance than to carry it home with me.

Eels, in the street.

And as I chewed them, I thought about the Frizzoni girl, this offered sacrifice who possesses 'the sight of a gnat' – Piero Sassoli's description on more than one occasion – this creature he'd singled out as a candidate for my affection. I thought of her family – such a 'sound' one. Good enough for Gismondo. I thought of her dowry. Some flinty patch of hillside to pass on to my heirs. To remind them of my beginnings.

Disgusted, I swallowed the eels without nicety; and the meek old man who sold them, seeing me devour his fare with so much apparent relish, was quick to offer me a second mess at an even smaller price. No doubt he longed to be rid of his eels and free to go home. So I paid and ate, more to delay coming home myself than from any remaining appetite, until soon the abhorrence I felt for Ser Frizzoni's bovine daughter gave way to anxiety.

An idle thought of Piero Sassoli's? Presenting me with a sweetmeat, as it were, which he'd hoped might suit my taste? Or had this morning's episode been a serious effort – the best he intended to ask of himself – to make some provision for me?

Could he think my merits so small?

Always, it comes back to this.

I flung the rest of the eels into the gutter, and had the satisfaction of seeing a cur and a boy – both sprung out of nowhere – ravenously sharing them.

I came home.

And as I climbed the stairs, the merchant surprised me; warmed by wine and a friendly visit from Ser Gaddi, he called out to me cheerfully, 'Have you eaten, Gismo? Will you join us?'

With the smell of fish on my breath I could only refuse, but the invitation was heartening. I gauged from the ease with which he spoke that, after all, this Frizzoni affair is nothing weighty. Lazy he is, but that he gives no deeper thought to my future is hard to believe. And if it was meant to count for so much, this morning – would he have cast it off so quickly?

It was, then, just an experiment –

Though not without the familiar barb, the taunt: for Frizzoni, perhaps, is one generation out of the soil – and Piero Sassoli never forgets where he found me.

No more than I do.

XXXI

A year after Gabriello was born – some months before the French king entered Florence – a country man came to Piero Sassoli. A man too well dressed for the average peasant, nevertheless I thought him shabby, and was quick to notice the black rinds round his finger nails. Like any peasant's, his face was walnut brown. His eyes were small, pinched, with long creases stretching out to the temples; and he held his mouth in a manner that somehow contrived to be stubborn and servile at the same time, the lips firm, as though he meant to succeed in his business, but also curved in a smile which the lines on his face betrayed as unfamiliar to him, and so one knew that he only smiled in the hope of looking more like a gentleman.

He stood facing the merchant across the table, feet apart and back straight – a stance to say that nothing and no one could shift him. But whenever Piero Sassoli spoke, this man would start nodding, which gave the contrary impression of someone most anxious to oblige. And more significant still, because he stood while the merchant was seated, he found it hard to resist a temptation that smacked of diffidence: he'd stretch his neck as he made his replies, lowering his head, and craning it out towards the merchant – which looked most pitifully vulgar, and took away any last doubts as to his breeding.

There was, in addition, an unpleasant tang of dust and sweat, all the worse for being half concealed by a cloying sweetness – and suddenly I thought of those wayside herbs which peasants use to freshen their clothes. This man also used them.

This man, who was my father.

He had come, he said, to take me back.

Summoned to listen, I'd let him embrace me stiffly; I'd suffered him to cry how fine I'd grown, and thump me on the chest. Then I'd stood aside, close to the corner of Piero Sassoli's table, so that the visitor, the merchant and I formed the three points of a triangle; and although I suppose I stood still, it seems to me now, whenever I think of the scene, that gradually I shrank towards the table corner. For in all the house there isn't a weightier object than that table, and no one man could hope to carry it away.

There we were. And at first this father, who'd come so far to claim me, eyed his son with ill-disguised bewilderment. But he was quick to recover. Then, turning from me to the merchant, in rehearsed and formal sentences he presented his case.

Lamentably, he began, since that day when Ser Sassoli had taken a fancy to young Gismondo here . . . when the family had been so honoured . . . In fact, in the present year . . . one of his sons had died. A promising lad. The one they called Jacopo.

(I found no sorrow in this news. Jacopo. Three years my senior and a great eater, who'd exacted a part of every meal on my plate.)

. . . Another, the eldest, had unexpectedly turned religious. God reward him. A heavy loss, for he was now a monk . . . So who was to help on the land? What could be done but fetch back Gismondo? He himself was growing no younger, and a man must face the facts. Ser Sassoli no doubt would agree . . .

But the merchant said nothing.

And I said nothing.

A sparrow had settled on the ledge of the open window, and from there it cheeped in at us.

The country man continued:

. . . But quite apart from the land . . . the practical issue . . . if he were honest, (and here his voice began to wheedle) he had to admit there was also the mother. The boy's mother. Who, since Jacopo's death, had made such trouble from morning to night with fits of weeping and reproaches that, in short, for a peaceful life as much as from necessity – and because he himself began to feel some remorse, as was only natural – he must take Gismondo with him.

He must have me back.

I listened. I watched his lips – they were cracked with dust; Piero Sassoli had offered no hospitality. While those lips formed words, they worked all the harder at a smile, and I felt a sort of amazed revulsion, as one might feel who sees for the first time an ape got up in silk and feathers. I sensed I watched a perversion of all that was natural to the man. A great pretence. By the time he stopped speaking, I had not the slightest fear that my father sincerely wanted me.

Not me, but florins. So much I knew. And yet all the same, I was afraid, because if he failed to wring some payment from the merchant, I thought he might take me with him for his dignity's sake – or out of spite. Only I sensed that he himself was still uncertain. He had no sure conviction of how he might best serve his interests . . . And all this I knew, although how I knew it when barely more than a child, I can't explain. But I understood. I saw he was too much a coward – or too much a peasant – to say openly those things he meant; and despite my fear, I blushed for him. This parent of mine humiliated me. Then that increased my fear, in case Piero Sassoli should be as disgusted as I was and, counting for nothing all those labours by which I'd tried to make myself useful, he might let me go quite lightly, with a flick of his wrist – to express his contempt for my father.

I considered that possible. I stood at the corner of the table, between those two very different men, and could put my trust in neither.

As for the merchant, he'd listened to all my father said with a worried, kindly expression, his eyebrows puckered, as if in the space behind them he weighed up every syllable; and the better to support such mental effort, his face rested heavily on the fat which even in those days had formed a pad beneath his chin.

But now and then he smiled.

And when my father had said his say, and after a suitable pause had followed, Piero Sassoli began to speak.

Of course! Of course! . . . The bond between father and son. Could any be stronger? Except, perhaps, the bond between mother and son? (Here his visitor nodded.) And to work the land in one's frail old age without that help which is right and proper – now there was a hardship, certainly . . . (More deep nods from the visitor.)

Piero Sassoli also nodded. Then he sighed.

Yes . . . Indeed . . . what could he do? Gismo must go if he wished! So much was obvious. It would never be said of Piero Sassoli that he kept a man from his duty . . .

On which fine sentiment, his eyes came round and regarded me, and, to my fright, I thought I saw laughter in them.

'Well now, Gismo,' he said gravely. 'Will you take to the soil, do you think? Do you relish the prospect?'

Then he waited in all politeness for me to reply. As if he had no comprehension of what I might feel. I could only gape. Had he put his question in Turkish, I couldn't have been more at a loss. Finally I asked, 'What do you mean?'

Piero Sassoli looked impatient.

'I mean,' he said, 'will you go or stay? You won't be pushed through the gate . . . but go, if you want to. The choice must be yours.'

– And he made it sound of no more concern to him than a hearty supper.

At that my mind fled. I stood at my corner, dumb, wretched; and after a while, he added, smiling, 'Think of your duty.'

I looked at my father. His own smile had vanished. Now his mouth formed a strange half-pout, while something like conflict had deepened the lines round his eyes, causing them to crinkle. When he saw me look, he repeated quickly, 'Yes, boy! Your duty! You'll have to come, unless . . . '

There he stopped.

One step in an honest direction, and all his courage was spent. A trace of panic crossed his features. His lips began to curve again with that hideous mock civility.

'Unless?' inquired the merchant, shifting a little on his seat and opening his eyes very wide. 'You were about to say, I suppose, something to do with compensation?'

'That's right!' Stretching his neck and jerking his head, 'I'm not a monster!' my father gabbled. 'If the boy wants to stay . . . but I must have something . . . '

'You would, you're saying, need compensation. Yes. I see.'

And now, gently, Piero Sassoli brought his hands together, pressing his fingers against each other, while his large face grew perplexed – an attitude as false as most of what passed in the conversation, though whether I sensed that at the time –

No matter.

Piero Sassoli looked perplexed, and our triangle filled with a massive stillness. On my father's cheek – his right cheek, for I stood to his right – perspiration glistened.

Then, softly, over the peak of his hands, like some cunning philosopher, Piero Sassoli said, 'But my dear Cavalletti. Here we encounter a problem. For you, it appears, require compensation if Gismondo doesn't go with you. And I . . . ' behind the fingers his smile was broadening, 'most certainly I shall require compensation if he does. Think of the training I've given him. All I've invested that's barely begun to pay. But perhaps after all . . . ' Now he looked hopeful. 'We have no problem? If you've brought back a part of that sum which I paid you six years ago . . . I'd consider half about fair . . . '

My father turned and left. He went with an oath thrown back at Piero Sassoli, and a particular curse for me. 'Damned' and 'unnatural' he called me; and as he was turning away again, his face, I thought, collapsed inwards under a weight of exhaustion – as if to leave without profit were not in the end so terrible, provided he left at all. He went with his head sunk low between his shoulders, and no pride in his step.

Smiling, Piero Sassoli watched till he was gone. Then he scraped back his chair.

'Well,' he said, 'why are you staring, boy? Haven't you work to do? But keep away from the gate for a while . . . '

And so this business ended.

My work, an inventory of the cooking utensils – since Monna Margherita's death some had gone missing – occupied me till evening. I worked hard and thought very little about anything.

But once night came, as I lay in the dark waiting for sleep, I allowed this fatherly visit into my mind, where it seemed to turn on a wheel, and no sooner was it fully examined than it began to turn again. And I noted, without understanding what

I should think of it, though it seemed a fact to scrutinise like a heathen object which might be either dangerous or precious – or both – that when I'd left my father's farm that day with Piero Sassoli, I had not been given away.

I had cost.

I remember holding that fact.

As for the rest – forget it quickly, that seemed safest. Throw it away, and sleep and wake, and sleep and wake, while months piled over the day as if it had never happened. That was my strategy.

But even so, there in the dark I know I asked questions. And especially I thought of 'the mother. The boy's mother.' Could there be truth in what he'd said – about 'tears' and 'reproaches'?

Questions like sirens. I deluded myself, and entertained them. I thought I was safe. I believed with the utmost faith that when I woke in the morning I'd already have accepted the answers, indeed, already have forgotten them –

No truth, not a grain.

XXXII

BUT memory is fickle. It squanders moments which pleased us, and countless of our valuable, most intricate perceptions – but it hoards like a miser events which were best cast out.

I never forgot those questions, nor how I'd answered them; and to the very word 'mother' I shaped in myself a hard indifference – one that became like a flint with an edge which, at the sound of the word, could sever me from all interest in a conversation.

I never forgot. My life filled with dread. I lived in terror of seeing my father again. Of coming from the warehouse to find him among the rogues and inventors who waited each evening for Piero Sassoli's attention. And often I'd imagine how the merchant would turn to me with a look of distaste and say, 'Isn't that your father? Ask what he wants. It must be you he's come to visit. He can have no business with *me*.'

The shame of it.

And if Gabriello were there, our smiling angelic infant, listening – how he'd sweetly approach me afterwards: 'That man with the dirty hands and the smell – why were you so polite to him?'

Dread.

Of callers, who interrupted a meal. Of strangers, who came to the warehouse and paused in the doorway, dark figures obscuring the sunlight. For ten years I lived in a sickness of expectation.

Then news came. And irreproachably. For it was brought not by a pedlar or wandering beggar, nor by some oaf who stood in the centre of the warehouse and bellowed out to everyone that he was my cousin. Instead, there came to my desk one day a timid youth, the soul of discretion, who bore a note from the priest of San Giorgio, a village at no great distance from my father's farm. And this note he delivered with so much reserve and respect that he drew no attention, despite his country looks and manners. Rigogli saw only an errand boy, someone he might have engaged in gossip but that he gossiped already: a man had come seeking a street, which none of us had heard of. And the errand boys, I think, took him for one like themselves – fiendishly skilled in the art of apparent diffidence, and ready to thrust out his tongue the instant my back was turned – so they ignored him.

But this courier was of another breed. As he gave me the letter his hand trembled, and I saw he was filled with a lively sense of how far I'd travelled from all that *he* called home.

I gave him twenty-five soldi, enough to bring a light to his eyes, and he left at once. No awkward whispers about the family. No hints that he'd hoped for advancement. He even spared me the knowledge of whether or not we were related. The soul of discretion. And thanks to this, the note provoked so little interest that I read it quite openly, there at my desk – to demonstrate that it was, indeed, nothing.

I read – and was overjoyed. A shackle fell from me. I moved like a man escaped from his jailer. Hurrying over to Piero Sassoli, I blurted out, 'My father's dead. He was buried two days ago!'

The merchant sat on a stool by Rassuccio, dictating letters; and when I broke in on his sentence, he looked up at me, incredulous. He frowned.

'What will you do?' he asked. Then I knew at once he expected something. Some – filial tribute. I lowered my voice.

' . . . pay for a Mass . . . '

'Good . . . Good . . . ' He nodded. His face relaxed. 'Everyone's mortal, Gismo . . . Well, you can't have too many Masses!'

After that, he went on dictating. Rassuccio's pen made scratching noises; I returned to my desk – careful, this time, to walk more slowly. I folded the note, and refrained from reading it again until evening.

I have it by heart:

> In the name of your brother Niccolò, your sisters Francesca and Ghirigora, and their husbands Matteo and Lorenzo, I, the priest of San Giorgio, write to tell you that your father has died, and was buried on the sixth day of this month. You are told because your father wished it, but your brother Niccolò desires you to know that your father meant him to have the farm, since Giovanni, the eldest, is a man of God, and you can have no use for it. It was also your father's wish that you give your brother Niccolò whatever assistance you can to improve the farm, so it may prosper. There is urgent need for a second donkey, and, since Niccolò is young, for the hire of a man to strengthen the ditches in order to save the olive trees.

Niccolò. A brother still in the womb when I left the farm. And Francesca. Ghirigora. The sisters I'd played with, baffling them with pebbles.

And their husbands.

Again and again I read this message. I followed the twists and curves of the words – and explored new shackles. New, because although I'd carried them always with me, I'd been so oppressed by fear of my father, that I'd scarcely noticed these other bonds. But now they threatened to tighten.

At dawn I rode out to San Giorgio.

I explained to Piero Sassoli that I felt I must see 'if everything was correctly done' – a tale he accepted with some impatience. He cut me short, and nodded to be rid of me.

'Quite right!' he said. 'Just as you will!'

I believe he resented it – a whole day wasted; one tribute too many. It was, in any case, not as I willed. But during the night I'd discovered such a horror of my shackles – that something I had to do.

So I rode to San Giorgio.

And on my way, the heavens broke open; a torrent of rain whipped my back, soaking and chilling me. It was a morning unblessed by the sun, when one longs to huddle for warmth with a pot of coals on one's knees – but despite that, I turned from the road, for I meant to take a longer route and avoid any glimpse of the farm. And I was appalled to discover that I chose my direction so promptly: I remembered the region too well.

At noon I reached the village. I sought out the inn – and that, too, was as I remembered it: verminous and dismal. A place of slops and grease, where the local peasants held their gatherings, and beggars pestered anyone who came near the door – beggars with the look of villains, who'd mark out a generous man to stab him in the night. A place where only the most ignorant traveller – or else a saint – would hazard his life in sleep.

From there, I summoned the priest.

Then I settled to wait. At a bench, with a flagon of wine. While the local men crowded together on the other side of the room.

My clothes being drenched, I shivered; but I sprawled to give a show of ease, and was gratified to see the effect I made: my best coat, which was green lined with vermilion, looked totally remarkable in such a setting; and my clean hands against the vileness of the table – these were precisely the advantages I'd hoped for. But the outer door stood open, and as the rain splashed past, and a cold draught ran across my shoulders, it was all I could do to appear indifferent to my discomfort. So I sprawled all the more, and even opened my coat, as if the room in some way stifled me. By all of which I meant to convey the impression that a man who could dress as finely as I did, and could boast of hands as clean as mine, had other, superior protection against the cold. Gifts of the intellect.

But in truth I suffered. Thank God I was fortunate; the priest came quickly.

He was a man of my own age. Young, half-starved, but with noble features, possessing a face such as one finds on a lawyer or a scholar. And I saw at once that I had need to be proud. For he was proud. He considered his life in San Giorgio a martyrdom. I knew it from his look, and the way he lowered himself to the grease-stained bench.

No sooner was he seated than I pushed ten florins across the table.

'My name', I said, 'is Gismondo Cavalletti. You wrote to me. You will give this money to my brother, Niccolò. And this I promise. If any of my family come hunting me down, swearing they never received it, I'll have you denounced for a thief. Believe me, I have sufficient influence. And although they won't be able to find me – I'll be in Spain for a time – if they trouble my patron, I'll hear of it. Then my friends will see that you're punished. And Niccolò, too, for paining the merchant who looks on me as a son, and dislikes this kind of intrusion . . .'

Then I set down two florins. For the Mass. A handsome payment.

Thus, by an act of contrition and panic, all the little I'd saved I gave away to loosen my shackles, shrink out of them, if I could –

And perhaps I succeeded. I don't dare believe it. Yet the years pass –

The priest chose to think himself insulted. While I talked, he pressed his lips together, disdainful, as if I were offering him rotten fish, and I saw that he pined to refuse to deliver the money. But since he knew I could have the Mass said elsewhere, and then he'd lose for himself much needed bounty, and since his pride was smarting, a fact he had to condemn – for he was manifestly saving his soul in all he did – his hand closed over my gifts, and he rose to go in silence.

It was then, when he turned from me, that I spoke without knowing it.

'And my mother?' I asked. 'Is she well?' – or words which must have meant the same, for he looked back stiffly and said:

'I know nothing about her. The man had no wife. Not in my time here.'

'And how long might that be?'

But he took his revenge. Pretending to be so preoccupied that he missed my question, away he went, hurrying into the rain.

Grey rain, forming a pool of mud by the door.

It hardly mattered. I couldn't have asked him a second time.

Dead ten years? From an excess of 'tears and reproaches'? Or earlier still, long before my father's visit? I could live without enlightenment.

I sipped my wine. The priest had left a tension behind him. I craved escape. The room stank of cheese and broth. Across from me at a table sat several dull-looking peasants. I sensed that they'd come together to celebrate some agreement they'd made – but now they said nothing. They eyed me over their dishes. To them, I perceived, I was monstrous – a thing like the freak that was born in Bartolo with a twisted body and the head of a goat. My clothes, my bearing, my face – every part of me was hateful to them. I soured their celebration. Did my sisters' husbands sit among them? Their chatter had died away while I talked to the priest. They'd heard what I said. But no one came forward. I forced myself to drain the cup, pour out more wine. Something, I felt, must happen. One of these men would get to his feet, come slouching forward, and claim his kinship. Or splashing in from the mud would come a sharp-eyed youth, secretly sent for, to cry out that he was Niccolò. I waited in terror for either event. But still I sprawled defiantly, so that no one should see my fear. Power and contempt. That was the message I meant to leave. That was the reason I'd conducted my business at the inn.

So I sprawled and drank, returning the stares of the men who studied me; and inside my terror an anger kindled – against the priest.

'The *man*,' he'd said. Meaning – my father. A sneer. A word to say: 'Your kind signifies nothing. The people you come from are little more than the dirt they dig. They're indistinguishable from each other. A man is a man among them, just as a stone is a stone, or a clod is a clod.'

He had more than matched my arrogance. I plotted a fresh encounter. I thought up choice phrases. My anger sustained me. I burned with it – and outstared the peasants. I compelled them to look away again and start mumbling over their dishes.

Only then did I leave.

XXXIII

TO outface our golden boy! Here's an event that's worth remembering!

Just now, when Piero Sassoli and I returned from Mass, we found Gabriello regaling his friend Andreuccio. They're seated together on the stairs. They have wine and slices of sweetmeat. And Piero Sassoli, seeing the cups and plates, grew as dark as a thundercloud – which Gabriello observed; so draping an arm round Andreuccio he cried, 'Now, father, don't be angry! I love him like a brother! Would you have me send him home famished?'

Shaking his head, the merchant hurried into the garden.

But as for myself, since they made no effort to clear a space and let me pass, I stood at the foot of the stairs, watching. They made a show of ignoring me. They talked about falcons. So at last I said, 'That sweetmeat . . . it was a gift to your father from Ser Romoli's wife . . . '

Gabby looked up.

'It was? What of it?' he said. 'If my father doesn't mind our eating it . . . why, pray, should you mind?'

At that I did push past. To have stood there defending Piero

Sassoli's sweetmeats would have been fatuous. They laughed as I came upstairs. But here's the point: normally I shrug this laughter off, whereas today, for once, from the top of the stairs I called back: 'You'd be starving by now if I didn't mind!'

Oh, terrible.

Gabby's face changed. His blithe smile slipped. Maybe he doubted if he'd heard. But smartly the answer came: 'People with friends have no fear of starving!' and again he embraced the grinning Andreuccio.

Even so, I saw he was startled. He knew there was truth in my words, and I count this exchange a victory.

XXXIV

THE moon – so bright, I can dispense with the candles.

Whether it's a world like ours.

Whether its people resemble us – except they're more graceful.

Or else uglier.

Or if the moon is truly Limbo – whether souls are visible. If so, what form? Wisps of smoke? Wraiths, that stretch and travel on moon-beams? Or mere sounds: tinklings and whisperings? Odours? Lavender and sandalwood. The sharpness of vinegar.

What constitutes the soul?

It seems strange to me that a thing so familiar as the moon eludes definition, and that even to say where it is taxes our wits. 'It's there!' we cry. 'There! Over Prato!' and in Prato: 'There! Over Florence!'

Everywhere. Nowhere. And no man has been there. Whereas, of heaven and hell, whose locations are also baffling secrets, almost anyone can claim that at least he has visited hell at some time or other, by his own road.

Piero Sassoli once told me that fashionable thinkers suspect the moon is a cold orb, and nothing more. A home to no living thing, nor spirit neither. That all it amounts to is rock and dust. 'Although', he said, 'there's speculation as to the dust. It may be the remnant of cities, built and lived in by angels before this world was created . . . '

A fine theory.

They're all fine theories, but perversely I have one of my own.

A disc of glass, the size of Rome. And through it, some wise celestial studies us. And as he turns his glass to peer in a new direction, so the moon wanes or waxes.

A great glass, through which we're watched.

It's a thought which Fra Bernardino would call 'iniquitous nonsense'. For our Deity (he'd say) requires no aids. He has perfect vision.

Then I might argue, 'You quote the Scriptures, how "God made the moon as the lesser light" – but countless objects useful to man have other uses for other creatures – so why not the moon? And why not a spying glass, used by some creature greater than us? Nature's devices are carefully husbanded. They rarely serve only one end . . . '

The old man would be sorely puzzled. Dimly he'd sense my meaning – that I spoke of a being essentially neither good nor evil, something beyond his seraphim and Lucifers. Something that thrived on knowledge.

Heresy. Oh, heresy.

The shadings, why do they alter? Mist on the glass? Ice?

And why do all men – not only poets – look to the moon? Why do we send out towards it our tenderest hopes and aspirations?

Surely this is an irony. For if those who live there are people more beautiful than we are, supposing we knew of them, could we find it in us to love them? And could they love us, who might look to them like so many grubs?

Or again, if the people in the moon were known to be hideous – could we love each other?

Worse, if in truth it's a place of spirits – is that anything more than a charnel house? Why yearn towards that? Or supposing the thinkers are right: a blasted Eden – is it the act of rational creatures to look *there* for comfort?

And if it's a spying glass –

From the observations of one outside the confines of our Church, and all our spiritual references – what mercy?

Questions. Questions. A teasing moon tonight.

And my opal: I have it by me, wrapped in its cloth, the knot still tied. My pale Madonna. Everywhere. Nowhere.

And from her – what mercy?

Now I open the cloth; the moonlight falls on her throat, and she smiles her indifference.

'*But only permit me to kneel before you, and you shall know the nature of a true desire. You shall feel it lapping around your knees like flames, as I burn towards you.*'

I should ask Rigogli – did he deliver my 'Moorish poem'? 'Speak the truth, and I'll forgive you! Did you – to embarrass me . . . ?'

Or one or other of the errand boys. Shall I squawk my question at them all?

'Who found my note?'

It may lie even now in a box, where she stores the vows of love that come to her from every quarter of Florence. One plea among many.

Her hands having touched the paper I wrote on. Her breath on my words.

This is the wine that writes. It's late.

We were unexpectedly asked to supper with Gino Salviati – a surprising gesture since this is a merchant who has lost much trade to us in the past, and whenever he meets Piero Sassoli in the street, he barely troubles to acknowledge him. But supper it was. A nobly worded invitation, which Piero Sassoli accepted with eagerness – for he looks to be friends with all men, even the man he ruins.

We went there at sunset. There were no other guests, but the table did justice to all the laws of hospitality. I particularly noticed the napkins – best white linen, freshly laundered. The meal itself was pleasing, and Ser Salviati excessively cordial. He claimed it had long been his wish 'to offer some token of amity', he bore no grudge . . . Indeed, he said, he admired a merchant who could better him . . .

This made for enchantment. Piero Sassoli was magnanimous. He had much to say about life's vicissitudes and the wheel of fortune. How this year, one man is up, and the next year, down. So on and so forth. He knows how to make placebos sound like philosophy, and I nodded agreement – although both of us know that when Ser Salviati loses trade, he has only himself to blame, being impatient and erratic.

How much more genial to slander fortune! Politeness and compliments flowed. We were excellent friends.

Then, after the meal, evidently wishing to amuse us, this impoverished merchant besought us to do him the honour of viewing a gadget. 'A contrivance,' he said, which he'd bought for his son's twelfth birthday. 'An extraordinary toy which in spite of itself shows some spirit of enterprise . . .'

We were eager to please. We rose as he rose, and followed him.

And there in the loggia, draped in cloth and steeped in moonlight, stood a thing that murdered Piero Sassoli's smile. A thing he would gladly have given his purse for. I knew it at once, and so did he. Nevertheless, when our host twitched the cloth aside, Piero Sassoli gasped.

It was the pedal chair.

A moment's silence. Then Ser Salviati explained the various chains and levers; and afterwards he asked, 'What do you think? Isn't it ingenious?'

But Piero Sassoli played his part with scant grace. First, he walked round this engine with his mouth a-trembling, and next he growled, 'A dangerous plaything! It's more like a death-trap! Why, look! It's unsteady. The slightest wind could topple it over!' – and seizing hold of the frame, he shook it till it rattled. 'Look at those chains!' he cried. 'They might catch round an ankle . . . And those wheels! They could easily overheat! It could all go up in a blaze . . .'

Ser Salviati listened and, as he did so, a smile of profound contentment spread across his features. He nodded, wrinkled his brow – and in the end he declared himself convinced. He was most obliged. This was timely warning. The contraption was obviously deadly. He'd see it was broken up , . .

Wretched Piero Sassoli!

XXXV

SON and father – a curse on them!

To calm myself, I've checked all the household accounts for the past eight months. Figures and totals. My sanctuary.

And this, too, I suppose could be taken.

For what is Gismondo but an ill-favoured man who sits by the ledgers? Not one of *us*.

The fellow's entirely expendable!

XXXVI

A mighty storm has gripped the city. While I write, the walls shudder as if iron talons were striking against them, and the air howls. The shouts of men who scutter through the streets sound like the squeaks of mice, miles apart from each other –

If it would all fall apart! Houses, streets, city – if we were clawed apart and, defying the laws of nature, could be hurled in thousands of different directions!

Piero Sassoli, caught up in his second best coat, bowling away clutching inventions to his breast, dwindling into the stars over Pisa.

And Gabriello: his plumed hat flying to the east, his fine cloak flying to the west, while the lout himself pitched and tossed through the clouds until, drenched with spew, he came down to Naples, and plunged head-first into Vesuvius!

And all those smiling, righteous merchants of the Porta Rossa and Calimala lifted up in their tunics and hose, nudged about by the tempest, and set down on the furthest reaches of Scotland, or some other barbaric wilderness.

And the priests! Fra Bernardino. Plucked from his cell, somersaulting over the convents, flung down at last in some Turkish palace of heathen women – and heathen priests even more 'pious' than he is.

And the brim of the world for myself. The extreme void.

A tile has fallen from the roof.

Would to God we were ripped apart!

Failing that –

We live. And offence is heaped on offences.

Why fear my family? Vulgar sisters, grasping brother – I've done with dreading them. Let them come. Let them flock to the gate, let them come crowding into the warehouse. I've no more blushes. I'd laugh in their faces. Let them shout it abroad: 'You know Cavalletti, who works for Piero Sassoli? Well, we're his kin!' It no longer concerns me.

Why should I fear exposure when even without it I'm nothing? Nothing.

Yesterday proved it.

Our golden boy –

One of his rare, unwelcome visits to the warehouse. Unwelcome, that is, to me, and also to Rigogli who has never forgiven him some prank or other: often the old man mumbles that he'll go beg if the Master sees fit to die before him, because he never could abide a trickster. Strange, since his stories are all of tricks.

But Piero Sassoli shone with joy at this visit and, abandoning his letters, he hastened to greet the prodigal, crying, 'How this pleases me! This pleases me!' Then he patted Gabriello on the arm – one would have thought a most perilous journey lies between house and warehouse – and Gabriello, too, looked vastly pleased. So pleased, indeed, that I thought at once: 'He's come with news. And the one to gain from his news is himself.'

Yet what could be of such importance that rather than wait till evening he'd carry it into the place of business?

It was a riddle – and I could see it delighted him, for while Piero Sassoli fussed and sent a boy to buy some comfits (we must be festive when great men call), Gabriello showed none of his usual impatience. He stood by quietly. He was so well contented that looking across to me, when he saw I'd raised my head from the ledgers he nodded – I'd have said pleasantly, if he'd been anyone else. I returned the gesture – the boys were watching – and he proffered me a smile, confident, no doubt, of the figure he struck, for he looks very fine in green. Heaviest velvet, as dark as laurel. It lends him considerable dignity. It accentuates his height and slimness – both of them legacies from Monna Margherita. It agrees with the darkness of his eye, and shows off to advantage his astonishing blondness. In short, he looked magnificent. He might have been the son of a Duke. There was even a most unwonted restraint as to brooches and medals, which increased the general impression he gave of good taste and breeding. No one could possibly have guessed that here was the son of a stout and red-faced merchant.

Gabriello. So benign! Smiling and dutiful, while his father prattled in a way which I've never known him tolerate. A sight as rare as a unicorn. 'This news', I thought, 'must be very precious. Bad news he blurts out. All his debts and quarrels and grievances. Or any boast of the common kind. But this is something he loves to hoard and anticipate the telling of . . . '

Finally, when Piero Sassoli had calmed a little, Gabby drew him away, coaxing him back to his desk and making him sit. Then, leaning close to the merchant's ear, he started to whisper.

There, in front of me. Even cupping his hand round his mouth.

Piero Sassoli, I thought, would object. At first he frowned and looked perplexed – but suddenly he brightened. He asked a question, and whatever he heard, it inflamed him with happy surprise, most avid interest. And the more the golden boy talked, the closer they brought their heads together, and once or twice they glanced at me –

They needn't have troubled! My ears aren't bats to fly the distance between the desks. And in any case I worked. The devil take their whisperings!

But Gabriello must have his intrigues: seeing me apparently occupied, he cried out as if he forgot himself, 'That's wonderful! I knew you would! Thank you, father!' – so that no one could help but hear, and knowing how it must startle me.

Thanks! The son gave thanks. Record it, ye heavens! The number I wrote lost all proportion. My pen blotched. Nevertheless, I kept it firmly set on the page while, flushed with secrets, he came bustling past. But as he drew level, my eyes looked up – not by design – and the smile he gave me dimmed the sunlight.

'How are you, Gissy?'

On he hurried to the door with Piero Sassoli close behind him, begging him to stay for at least the rest of the morning and 'take an interest'.

'I'd have liked to, father, but you know I can't. Not today. I must go a-visiting!' – brushing aside the boy who'd come back with comfits.

Then the final insult.

As he left, he turned and waved to me – and with such an appearance of candour that for once I was tricked. I actually waved back.

The errand boys grinned. Old Rigogli coughed. Even Rassuccio, who'd raised his nose from his papers as a mark of respect for the princeling, stared at me. I wiped my hand on my sleeve. Everyone grinned all the harder. My face burned. The ledger before me seemed to turn to ash. If I tried to write, I felt that the page might crumble –

To have made such a display of excluding me! Oh, I understood it. He could have taken his father aside, suggested a turn in the street, discreetly requested to talk in private – but there, with everyone watching – and cupping his hand round his mouth, as if I were some notorious spy!

And Piero Sassoli to allow it.

Then after the injury, the fulsome greeting to bear home the message: Don't think that you've won my father's confidence! See how easily I make him forget you. We'll suffer you thus far, my father and I. Not that we feel the need, but if you know your place, we'll grant you a living. And being sensitive souls, we shall all be polite. 'How are you, Gissy?'

The merchant was speedy to make amends. Poor amends, since he was less than honest.

He approached in a flurry, mopping his face with his handkerchief.

'Well now, Gissy . . . ' – never before has he called me that – 'well now, Gissy, here's marvellous news! Our young buck's made an impression, and one where I least expected it. A very considerable gentleman. This opens up prospects! And to think how I've worried! There's a fortune in it . . . But slowly . . . slowly . . . Nothing must be rushed! When the right time comes, we'll hold a banquet, that's the thing. We must entertain this gentleman. Just a family occasion – but good enough to show that we're not from the gutter! We must all be there. Margherita's brother. My sister's family – I'll send for them. And you, of course . . . '

'Will not be there!' I finished for him.

'What?' Piero Sassoli's face looked soft and shocked; and when he spoke again, I could hear the stammer which has troubled him in recent months. 'But Gabby specifically . . . my dear, good fellow . . . Gabriello most assuredly . . . '

'It wouldn't be fitting.'

And to show the merchant how tranquil I was, I dipped my pen in the ink. Then I had no choice but to set it down, as my hand was shaking. To keep him from making too much of this, I looked up at him quickly, and found he was watching not my hands, but my face.

'Why?' he sputtered. 'I can't think you mean . . . '

'Oh, you know why.'

– I don't belong. It's not the work of a father to whisper to one son in front of the other, and expect to be asked no questions. I'm no more than a lackey – These are the things I meant to say. But I felt contempt. Trust, respect, affection – where's the value in gifts that have to be clamoured for? I scorn such gifts. So all I said was, 'Oh, you know why.'

Piero Sassoli's chin dipped and his mouth sagged. He began

to gaze at me so intently that one might have thought he'd been blind for years, and was only now vouchsafed his sight again, that he'd only just noticed how large and dark my blemish had grown, and that despite his pride in da Vinci's interest, he was thinking what a ruinous spectacle I'd make at his family gathering.

Then, seeing that I watched him study me, he was greatly confused. His colour heightened. He shook his head and turned from me muttering, 'I'm not going to argue . . . '

'I congratulate Gabriello,' I said, 'but as for the banquet . . . '

'Just as you will. Do as you will.'

He escaped to his desk, snatched up a sheaf of papers, and busied himself.

That was the sum of it. No more inquiry. No protestations. Whereas in the past, no matter how reluctant I've shown myself, Piero Sassoli has always insisted I sit with the family on any important occasion.

– And now I've created a precedent! I doubt if ever again I'll be counted among the Sassoli. I've exiled myself.

Or else – now here's a thought sprung up like a poisonous toadstool – was I manoeuvred? Did Piero Sassoli secretly wish it? In his mind did he say, 'This suits me well'?

I can easily believe it. Why else should he hurry away, without wishing to know my reasons – even demanding them?

No matter. In truth, I profit from the merchant's dishonesty, for my own position is now made honest. Now I'm placed outside, which is precisely where I've always been. By rights, I should glory in yesterday. Refusing my place at the banquet – that was an act of honour.

And yet the pain. He needn't have agreed so readily.

Today – nothing, not a mention; although one of the errand boys, when he thought my back was turned, waved at me. And all day long, Rigogli was sullen. Piero Sassoli, on the other hand, was amiable and generous with compliments.

'Here, Gismo, may I trouble you to read this? From Guido Migliorati. About French linen. No one could quarrel with his price, but his last consignment – weren't we somehow disappointed? Some problem, I forget . . . But you, I know, can hold these things in your head far better than I . . . ' And afterwards:

'What a splendid memory! I'm obliged to you, Gismo. Thank you. Thank you.'

So I came away thinking that perhaps I'd made too much of yesterday's incident.

I came back alone. Despite the storm, Piero Sassoli has gone to visit Simone Noseda. And as I forced my way through the streets, pushing against the wind, I felt in an excellent humour, calm and lightened. My grievance, I thought, might be scattered on the air like rags and papers. I was willing enough to let it go –

But then I entered the house, and in the hall I found an inventor: a fool with a lamp which he claimed changed the colour of its flame in the presence of spirits, and it took such trouble to be rid of him that I became pained by everything – the tick of that monstrous clock, the chatter of the women in the kitchen –

I retreated upstairs. I sat here and listened to the storm. I discovered a curious satisfaction in hearing its blows on the walls. The house groans. It creaks. My supper was brought, but I've barely touched it. I entered an item in the accounts – and all the time my anger was mounting.

Compliments. 'What a splendid memory! I'm obliged to you, Gismo.'

Am I an ape, to be schooled in bows and grins whenever I'm offered a honeyed comfit?

Rage on, storm! My blessings on you. Howl your worst. Bruise this city. Tear her, humble her!

I thank you kindly.

XXXVII

'*ARE we never to smile again, because you have your cross to bear?*'

And another time he said, 'How you cherish yourself, Gismondo! How minutely you examine every misfortune!'

And at dawn this morning, when I went to him, and found him with another in the cloister garden, before I could open my mouth to speak, he smiled and said, 'But here comes one who bears the world on his shoulders!'

Thus he proves his complacence.

Friars – isn't it they who cherish themselves? Don't they withdraw from the rest of us to nurture their tiny souls? Don't they bear their cross with greater pomp than anyone else? Isn't it they who believe they shoulder the world?

– But I chose to contradict him only by my silence, and Fra Bernardino seemed pleased for that, saying as one might to an infant grandson, 'You're welcome, Gismondo! Come, walk with us. After last night's storm, Fra Filippo and I are looking about, as you see, and reckoning the damage . . . Those shrubs over there, for instance . . . and the figtree, all but uprooted! Even here, in so sheltered and holy a place as this, the world wreaks havoc. From this we may learn . . . '

'I've no time, Father. I must make my confession.'

'So urgent, Gismondo?' His voice was sharp with reproach, for he likes his sermons. None the less I'd silenced him, and without more words he led the way to the chapel.

Then I described my anger. How I'd lain awake in the night, and refined schemes: setting fire to the house, or creeping with a knife to the slumbering Gabriello – ideas which in the light of dawn had horrified me. I described them all, and when I'd done, he patted my wrist, just as usual – but his hand shook, and he said nothing.

So, smiling, I asked him, 'Am I to hear none of your admonitions?' – and this increased his discomfort. His eyes turned from me.

'My son,' he said, 'consider. Our Lord may wish you to find salvation by other means. I'm a simple man, and very foolish. There are confessors more learned than I, and far more able . . . '

'Oh, you suffice!' His sudden timidity disgusted me. 'Listen,' I said, 'if God so fervently wishes me saved, even the weakest of His instruments – even you – ought to suffice. Isn't He omnipotent?' – and immediately I came away. The old man clucked most woefully behind me.

It was a beautiful morning. Birds sang. The sky glowed like the stem of a candle that burns with a soft flame. A scent of foliage, young and cleansed by dew, hung on the air. The storm was truly over. I regretted my words to Fra Bernardino.

A storm is not the whole of life.

And he means well, after his fashion. He's not to be blamed for his small wit. The blame lies with his Creator.

Piero Sassoli didn't come home last night. It had made no sense, he said, to battle his way through a whirlwind. So today he came late to the warehouse, white in the face and red round the eyes. He declared that Noseda's best bed is as damp as the Arno and full of lumps, and the shutters had clapped and banged incessantly.

XXXVIII

THIS great supper – this banquet! It stirs the air in the house as a child might ruffle a cat's fur. Every corner bristles with expectation! Everywhere there's a breeze, a fluttering talk of this fine occasion!

A most considerable gentleman, one who sees merit in Gabriello and promises sure advancement – although precisely the nature of this advancement no one as yet seems to know, nor even the name of the gentleman. But at all events, a magnificent supper, the like of which has never been held by Piero Sassoli, with two cooks borrowed from friends to supplement the labours of the household cook, and the best musicians in Florence to be hired, and a cousin to be fetched from Genoa, and Piero Sassoli's own sister to come with her gouty husband from Padua, though she hasn't been back to Florence in thirty-four years of marriage. A feast to encompass the entire family.

XXXIX

PIERO Sassoli behaves like a guilty taverner who has once too often fed me on dog-meat! He continues his efforts to be amiable, and this evening – a rare thing when he has company – he begged me to take my meal with him. I was willing to do so, for despite all I feel, I find it gives me no particular pleasure to cause him pain.

And this guest he has – here's an unlooked-for development! An eminent physician from Venice, one Maestro Ruccelli. Laden with recommendations and sent, it seems, by the merchant's agent to do what he can for Piero Sassoli's stomach. It has all been kept the closest secret. Not till this afternoon when a boy came running with news of the Maestro's arrival did Piero Sassoli enlighten me. And then he looked half surprised himself. He drew me aside.

'This is Francesco's doing,' he muttered. 'He's always meddling! I happened to mention at the end of one of my letters how I was troubled by indigestion, and he wrote that he knew just the man to cure it. But when to expect this Ruccelli I'd no idea. I suppose I might have told you about it, but I'm aware you worry on my account – and you see, it's nothing. Francesco's only stocking up credit . . . Well, Gismo, you must sup with us.' And then he added hopefully, 'There must be someone who can cure it. Such a commonplace ailment!'

Maestro Ruccelli perhaps. If any physician is more than a quack, this man might be. Even at supper he worked, watching his host, as if the merchant's every move were a coded message. And Piero Sassoli, sensing those eyes upon him, ate much less than he normally does. Straight-backed he sat like a maiden, and scarcely appeared to notice his plate, until at last the good wine came to his aid: then he relaxed enough to gaze at the food with longing, and to break off a piece of crust from the pie he'd refused – but half of that he left on the table.

By all of which I perceived that this visitor is welcome. The merchant has little faith in his Florentine physician – a murderously short-sighted, windy individual. His last prescription was an evil paste to be smeared twice a day on the belly, but it stung so much that after a single application Piero Sassoli himself took the pot into the courtyard and smashed it. So now his hopes must rest on a stranger. It's a circumstance not unlike mine that time I tried to sell the opal, and the craftsmen of Rome formed a league against me. Florentine physicians know the same trick. They'll come in their droves to secure a case, but once there's a treatment under way, none can be found who'll give his opinion against a colleague. So much they pamper their interests, these quacks, and call it the ethics of physic – and God succour the patient! All he can do is suffer – or bring in a man from somewhere else.

And so in this – as in most things – Piero Sassoli has told me less than the truth. I believe he sent for this Maestro himself. Otherwise, how strange, that he takes a whim of Francesco's so seriously! What a curious chance that this visitor comes only two days after I'm told to buy fresh veal and pork, and have Rumanian wine brought down from the farm.

Just one more deception. A small one, true: I'd have called it a trivial irritation – if there hadn't been a sore already.

But the merchant, housing a physician! The fact that he feels the need of it – that transforms all annoyance into worries, speculations. There's a warning in it. While I sat at the table, repeatedly I told myself, 'Beware, Gismondo! What's happening tonight is like a bell tolling away your security!' Yet my mind was ever perverse. I've found much pleasure in the evening.

For one thing, Gabriello was absent – gone to Rome, where he hopes to find 'a suitable gift' for his fine new patron. And then, this Maestro Ruccelli: he's a person of more than common intellect; a gentleman of such perfect manners that he made no distinction in how he spoke to the merchant and how he spoke to myself, beyond that which is natural to acknowledge one's host.

A gentleman, moreover, who possesses a fund of entertaining information, for he's travelled far, and as he spoke of the countries he'd seen, he described the peoples and their ways with such shrewd, exact observations, that even those places long dulled for me by over-much hearsay became new again, and vivid. So I assessed him: 'Here's a man who goes about with his eyes wide open, and blinks at nothing.'

After a while, he spoke of earthquakes – he'd witnessed the misery caused by one in Portugal – and he offered us this theory.

The earth, he suggested, is alive. Like all living creatures, she must breathe, and from time to time she falls ill. Then she writhes and vomits, or breaks out in blisters – those manifestations which we call earthquakes, landslides, eruptions.

'Now, if we were willing to study the air,' he said, 'which I take to be the breath of the world, we should know in advance of earthquakes. For just as with men and animals, so with the earth. When she falls sick, her breath becomes foetid, hot and irregular – symptoms it's possible to recognise, and by learning to know these signs when they came, we might avoid catastrophes. Towns and cities could be emptied in time. Countless lives could be saved.'

A healer's notion; so much a physician's, that I couldn't conceal my smile. I was put in mind of a baker I once heard maintain that the earth's a pudding, and it overflows in its dish whenever the oven becomes too hot. 'Which is why', he asserted, 'the hottest countries are worst afflicted by earthquakes. Even a child could see it!'

But Maestro Ruccelli took no offence at my smile. Instead, as if he guessed my thoughts, he smiled also – in a manner that made it plain he treated himself with no great reverence.

Piero Sassoli, on the other hand, was deeply impressed by all the physician had said, and I saw his face lengthen. Then, leaning across the table, he spluttered, 'But if you say the earth's alive – you make it mortal! All that lives . . . we all have to die!'

'How do we know?' said Maestro Ruccelli: and when he received no answer – 'Ser Sassoli, I put it to you, where can we find the evidence? If you passed an immortal in the street, do you think you'd be aware of it? Do you suppose he'd look so different from other men?'

'I can't imagine . . . ' Piero Sassoli wiped his mouth and energetically crumpled his napkin. He's ill at ease in a philosophical conversation, but he meant to pursue his subject and, blinking, he asked: 'You're not implying such people exist, are you?'

At once the physician shook his head.

'I imply nothing. Perhaps there may be secret beings who somehow contrive it. They may hoop time's changes into a cycle – so that they grow from youth to age, then back from age to youth . . . and so on, for ever. I don't say such exist, only that I can conceive of them. But that any could go untouched by time, never changing – that, like you, I can't imagine. In everything there's change. In the very earth it's everywhere. We quarry stone from the hills. Rivers alter their courses. Where there were fields, a town springs up. Where there was once a town, now we find rubble . . . Time, like faith, can move mountains . . . '

And suddenly he fell silent, as though the Alps were turning to dust before his eyes.

'Yes,' said Piero Sassoli.

Maestro Ruccelli raised his wine cup.

'Forgive me,' he smiled. 'Any physician takes an interest in time. My tongue runs rather too easily on the subject . . . '

'Oh, please! Most fascinating, please!' cried the merchant, reddening, as if he feared to be thought out of patience; his hands began to flap like pigeons over his plate – and it seemed to me that his guest took careful note of this agitation before he continued:

'Physicians are closely concerned with changes. The infant forming in the womb, the strong man daily growing weaker, the scar that slowly heals – all are changes wrought by time. It's a force we must learn to harness . . . which reminds me, Ser Sassoli – what a magnificent clock you have in the hall! I'm very glad you own one. A most valuable aid to healthy living. It promotes routine, and routine is good for the body.'

Praise. Praise. At these acceptable words, Piero Sassoli visibly relaxed, while Maestro Ruccelli, seeing that his host was soothed, went on to describe the famous clock in Pavia. A mighty engine of dials and chains that does, in truth, appear to harness time, confining it, controlling it in days and months, years and feast days. And as the physician spoke, his voice became mild with delight; it warmed with a cautious allowance of excitement, and I found myself trembling. He described this clock so intimately that I seemed to walk about inside it. For the space of a breath, I shared his vision – this harnessing of time, this knowing it down to its smallest part, and all its power somehow brought to use. It's not my personal vision, but close. Instead of time – mathematics. Where his units are days, weeks and so forth, I've only to substitute numbers – a machine to harness the mystery of totalling and subtracting, of dividing and multiplying in all their possible combinations – and our dreams would be the same. Then, as I listened, two remarks occurred to me: one I kept to myself and one I didn't.

The silent thought was this: what a mercy to have a clock in hell! Any, provided it came from this world – even the monstrous thing which Piero Sassoli owns. For no two sounds from a machine can be identical – the metal must wear – and even eternity would be less daunting if we could hear it broken up, moment told off from moment. We could say in our anguish, 'The pain I'm suffering now is not the pain of a moment ago, for that time has ended, and taken my feelings with it. And this moment must also end, and take this feeling with it.' So, even in hell, we might have a sensation of change.

The other thought I spoke out loud, without fearing for the consequences – a compliment to Maestro Ruccelli.

'How fine it would be', I said, 'if we could all carry a clock about with us! In our purses, or hung on a cord round our necks. To know at a glance, no matter where we happened to be

– in the street, or the office, even on a ship – the point at which we stood between yesterday and tomorrow. The exact point! How that must heighten our sense of life, and strengthen us in our purposes!'

At this the Maestro laughed – not in derision, but rather with pleasure.

'Portable clocks for us all? One to each man? And the women?' he asked. 'Shall they have clocks to gauge how long they've gossiped?'

'Even the women,' I said.

'Wonderful! Though – as a physician, I can't approve. Carrying such a weight all day would never do. The servants must do the carrying – and take it in turns.'

'Oh, no . . . ' Then all at once I saw my idea clearly: I selected a cube of sweetmeat. 'I was picturing clocks so small, they'd weigh no more than this!' – and I held up the cube to the candlelight, so that the fragments of cherry in it glistened. The Maestro gazed at it in surprise.

'Now, if that could be done,' he said, 'how nicely we could keep our appointments! With what ease we could measure whether our skills increased or diminished. We could portion our day exactly according to our priorities . . . '

'Utter nonsense!'

Piero Sassoli gave a snort; and after that he reddened again, having unintentionally broken in on his guest, when all his venom was meant for me. Perhaps he was out of sorts because he hadn't eaten his fill, or else – and this is just as likely – it displeased him to see me making so free with conversation. At any rate, his policy of sweetness towards me was forgotten on the instant, and he glared as he scoffed, 'You and your crackpot notions, Gismo! Every man with his own clock! And gardeners too, I suppose? And potboys? And what about porters and water carriers? Or will you draw the line at respectable shop-keepers? Utter nonsense!'

He chuckled, and reddened even more – an embarrassing outburst. I stared at his chest rather than gape at his face or be so weak as to look away, but Maestro Ruccelli, I think, was watching him closely.

Then it came to me that if every fool were to carry a clock, where would be Piero Sassoli's pride in possessing the brute that stands in the hall? But mostly I think he disliked my talking so freely.

Yet if I'd said, 'Speaking of engines, I have this idea . . . this device for sharpening hundreds of needles . . . ' What then?

Would he have cried, 'How brilliant!' – or would it still have been, 'You and your crackpot notions, Gismo!'

But I hadn't meant to complain. Maestro Ruccelli turned us from any unpleasantness, saying quietly, 'Innovations, all the inventions of the future – how they perplex us! Undiscovered discoveries – we're surrounded by them. Why, in ourselves we carry such intricate machinery of flesh and sinew that a man can study it all his life and still know next to nothing. A good physician admits this . . . '

The wise ones, maybe.

I like this Maestro Ruccelli. He treats me with respect. In his face, there's interest when I talk to him, an honest attempt to assess my intellect – such as one permits to be seen only by an equal, inviting them to show the same. I like this more than I can tell, I've encountered it so seldom.

The shutters are open. While I've been writing, rain has fallen. The air smells pure. The moon shines on the neighbouring roofs, laying a white and snow-like path across the tiles, a path that ends in gleams on the shutters – and the water droplets clinging there. I've studied these droplets. No one could call them truly round. Where they hold to the wood they're flattened, and they're fullest at their lowest point where they collect inside themselves, straining for freedom. They shine, they're beautiful – but by the artists' rules they're far from perfect, their shape being hardly any shape. If I breathed on them, they'd quiver. They're almost insubstantial, nothing more than trapped moonlight, and yet if I touched one I'd feel the moisture on my finger. And so, to prove they exist, I'd have destroyed one.

What's to happen? Either they'll fade in the early sun, or break free, be shaken free – and smash upon the tiles.

The moon tonight – that's also far from perfect. Two-thirds formed, neither a sphere nor a crescent.

'*Changes*', said the physician, '*wrought by time*.'

I feel unlike myself. Alert, and very willing to smile. Ridiculous. It seems tonight, sitting in this room, I'm happy. Even the thought of that feast for Gabriello is little, very little – a black roach I could crush with my heel.

Even Madonna – tonight my pain when I think of her is strangely separate from me. It's as if I'd turned it outwards to send wherever I will, like a barb.

Why this joy in me? It makes no sense. Yet why deny it?

May Maestro Ruccelli tend the merchant well.

XL

TODAY I went alone to the warehouse.

After I left last night, Maestro Ruccelli said several things that greatly alarmed the merchant, and this morning Piero Sassoli lay late in bed. Not that he slept any longer than usual; I was barely dressed when he sent for me. At once I sensed the truth, but I made up my mind to appear amazed, because nothing else could be tactful: Piero Sassoli has always scorned the thought that he might be ill in earnest.

So I hurried to his room. There he lay, propped up on pillows. His bed-cap had slipped and was hanging low on his right ear, exposing the dome of his head on the left – a spectacle so extraordinary that I failed to think it comic. Indeed, the whole sight I found extraordinary, his belly whaling up beneath the sheet, his fingers twitching on the covers. Never before had I seen the merchant lying on his back, and I observed for the first time how very short he is, and how long his bed.

When he saw me, he smiled – but such a timid offering that I lost confidence. This I hadn't anticipated: he was abashed. I stopped in the doorway, uncertain how to behave, except that I felt my face must convey only amazement and solicitude – and this proved sound instinct: I passed some test. His manner changed. He waved me forwards.

'So!' he cried. 'There you are! And here, as you see, am I!' – indicating the bed, like a conjurer showing his strangest trick, and his smile grew sharp – as if now that he lay prostrate and the truth was out that Piero Sassoli's ill, he expected the fact to pay some dividend. But what did he want? Cries of distress? Wringing of hands? Weeping on my knees?

I could only hold up my mask of solicitude – though it might have been more than a mask, but he seemed so unsure of his own role. Ruddy-cheeked and amply fleshed, cosseted on his pillows, and yet so nervous – he reminded me of one of those scoundrels who decides the world has neglected him, and so he claims to have talked with the Holy Virgin as she hovered over his henhouse; and now he smiles, implying that the vision was vivid enough, but he found it in a wine flask, and now he holds his head up high as though to say he saw this thing in sober honesty; and now his eyes are full of taunts since no one can prove he lies if he himself is ignorant of the truth: what may not count for a vision?

Or for an illness? It's little different with Piero Sassoli. Maybe he's dying. Or ill, but will soon recover. Or this business may all be nothing. His smile this morning, just like a scoundrel's, was self-important, yet not without some sly apology.

'Now then, Gismo,' he said, pulling a face at the covers, 'you see what I'm brought to! But you mustn't think I willingly play the sluggard. It was no idea of mine! This, I'd have you know, is Venetian physic. Soft and easy as you'd expect. Maestro Ruccelli will fuss like an egg-bound goose if I stir from here before noon. But the worst of it – I'm to be kept from the warehouse for two whole weeks. I'm to swallow great draughts of rest and slumber. How will you manage? *Can* you manage?'

I said I thought I might, and Piero Sassoli grunted.

'I'm to go to the farm,' he said. 'I'll go tomorrow. You must write me a daily account of everything. Don't forget our payment to that fool Mazzetti . . . and my meeting with Bellozzo . . . Send his documents to me . . . And those instructions for the taffeta . . . Oh, I'm going to worry!' he promised. 'I can see I am!'

I believed him. A fixed desire to think I'd come to grief without him is very natural in the merchant. And yet I noted a contradiction in his voice – one I know well: there was a hint that I should somehow lighten his load.

I did what I could. I said, 'The more you worry, the more you'll need this Maestro Ruccelli. So why not lay aside your cares for a while? Forget the trade . . . '

'Forget it?'

He stared at me in horror. I'd accepted his illness too readily – I realised that as soon as I'd spoken. Now he saw me as a usurper – or else an executioner – hastening him to his grave.

'Easy to say, nothing to you . . . ' he muttered; and then, more fiercely, 'Well, let me tell you, that's what it is, nothing! So we'll have no more hospital talk . . . this laying aside of cares! In heaven's name, man, how sick do you take me for? All I have is indigestion. It's not a physician I need . . . I should have sacked the cook!'

I thought it wise not to comment, and soon he added, 'I've a mind to get up!' – after which he lay back quietly, waiting to be appeased.

'As to the cook . . . '

'Well?'

'About the banquet. Now you've set the date, you can't very well sack the cook. A new one could never be found in time . . . I take it you still mean to have the banquet?'

'Of course!'

'All the more reason to look to your health. You don't want this trouble of pains on the day. How would it be if you had to take to your bed? Gabriello . . . I'm thinking chiefly of him . . . '

'No you aren't!' said the merchant. And then, swiftly, 'But yes, you're right! I must be fit for Gabby's banquet. I know it, so you can spare me the sermon. I'll do as Ruccelli says. It's cruel and an inconvenience, but I'll rest, God help me. These things must be viewed in a right proportion . . . '

Perspective, I think he meant.

I left him to find such a view, if he could.

So today I went alone to the warehouse; and tomorrow the

merchant goes to his farm with Maestro Ruccelli. There, for once, the beautiful slave may be denied him, but he'll stroll in the vineyards and eat plain fare, and hope to mend.

Maestro Ruccelli –

He combines a wealth of sense with his learning.

By the time I came home, he'd already achieved the impossible: tranquillity throughout the house. And this had been done without offence to Piero Sassoli – for he hadn't shut the gate. The merchant despises a shut gate. I've heard him say there are only three sufficient reasons why a man may shut his gate in daylight, and all three reasons are drastic. He may do it if there's a death in the family, or plague about, and he may do it if the city's invaded. No other pretext. But when he had his 'sufficient' reason – when Charles the homunculus came with his mercenaries – even then he chided himself; and after the French had gone, he went about for weeks explaining to friend and stranger alike why he'd felt compelled to shut his gate, deploring the fact, although every propertied man in Florence had done the same.

So here was a problem. How to procure the peace which Piero Sassoli needs when he himself believes a house should resemble a market, with access for everyone?

Maestro Ruccelli found the answer.

When I returned this evening, the gate was open as usual, but Bruno the stablehand stood on one side and Filippo the gardener on the other. Dark-visaged fellows, strong in the shoulders, with stout legs – both are admirably suited to the task they'd been given, and I think they enjoyed themselves. While I was still at a distance, I saw them turn away a would-be visitor – a man who clutched a roll of papers to his breast. This individual argued loudly. Though more than twenty paces distant, I could hear him declare that great men often lose fortunes on account of their servants, and if he could only speak with Piero Sassoli . . .

The guardians of the gate looked unimpressed. They smiled discouragingly, and Bruno said something – but whatever he said, the inventor – for such he was: I recognised the breed – chose to ignore it. He stood his ground. He started to coax, to wheedle, his voice rising like a chorister's . . .

Then Bruno and Filippo came slouching forward, and their smiles had turned into grins. Fearing they meant to be rough, I hurried to close the gap between us. Piero Sassoli, I thought, would never forgive them; he'd fear for his reputation – but by the time I reached the gate, the visitor had thought better of his stubbornness, and though no one had touched him, he was scampering away up the street. Bruno and Filippo gazed delightedly after him.

'That was skilfully done!' I said.

They looked at me, and their smiles slipped. There was about them a satisfaction which, try as they might, they couldn't conceal – but neither said anything.

How clear a sign of disliking a man! My compliment had marred their pleasure.

I walked past, as if it didn't concern me.

Inside the house – a profound hush, so rare in the late afternoon that I stopped in the hall to listen, and my heart beat fast. It was silence overlaid with sounds: the clicking and creaking of the clock; pots and kettles being moved about in the kitchen; bowls placed on a wooden surface; a liquid poured from a jug, and the women – whispering.

I felt unnerved. There was none of that babble of strangers, nor the merchant demanding what, in the name of the blessed St John, might this thing be? And what was the price? Such a hush. It took me back to the day on which Monna Margherita had died. All it lacked was the wailing of a new-born infant.

I began to climb the stairs.

At the top – Maestro Ruccelli. He'd come from the merchant's room, and when he saw me, he wished me good evening, then added, 'Ser Sassoli's taking a rest. A pause before his meal – it's the only infallible aid to a man's digestion. I hope you needn't disturb him?'

'I needn't,' I said.

'You have my thanks.'

Still he stood there; so did I. It appeared he wished to detain me, and while I was wondering whether this really was his intention, or whether to bow and pass, he spoke again:

'I'm told this house is seldom quiet,' he said. 'That at the end of his work, Ser Sassoli takes pleasure in visitors, marvels, inventions – day after day. Over-exciting his mind, and overheating his blood. Really, a life for a Hercules.' He laughed. I smiled. The door to the merchant's room stood ajar, which kept me from laughing with him. Maestro Ruccelli seemed to understand. I believe he noticed my glance at the door, for immediately he changed the subject.

'A milder evening.'

'Yes. It's almost spring . . . '

'I was about to take a turn in Ser Sassoli's excellent garden. If you could spare the time . . . '

If I could spare the time, he'd be glad of my company.

I went with him, and willingly. I can detect in his manner towards me nothing of condescension, although he knows my place in the household – Piero Sassoli makes it plain to everyone. And apart from that, my blemish he can see for himself. But he never behaves with less than perfect courtesy. I've had none of those long, cold stares. Not a single word that was patronising. I feel comfortable with him.

How unlike da Vinci he is!

I find myself comparing them, because Maestro Ruccelli possesses the nature which I'd hoped would belong to da Vinci; and so it's impossible not to wish that, being by far the more benign of the two, he were also the greater man. Of course, I can see that he isn't. His mind, although it looks about and inquires, has none of that power which one feels in da Vinci. This physician broadens his view, but makes no attempt to forsake it, whereas – it seems to me – the minds of the great work in a different fashion, and rather than run the risk of fitting a thought too snugly into their understanding – they'll shatter their concepts like useless moulds. How else could they constantly startle us? Setting before us work of astonishing novelty, which nevertheless, the instant we see it, we know to be truth?

These ideas, which have long been vague and scattered in me, refine themselves and come together tonight.

But as for Maestro Ruccelli – now there's a thorn of perplexity! For to wish him great must be the act of a fool. Would he be courteous then? And besides, I see he's content. He accepts himself as he is, and all of us, in so far as he understands us, he seems to accept as we are. He conducts no quarrel with the universe. Rather I think he treats it like a book, written by an infinitely higher mind, a thing from which he knows how to take interest and pleasure, both in proportion to his abilities. And if one should comment: 'But here is meant much more than you've perceived!' he'd probably only smile and reply, 'I expect you're right!'

It's a gifted, fortunate mind that can come to this, for all it's not a great one.

And yet it's not a great one.

Well, we walked in the garden, between the rows of lavender bushes which long ago Monna Margherita chose to have planted – and he spoke of Piero Sassoli.

'Since his son's away, and also because I gather that you're the one who keeps things running smoothly here – I think you should be warned. Ser Sassoli suffers from more than indigestion.' He looked at me. 'But I suppose you knew?'

'I'd guessed as much.'

He nodded. We walked, and while he spoke, I was careful to keep my eyes from his face. I felt I'd be wrong to watch him closely, as if I searched for signs of half-truths.

The air was cool but pleasant, and rich with the odour of damp earth.

Maestro Ruccelli gave his opinion plainly, unhurriedly.

'Any shock, or bout of anger – even an excess of pleasure – and Ser Sassoli may lose his life in a trice. Rubbed out, like a taper. The pains he suffers come from God. They're reminders of his mortality, and so I've told him. Any man of sixty-five should know it's time to face a reckoning – '

Here he paused, stretched out his hand to a shrub, and broke off a leaf. I distinctly heard the crack of the twig. He rubbed this leaf in his fingers, and smelled it. Then, seeing me observe him – for I'd turned my head at the sound – he said with a smile, 'An agent of healing. During my travels I've often seen the local people make use of some plant that grows by the roadside – plants I've passed and never suspected of medicinal properties. It has taught me a lesson. Now, wherever I go, I pluck and sniff like a savage . . . But concerning Ser Sassoli,

I've also told him – and it's true – that he needn't die for years. If he rests, and orders his habits, and will keep to the diet I've prescribed . . . who knows? He may yet see you and me to our graves!'

Strange. That image of the old, sick merchant standing over my grave.

Oh, I felt relief. More time. New hope. Piero Sassoli might yet live for years. A pale and modest joy immediately kindled in me, and by its light I saw what a darkly tangled thing my dread had grown – how it had choked my mind. But almost at once the flame died down, the relief I felt began to settle, and lurking in the ashes of my dread – I found outrage.

Perhaps the notion offended me – Piero Sassoli, standing over my grave – or else was there shock in the thought of time, years still to come, with nothing changed, except that the merchant grows shorter-tempered and more demanding? I can't tell. It's only now that I ask the question. But I felt my face contort and the harder I tried to control it, the more this indignation rose, twisting my lips. Quickly, before Maestro Ruccelli could notice, I asked: 'And this banquet? Has he told you, he plans to hold one for his son, to honour a patron? But won't that over-tax his strength?'

'We've already discussed the matter' – he continued to examine the leaf he held, and while he did so, I struggled to make a better countenance. 'I've found', he said, 'that nothing could vex Ser Sassoli more than to fail his son in this banquet, so I've given it my blessing. But never fear . . . ' His eyes came round, and he laughed, 'by the time you hold these revels, I'll have worked him into an awe of his stomach. He'll eat no more than a sparrow's portion, and he'll ration his cup, sip by sip, I promise you! He also agrees to retire at a decent hour. I may count on you, I suppose, to give a discreet reminder on the night, if you see he forgets . . . '

'I regret I shan't be present.'

'Ah. Now that's a pity . . . '

This, with no curiosity. He made it sound not as though I, Gismondo Cavalletti, lacked the importance to be at this banquet, but as though a family gathering naturally couldn't displace any weightier business I had in hand; and for this tact I warmed to him the more. Possibly he sensed it. He began to talk of other things: of festivals in the East, of silks and their brilliant colours. He inquired about the various dyes we use in Florence. And so our garden stroll went on agreeably, until, as we turned back, he said, 'There was something else I wished to mention . . . ' But then, as luck would have it, he looked towards the house, and what he saw swiftly closed our conversation.

At the doorway, with a sort of nettled eagerness, stood Piero Sassoli.

Maestro Ruccelli shrugged: 'But I see we haven't time,' he said. 'We keep my host from his supper!' And we began to walk more quickly.

The merchant, in that way he has when he seeks to right a balance, greeted one of us very gustily and the other not at all, exclaiming, 'So here I find you, Maestro! Here you are!' He drew the physician away. Maestro Ruccelli, however – as if to show that Ser Sassoli might do as he liked, but such behaviour was not his own – turned round to me and inclined his head, and so took his leave very civilly.

I'm obliged to him. It was awkward enough to stand there, excluded, barred from their supper. For dignity's sake, I was half inclined to follow. In the presence of such a guest, I thought, I could hardly be sent away – and how many times has the merchant said I'm always welcome? But that belongs to the past. Nevertheless, I was tempted to follow –

And yet, the fuss! The flurry! The fetching of extra plates and a cup! The sending for food already dispatched to my room! All this offered so great an embarrassment that only a lunatic would choose it.

I came away.

And tomorrow Maestro Ruccelli goes with the merchant. And from the farm, he returns to Venice. It's likely we've talked our last, and I'm never to know what it was he 'wished to mention'.

No sleep. I'm much too agitated.

First, there was the physician's voice trapped inside my skull, saying, 'Rubbed out, like a taper! But he needn't die for years. I may count on you, I suppose, to give a discreet reminder . . . '

This went on until I sat up straight, staring about me. I looked across the room. I saw this table, the ledgers – slabs of black piled together – and they were oddly comforting. Lying back again I told myself, 'There's plenty of time. If Piero Sassoli rests, you'll have years in which to plan your actions. Calm . . . calm . . . '

But it was futile. That unaccountable anger which had assailed me in the garden seized hold again, and this way and that I tossed, helpless. Then at last a stillness came; I drowsed. 'Soon,' I thought, 'I'll fall asleep.' Mere pretence. I lay as rigid as iron. I waited behind shut eyelids – worrying.

This advancement Gabriello hopes for – what's the bearing of it? Who is this 'very considerable gentleman'? Do they plan to merge the Sassoli trade with some other, greater family's? Or perhaps he'll go to court, our golden boy? Has he pleased the eye of a Duke? Now there would be a gift from heaven: years of his absence! But no. It's a sin to wish too much. And yet he'd suit a courtier's life. How subtle he'd be at intrigues. How masterful at extravagances. So skilled in the art of appearances, false modesty – skilled enough to attract a noble wife?

No. Not that. But what else does the fool take an interest in?

Why, all that's easeful! Endless wealth. New delights for the senses – and flattery. How he loves to feel the regard of those who count as important – or those who crave to give. Could he have charmed some doting Croesus? One of those simple-headed beings, who give away horses and farms to beautiful men – much in the way that most of us might hand a few almonds to a child?

No. It's something more than a farm, or why would Piero Sassoli be so excited? This 'gentleman', whoever he is, secures the future – our dearest Gabby's – whether the merchant lives or dies. What else can it be but a merging of trade? And if that happens, where shall I fit?

Questions. I almost smothered in questions. They rose and writhed like those shapes of dust which are spirited up in the road on a windy day, stinging the eyes, burning the throat – and they stifled all hope of sleep. I'll have none tonight.

And the night stretches.

Back I've come to these notes. I'm filled with impatience, a need to be writing, but what to write apart from questions? The present crowds at my heels, the future comes close behind, and I'm not yet done with the past. My mind is baffled. I feel an urge to set down thoughts at random – but that I won't do. Nothing can be gained from panic: a torch, set to the straw.

So how to lose these hours? Sleep may be impossible, but when I think of the past and what remains to be written, my eyelids droop; and when I think of the present, this impatience helps me to panic.

The fish for supper tonight. Three good lire, and mangled rather than filleted. In every bite, a crop of bones, small and sharp like pins. I'll speak about it tomorrow. I must. If something like it found its way to this banquet – but of course it won't! A special effort will be made. Gabriello was ever a favourite in the kitchen, although I can't see why; he ignores them completely, except to demand some special sauce or pie for supper. Oh, but they'll make an effort – not least because there'll be rival cooks in the house.

But tonight – the bones: there's no excuse. Any half-wit can fillet a fish. And those parts which were served to the merchant and Maestro Ruccelli – were they also rich in bones? I must ask the travellers before they leave in the morning. I must anticipate any mention of the subject, and yet not make too much of it, so that I can neither be blamed for tonight's poor quality nor seem to complain myself. For strange food comes from the kitchen. The cut that was served to me may have contained every bone in the fish.

It's so. And once, in the days of the Heretic, I'd have known that such an arrangement must be the work of Providence, to better my soul. Whereas now I know otherwise.

The Heretic. Well, there's my subject. I yawn. I fidget. But no matter how I resist, I sense him waiting. I must set him down. And if I'm obliged to watch the night out – what more fitting subject for the hours of darkness?

Fra Girolamo. Why did he happen to us? Dominating Florence. He reshaped lives, inspiring us with the highest joy – and terror, and misery; all of it to be swept away, so that now, when eighteen years have passed, the city appears to be much as it would have been if he'd never existed. What does one call this? A waste? A mistake? Good intentions twisted into delusions? Should one think of him as a reed – a puny, incidental thing round which the people's madness gathered, layer upon layer, until they had made for themselves a disciplining governor as strong as the one who died – as strong as Lorenzo de' Medici?

Or even stronger. For the Heretic was absolute. Our penalty for every fault and transgression was never a fine or a simple whipping – though these might also have been incurred – but torment in hell, and long leisure in which to anticipate it. And when he spoke of our punishments, the horror was visible in his eyes – the way they blazed, full of unspeakable fear and pity, so that no one could doubt he saw us burning already, our sins sending up a foul smoke, while our bodies roasted, and yet refused to perish.

How he trembled for us! And we – how we trembled with him!

He was intimate with every part of hell. This graced him with a strength of conviction not vouchsafed to the rest of us, and so we were drawn to him. We flocked to his sermons, not to learn from his words, but to be stirred by the passion with which he uttered them – to see what it is, to be convinced. As he spoke, his body quivered. His harsh voice, no more tuneful than a raven's, would croak the command: 'Listen, and be saved!' Then he'd bare his soul, screeching out his agonies, his dialogues with the Everlasting, his tortured insights – and the cynic's smile would be wiped from men's faces.

He trapped us in a web of guilt. When in a sermon he pictured hell, it was everyone's hell. From the distress of those who listened, even the dullest Turk could have seen that this hell encompassed the secret terror of each of us. And when he spoke of sin, again and again he'd illustrate the evil with some instance which made one gasp, because it came so close to one's self, and – as it seemed – particularly one's self.

Ladies would faint at a glance from him. They renounced their rouge pots and mirrors, their fur trimmings. They wore sombre colours, and their eyes grew dark from nights spent down on their knees, earnestly praying for redemption. They were terrified of Fra Girolamo – and worshipped him. During his sermons, their upturned faces received from him a sense of shame, like sunlight. Greedily. *Mea culpa.* They hungered for him.

– But that I note with hindsight. All I saw at the time was his power. I'd listen while he berated Florence as a nest of idlers, a den of whores. I'd look about at the timid assembly, and feel a soaring pride that this man, so small and lacking in appearance, could hold a city in his fist. And because he dealt with a God of wrath, who had nothing gentle or mawkish about Him, I, who had never felt compelled to make obeisance while any priest was raising the Host, felt in this Fra Girolamo a Presence to whom it was natural to bow. A deity of perils, and all the powers of austerity: a God to suit the future which I thought would be mine. Monna Margherita was dead. The cries of a child rang through the house. And Fra Girolamo presented me with a plausible God.

Each month increased my devotion to Him.

Even in those bands of children – 'blessed' brats, who roamed the streets, chanting hymns, and spying out every ungodly act among their parents to report it to the authorities – even in those I acknowledged the will of God. For Gabriello was scarcely weaned before he began his spiteful prattle against me, and it was all of a picture. Fra Girolamo interpreted it. And if, when I saw them in the street, I envied rebellious students their drunken revelling, none the less I shuddered for them. They would be damned; I would be saved; and none of it seemed preposterous. I'd elected to live in virtue. I kissed the hard heel of salvation.

– But contradicted myself. For I still desired the merchant's praise, and I laboured to win some sign that he cherished me. This, despite my knowledge that Piero Sassoli had no real love for the Friar's God. But I put that down to weakness in him. To a man like the merchant, I thought, the accepting of heaven-sent discipline must be a task of the greatest discomfort, so I troubled myself for his welfare; I prayed for him. And mingled with my concern, because I saw he was weak, there was contempt.

Yet I worked all the more to do his pleasure, and prove that he couldn't spare me; I longed for a single word that would show his approval – and what was that but a contradiction?

In the early days, before the Friar became well known, Piero Sassoli would laugh about 'the passionate Dominican'. And once I overheard him saying, 'Fra Girolamo was born too late. He'd have found the world much more to his liking two or three hundred years ago!' That was the year in which Monna Margherita conceived; he spoke to a fat, luxurious German merchant who came to supper, and as the words of adults will sometimes stay with a child – I remembered them.

But later, Piero Sassoli went along to sermons with the rest of us, returning home white-faced and sober. And when servants asked if they might go to see their confessors, he sent them off with alacrity. I remember his copious instructions that none of the needy be turned from the door, and how, 'We must all keep a decent limit on our comforts.' So far he tried. He even took to wearing muted colours himself; and a certain greyness affected his speech, so that – for example – he might say to someone from another city: 'Of course, when the Magnificent was alive, I could have shown you a different Florence altogether. But, well . . . well . . . every time has its merits. Now, as you see, we have clean streets. Clean streets . . . '

Oh, he was cautious.

Except for the suppers. They were no more subdued than they'd ever been. When he sat down to table with a company of friends, the music struck up, the wine flowed freely, and I'd listen from the staircase, amazed – shocked – by the easy laughter.

In addition, he collected even more zealously: treasures of art, inventions – shaking his head at the 'frivolous nature' of many, but insisting a man must look to his business, and that all these things made 'sound investments'.

So time passed us. Charles of France with his army came and went. Fra Girolamo's grip on us tightened. His precepts became more severe, his blessings indispensable; and it seemed to me that most of the people rejoiced in him. For the closer men drew to the Friar's exacting God, the more clearly they saw all the sloth and sin in themselves, and the louder they clamoured to be saved.

Though there were some who didn't.

– Which brings me to a slight, but extraordinary incident. One I think Piero Sassoli has never forgotten – and neither have I. In fact, I believe he resents it still. I've no reason to think so, since it's a thing never spoken of, but I feel it between us. Something of it remains.

And yet it was nothing.

In the year before they burned him, Fra Girolamo arranged a bonfire of his own: one of those soul-scouring carnivals when every person in Florence was to give up something – some much-loved possession – to be burned to ashes. An ornate comb. A mirror. Too lavish a set of brushes. A dicing board. All to go up in a blaze amid general applause, with a fanfare of trumpets, and choirs singing 'Alleluia!'

It was not the first event of its kind – I remember that, too, and the people's astonishment – but this time, the day was awaited with secret pleasure, an eagerness wrapped up in silence, because men had discovered these fires released sensations for which they could find no common name, only an appetite.

The preparations were elaborate. They took the greater part of a week. In the centre of the Piazza della Signoria a scaffold was erected and, at a little distance from it, a heap of rich and valuable things accumulated, to be sorted by those with authority and placed round the scaffold in appropriate layers. Night and day this heap was added to, people hastened to fling upon it their prized belongings, then hurried away without so much as a backward glance in case anyone should think they sought approbation – a fear so widespread throughout the city that more people took their offerings along by night than during the day, so exceedingly careful they were for the health of their souls.

And no one more careful than Fra Girolamo. He cared so much for every soul in Florence that he hit on a plan to encourage the most reluctant Christian to contribute something. He appointed special Collectors; and these, followed by a cart in which to bear away the goods, went up and down the streets, going from house to house, politely requesting 'some small token' from everyone who lived there.

So it was that most of the well-to-do contributed twice: once by carrying a possession to the great mound in the Piazza – for a man should be seen to do his duty willingly, no matter how discreetly – and once by giving up something to the meek but sharp-eyed Collector who came to the door.

But as for Piero Sassoli –

With considerable pomp he called his servants together, cook and maids and stablehand, even the potboy, and he made it plain that he wished them all to show a correct disposition by taking something to the Piazza. He needn't have worried. Every bead and bangle had gone from the women; the stable-hand had given his comb; the potboy had surrendered the feathers he collected from the kitchen floor, and which he loved to keep in a sort of bouquet – all this I knew: the cook had talked of nothing else while I was in the kitchen, listing some produce that had come from the farm. I suppose she wished me to know that others feared God as much as I did.

But Piero Sassoli never thought to inquire what had been done already. He simply gave his orders that everyone should give up something.

Next he bethought him of his trade, and himself. He declared that on the following morning Rigogli and I should accompany him 'to make a gesture for the business. And also a personal one. We must each of us make a sacrifice . . . '

This we did, taking a roll of good, rich satin from the warehouse – there was little demand for such a cloth in those days – and old Rigogli took a box, a dainty thing that was made of bone, delicately worked with patterns of flowers and leaves. And the silent Rassuccio, walking along beside us (although no one had asked him), bore in his arms a bird carved in pine wood, an eagle, wonderfully life-like. And the merchant carried a purse. Sewn in brilliant reds and emerald, it was one which I'd never set eyes on before. And I took my silver cup – a diminutive, childish thing, but still very precious, which Monna Margherita had given me. And seeing me fling this on to the pile, Piero Sassoli grimaced – but he made no comment. Not a word did he speak until we'd walked back across the Piazza. Then he exclaimed, 'So that's that!' – sounding very relieved.

Only, that was not that.

The next day brought the Collector. He came before supper, while Piero Sassoli was considering the talents of a youth from Mantua, who built strange weapons. I remember a gun that bristled with sword blades and stabbing blades; it even boasted a groove through which an arrow could be fired, and Piero Sassoli thought it a marvel. He was shouting out that we must adjourn to the garden, where he'd trouble his guest for a demonstration – when in at the door came the dark-robed Collector.

An individual of forty years or so, thin-lipped and sallow. His hands were piously hidden away in his sleeves, and he wore an expression of godly rectitude.

The moment I saw him, I bowed – but no one else did. He acknowledged my action by watching it.

'God's blessing on this house,' he said gently. 'I come on His errand.'

Then he inclined his head towards the merchant, who stared in silence. The Mantuan gaped; Fra Girolamo's men always bewildered outsiders. I myself was humbly attentive. So we stood there.

At last, Piero Sassoli laid the gun on the table, and returned the greeting with a bare 'Good evening' – which came out as a snarl. He was like a schoolboy called from his play; he made small effort at courtesy.

'What do you want?' he demanded.

The Collector took no offence.

'I've come', he said, 'to free you of your burdens. Any earthly object which you suspect you treasure above your soul . . . I beg you, lighten your loads. Give your worldly goods to the flames. Fra Girolamo has sent me, for his love of the people . . . '

'But I've already given!'

Piero Sassoli turned red. I was alarmed by his tone. The Collector regarded him steadily. He blustered on: 'We've all been to the Piazza! Myself, and all my people! We know what's right . . . I've given a most expensive purse . . . and silk from the warehouse worth at least two hundred florins! I think that's more than enough.'

'Indeed?' The Collector's eyes moved. They took careful note of a sumptuous painted chest which was a feature of the hall in those days – the one now kept in the guest-room – and then they came to a rare and costly vase, a beautiful thing of glass, deep peacock-blue, from Damascus, which stood on the table. The merchant had bought it only two days previously. 'Indeed?' the Collector said.

Piero Sassoli followed the path of his gaze. He opened his mouth to speak, thought better of it, and looked at me beseechingly, so that all my stored contempt and pity welled up together. His fists were clenched, a sure sign of his stubbornness, and in the struggle to overcome his greed, I knew that someone would have to help him.

So I unclasped the belt I was wearing – a handsome gift from the merchant himself – and held it out.

'Take this, I beg you.'

'May you find your reward in Heaven.' The Collector received it without emotion. His manner plainly expressed that the item was nothing. Its only value lay in the giving. Then, taking my hint – I mean, to shame the merchant – he turned to the gaping Mantuan: 'And you, sir?' he said. 'Do you wish to give anything?'

'Me?' the inventor gasped. 'But I don't belong here!'

The Collector smiled. 'We're all God's children. We all have souls to save.'

And our Mantuan hastily plucked the brooch from his cloak. Then Piero Sassoli was disconcerted – though no less angry – and with a terrible frown at the youth, he blurted out, 'I've given enough, I tell you!'

Fra Girolamo's man bowed. He was very calm and softly spoken:

'As you please. Nevertheless, I shall wait at your gate a while. To give you time to be quite certain. And so I wish you a pleasant evening. God be with you, gentlemen.'

After he'd gone, Piero Sassoli swore vividly.

'Leeches!' he cried. 'Blood-sucking leeches! Waiting in the street, for all the world to see – he knows I'll have to give something! Devilish succubi! Vultures!' – and he banged with his fist on the table and swore again.

The Mantuan greyed with embarrassment. He busily adjusted his cloak. But I could only watch, and condemn. The merchant's resentment showed like a knife that has long been wrapped in silk and lain hidden in a household chest, and all at once the blade has sheared through the cloth and comes to light – a sharp, malicious instrument lying among domestic things. And seeing it, I knew that Piero Sassoli had never attended a sermon from any spiritual prompting, nor was he anxious to be reformed. Nor was it just weakness of the common, wavering sort, as I'd supposed, when he held his excessive suppers. No. His ranting came as a revelation. At last I perceived that he cared not a jot for Fra Girolamo's God, nor for the saving of souls, nor for the glorious rebirth of Florence as an earthly Paradise. These things concerned him only as threats to the life he desired, and all the rest was sham; the pretence of one who hopes that time will change.

I was horrified. A measure of my innocence even then.

To be so damned. To be insensible as stone to the power of Fra Girolamo, the Presence in him.

While I watched, doubtless with a long and sorry face, absorbed in these thoughts, Piero Sassoli continued to rant until, out of a kind of sympathy – or else because he hoped it would sell his gun – the Mantuan offered a nervous suggestion.

'Pardon me . . . ' he said, ' . . . but, Ser Sassoli, couldn't you send out . . . something that has no value . . . ?'

And the merchant stopped with his mouth wide open, as if a dart had pierced his temple. Then: 'That's right! That's what I'll do! Here, Gismo – take him this!' – seizing hold of a lump of wood that weighed down papers on the table, a crude piece shaped like an orange, which had been worked for him by the son of a friend. 'Tell him I cherish this above everything!' And he thrust it at me.

So –

Now we come to it –

I walked to the table. I took this object, but as I did so, I looked at Piero Sassoli, and something – horror, perhaps, or contempt – must have shown in my face, and shown completely. An extraordinary pause occurred – no longer than it takes a man to count to five, and maybe not so long – while my hand closed round the paperweight. Then Piero Sassoli's eyes flickered, his lower lip trembled; he looked down, as though my gaze had stung him, and in another moment he hissed, 'This, too! Take him this!' Picking up the Damascan vase and pushing it at me. 'Take it! Take it!'

I obeyed. I said nothing. I was much too surprised to speak.

At supper that night, Piero Sassoli was genial. He abruptly dismissed the Mantuan but kept me late at the table, talking about his farm, about orchards and olive trees, so that I knew he was doing his best to prove that nothing untoward had happened. All this I suffered, but I remained surprised, and only after I reached my room did I dare to perceive the reason: not shame, but fear. When I'd taken hold of that paperweight and looked at him, Piero Sassoli had been afraid. He'd recoiled from me! Yet I'd intended nothing.

It's a memory ringed with astonishment, and one which serves no purpose. I seem to find it pleasing, but really I've no use for it.

Besides, it was contrived by the times. By the merchant's guilt, and his secret terror of the Heretic, not by any lasting fear of me.

But – what did he think I might do? I, who have always laboured to win his trust, and am vexed whenever he shows a lack of faith in me?

And why should the memory please?

Dawn holds back. I ache. There's a price to be paid for tonight – yawns, and pains in the head, the figures swirling in the ledgers. By this afternoon I'll regret it. And Piero Sassoli gone to the farm – that's twice the work. Written reports of everything.

XLI

IN the end, I extinguished the candles and drowsed, here at the table, resting my head on my arms; and when I came to my senses, I found I was reading: '. . . twice the work. Written reports of everything.' The words were plainly visible. Dawn had come.

At once, before I could feel the need to stretch out in bed, I knew I must busy myself. Down I went to the kitchen – an unwelcome intruder, for the women had barely risen: the cook, still in her shift, was rubbing her eyes into smudges. She, in particular, looked annoyed to see me, so I demanded – and got – a cup of wine. I said nothing about the fish for supper last night, since I meant to speak to the merchant first. Instead, to give my visit some purpose, I inquired about the arrangements for Piero Sassoli's journey, as if I'd forgone my sleep on his account. And there was need for inquiry. To save themselves a chore this morning, the women had filled the flasks before they'd gone to bed so that all the water was stale. I obliged them to empty it out and fill the flasks again.

Thus I was vindicated.

Next, I went to inspect the horses – and came upon Bruno sprawled in the straw, vigorously snoring. I let him sleep. It was a pleasure to stroke the beasts, and murmur the nonsense they love to hear, without a sense of Bruno's grin at my back.

After that, I walked in the garden until the sky was a delicate white – the colour of eggshell. Then I returned to the house.

In the hall was Maestro Ruccelli, examining the clock. He was peering closely at the wheels, and seemed to concentrate so gravely that I thought to pass in silence; but he straightened up as soon as I softened my footstep, and wished me good morning. Indeed, he did this so heartily, I couldn't escape the impression that he'd waited there in the hope of seeing me and, because I was pleased, I behaved like a fool: I wished him farewell, before I'd properly returned his greeting.

'Maestro Ruccelli! . . . I hope you have a pleasant journey . . . It's a good ride, but not too far. I hope you like the farm. I think you will. The house itself is beautiful, though simple. And the land's quite favourably situated . . . '

'Thank you. Yes, I expect to enjoy it – providing my patient co-operates!' The physician laughed; and seeing me look about, he added, 'Ser Sassoli's still asleep. I gave him a draught. Not a powerful opiate, you understand, simply a mild persuasion – and Nature does the rest. I'm confident he'll wake before noon, but as to when –' He shrugged.

'In that case, would you convey a message to him?'

'Certainly.'

'My wishes for his quick recovery. And – I'll write as directed. Every day. For I know he'll worry otherwise.'

This, I felt, was my wisest course. It would only have irked the merchant if I'd kept from the warehouse, squandering all the morning just to be at the gate, waving him off. But I also knew he'd grumble at finding me absent. He looks for a ritual at his departures.

Maestro Ruccelli nodded, and from his smile – the deepening lines round his eyes – I thought he could see my dilemma. I thanked him and bowed. Nothing was left to say. I made to leave. Then he called out, 'Excuse me! If you can spare a moment . . . ' I turned back, and he lowered his voice: 'There was something else I wished to mention. Although it may not be welcome.'

'Please.'

'I'll not – dance round the point,' he said. 'Would you care to hear a physician's thoughts concerning yourself? Your own welfare?'

And once he'd said that, he waited. Not, I knew, for courtesy's sake, but truly for my answer. Only I had none. I'd already guessed his subject.

'My welfare.'

'Yes. I refer, of course, to that growth on your face.'

So. That was honest – and I was grateful for it. All the same, my cheeks began to smart.

'What of it? Say whatever you wish.'

I gazed past him at the clock. Perhaps from tact, Maestro Ruccelli moved to the table and picked up a cup of wine that stood there. From the corner of my eye I watched him.

'Since you allow it,' he said, 'I've some observations to make. In the first place, you have remarkable features. Apart from the growth, an altogether excellent appearance. In fact, you're possessed of most of those attributes which we consider desirable – height and proportion, keen eyes, and – if I may say so – intelligence. Now, in the way of my profession, I've discovered that where there exists a single blemish – as in yourself – it often causes greater distress than several blemishes cause in others. So I can't help but wonder if you've ever been troubled by this – excrescence.'

I was dumb.

As he'd spoken, I'd forced myself to look towards him. I felt I was smiling in a soft, poetical way that was unnatural to me. I stared at the cup he held.

Maestro Ruccelli continued:

'I suppose you've considered removing it? Of using a blade, or a flame, or else some fiery paste or liquid? And if you've resorted to none of these, I'm sure you've known your reasons, but – forgive me if I seem presumptuous – a man may act with sense and restraint yet still have his doubts, which is why I decided to speak of the matter. I can claim some knowledge on the subject, and I wanted to say, you've acted wisely. You were right to leave this growth alone. Destroy any doubts.'

He paused, and I made shift to thank him.

'I'm glad to have this confirmation of my instincts.'

'Good. These growths are treacherous,' he said. 'We tamper with them at our peril. Remove one from the surface of the flesh, and it grows again – but inwards, eating into the bone and consuming the very life of the patient. Or else it multiplies, and where before there was one, afterwards there are three. At the very least the removal leaves a scar just as disfiguring as the growth. It's folly to tamper – and for what? A little vanity? It doesn't impede your vision?'

'I see it all the time,' I told him – and now I found I was speaking to his face – 'but generally I look past it. Like a speck in the eye.'

'Good. It doesn't pinch the nostril, and restrict your breathing?'

'No.'

Not yet.

'But is its size increasing?'

'Yes.'

He nodded. 'Leave well alone,' he repeated. 'A dangerous sort, and after all, it's a very modest flaw! Any day of the week a man sees worse. Not only more conspicuous and inconvenient, but ones that tell the most shameful secrets about their owner. Whereas yours is a blameless thing. It's the kind that settles on one man and not on the next for reasons none of us understands . . . I mention this, because I know there are righteous fools who gossip and choose to see the signs of vice in every defect. But a commonplace blemish like yours – you need never fear it reflects on your character.'

'Commonplace?' I wince to think of it, but I stressed the word as if I'd been insulted. In truth, I was only remembering da Vinci's eyes – how they'd greedily studied my blotch, seeing, as it were, a freak, a miracle.

Maestro Ruccelli looked amused, as well he might.

'Most assuredly it's commonplace! Kings, cardinals, lawyers and beggars, ladies and soldiers . . . Don't think you bear the mark of a single station in life! . . . Well . . . now I've said everything I hoped to say. I trust I've given no offence?'

'None. None.'

Again I thanked him. And then I was glad to have reason to hurry, being already late for the warehouse.

I thank God for this physician.

How quiet the house is!

Before supper this evening, I walked from room to room. Piero Sassoli's bed, which only yesterday I thought too large for a man of his length, today looks small. The crucifix that normally hangs above is missing. A naked nail juts from the plaster. Piero Sassoli must have taken the crucifix with him. A thing unprecedented.

In the room where he keeps those pledges left by inventors – models in wood and rope, glass and sinew – a layer of dust rests on everything.

But the door to his 'most valued items' is locked – as usual – and only he has a key. If the house catches fire, I'm to axe my way in, and save what I can – yet we keep no axe for the purpose, in case some thief should discover it and think it an invitation.

Our golden boy's door is also locked. Once, forgetting his own sealed treasury, Piero Sassoli asked his son, 'Don't you trust the servants? Isn't this house your home that you bolt and bar your door like this?' And Gabriello replied, 'Oh, it has nothing to do with the servants. But I certainly don't trust outsiders!'

Meaning myself, of course.

So be it. An outsider. And both the masters away.

Tonight, throughout the house I sense a slackness which I can't condone, but neither have I a mind to harass the servants. In this slackness there's a threat. I sense they could be quickly provoked into breaking things or mislaying them, and making issues out of nothing. They look for a grudge. So I intend to be as unobtrusive as possible.

I've little choice. When I returned today, Anna the maid had come from the kitchen and was taking advantage of the evening sun – the first warm evening since last autumn. She sat in the courtyard, her head thrown back, her throat exposed and eyes half-shut – but even so she saw me coming, and while I was still some paces away she was up with a flurry of skirt, back to the kitchen before I could scold her.

Not that I'd meant to say very much, if anything.

The truth is, I tire of being unpopular.

I tire of solitude.

XLII

THE merchant's desk – quite uncluttered. Now, whenever I glance at it, I picture a stranger sitting there, some agent appointed by Gabriello, and immediately I seem to draw into myself all the stifling speculation which fills the air in the warehouse, so that I long to escape into the street.

Never have I seen Rigogli so subdued. He begs me to send his humble greetings in every letter I write to the merchant, and assures me he prays on his knees each night for Ser Sassoli's health. He lights candles in Santa Croce. He solicits the saints.

Rassuccio, in contrast, is silent. He works much as usual, but raises his head even less – as though to express an opinion that the ills of life are rarely prevented, least of all by seeing them coming, and when one approaches, the only course a man can take is to ignore it.

As for the boys, they fidget, they whisper; they work in fits and starts. They expect a holiday – and fear dismissal.

And all these thoughts and apprehensions trouble me – Rigogli's more than the rest: the very sight of him draws a sickness to my stomach; his eyes shine dimly with the light of imagined funeral tapers, his mouth is a-tremble with stored-up speeches of grief.

And yet Maestro Ruccelli spoke plain words. The merchant is sick, but he may live for years. So why be brought to the edge of panic by a quavering dotard – and one who knows nothing?

This is wonderful folly, to be half convinced by a man who knows less than I do!

XLIII

ALL that's probable reversed! How else can I think of it?

Accompanied by her steward, coming from the Cathedral, Madonna. I stopped the instant I saw them, and then, because I must, began to walk again: the space between us diminished. Naked I felt, as a new-born babe. Unprepared like this, was I to greet her? Would she acknowledge me? Offering a smile, perhaps, like the one with which I was almost favoured at Mass on Christ's Nativity – so close to mocking? Or would she pass without a sign and leave me bowing at her back, ridiculous?

And the note: had she read it?

'*I beg to bring myself to your attention . . .*'

I turned aside.

I began to escape across the Piazza but, as I did so, I saw Madonna stop; she spoke to her steward, and the breath snagged in my throat as he came briskly forward, apparently meaning to cut across my path.

'No! You're deluded!' I thought. 'Whatever his purpose, it has nothing to do with you!' – so still I hurried, and still this lean and sober person bore towards me, his eyes like rivets aimed at my face – until in the end I was brought to a halt.

'Ser Cavalletti?'

I bowed, and so did he – with no remarkable suppleness. And then his words came out as though he wished to set them up as stakes, enforcing a distance between us.

'Ser Cavalletti – my mistress, Madonna Lucia da Fano, has expressed a desire to speak with you. Perhaps you failed to see her?' – here he made the slightest movement of his hand towards where she stood waiting.

I had no words.

Again I bowed.

The note. Seeing her now, the first time since my indiscretion, I could think of nothing except the note. For my presumption – a rebuke? A hint that if I plagued her further, she must apply to Piero Sassoli?

Her steward and I walked back together, and as we went I found that she was watching me, so to help compose my countenance I said to myself, 'This has nothing to do with the note! She could never have received it. This is some message for the merchant . . . ' and all the while, I trembled like a man in a fever.

Then as I came close, she smiled, so secretly. Immaculate.

I bowed, with all my soul.

'Ser Cavalletti – this is good of you.'

So then, not anger. I blushed at her throat, for my eyes would look no higher. My courage was lost, quite lost.

'I hear that Piero Sassoli is ill. Can you tell me how it is with him?'

So then, utterly simple. In my relief, I started to babble:

'Oh, he's better than he was. He's at his farm, resting. A physician is in attendance, and we have good hopes. It seems he improves . . . I keep him informed of all transactions, and all inquiries, you may be sure . . . '

Sounds, tumbling over themselves. I glanced up, by way of apology, and my eyes met hers.

At once I was silenced. She gazed at me with such particular interest. She listened to my words, and yet I felt that what I said was insignificant. She observed this man, this Gismondo, in part so repellent, so divided –

'The rumours I've heard,' she asked, 'they're exaggerated?'

'Oh, yes!'

'When you write to him, will you say I wish him soon recovered?'

'Yes, I will . . . most certainly . . . '

And here, I thought, was the end of it. So I bowed again.

But Madonna still watched, and now her eyes were on my blemish. I coughed. I looked at her steward, but he stood like stone. I might have been crucified and he'd have stood by unheeding – unless she'd required him to hammer home a nail.

Then: 'Gismondo. Gismondo Cavalletti.'

Thus she spoke it. My name. And her voice had altered. It smote at the life in me. I was suddenly terrified.

'Yes,' she said, 'I hear you're faithful. A message entrusted to you is safe indeed. I imagine you're skilled in the art of messages.'

'Madonna?'

'You'll do me this favour?'

'Willingly . . . '

'Thank you. And would it pain you, Ser Cavalletti, were I to need your services in more than this?'

Stricken, I stared.

Then openly she smiled. Never have I seen on her lips such a smile.

'Well,' she said, 'we must be patient. I wish you good day . . . ' – and even while I floundered with my bow, she went from me.

I sleepwalked here.

The words scatter from my pen in demented shapes. I'm stupefied by hope – a surfeit of hope – while what reason I have is in rebellion.

How could she have come by the note? Did they deliver it, the thieves? Surely. I think so. But is it likely that I'd find grace?

It isn't. And I misinterpret –

Yet what was her meaning: 'I imagine you're skilled in the art of messages'? And ' . . . were I to need your services in more than this'? And 'Patience'?

Patience! Sweet saints, am I mad? How else to interpret it?

I must be ready. She may ask not the homage I crave to give, but the doing of some – chore, some poor fool's task. Yet why? Why single me out, if not to test my devotion? Patience, she said. And why should she say that, unless, having read my note, she hasn't completely rejected me?

I have by me the mirror.

It's true; the blotch increases. Yet Maestro Ruccelli talked of it as if it were nothing. Is it indeed such a 'modest flaw'?

And could it be said, 'Now here's a man who's worth employing'? or – 'This is a man who merits a higher station in life; the Sassoli are wrong to keep him down. Anyone with a head for business would gladly appoint him their agent. Why, anyone who can discriminate would gladly receive him among their acquaintance. He's intelligent, honest, and apart from the growth – such a modest flaw – his appearance is excellent. A mystery that he waits so long before looking about for a wife. He may look where he pleases – '

Could it be said?

Shall scales fall out of my eyes, and I discover a world in which these things aren't monstrous?

Shall I hope?

Courage, Gismondo.

Yes, but the folly of hoping too much –

'Patience,' she said.

Patience. Patience.

I must calm these thoughts, wait. And yet – look outward, eyes.

XLIV

'AND Gismo,' writes the merchant, 'for Gabriello's banquet, try to devise some small distraction for the close, a touch of special elegance – '

So I consider turtle-doves, and how to set them free from dishes on the table; or day-old chicks, and how to contrive their breaking out of gilded pastry eggs, with tinkling bells in their beaks. And my mind is more than content to engage in these inanities – to think of anything, except Madonna. What she said, and what she meant, and the hope I felt – though these are treasures no further away than yesterday, today they're hidden from me.

Here's a curious state to be in! I'm numb. Like a stroked fish. I'd never have thought it possible. No joy, and no impatience. All my hope I seem to have so scrupulously concealed that I'm puzzled to know it's there, or any kind of emotion.

Only one trace of it remains: outlines of objects are sharper, and their colours are heightened. Somehow an intensity has sprung from the core of things.

XLV

BUONARROTI'S David. Today I stopped to look at it. A manifestation of skill and grace known to all of Florence. And everyone knows it was cut from a block of marble which some oaf had desecrated, hacking a great hole in it. Now it stands in the Piazza della Signoria, a faultless work. Ten years after he built a figure in snow to satisfy his proud Medici patron, Buonarroti sculptured this: a durable counterpart – but with this difference: the adolescence has gone. This Israelite keeps his strength on the inside. There's no need here for urgent attitudes and straining. Unlike the Grecian warrior, he hasn't even taken aim. Not yet. But the onlooker knows – a single glance suffices to tell him – that when he does take aim, failure is impossible. Wherever he aims, this David will hit the mark. It's a truth that's so self-evident one raises no voice against it, no logician's specious argument. When the right time comes, this human form will move with the speed of thought, the purity of light, and we who look on concede as much in awe.

But the glory of it seems to belong neither to David nor to the sculptor; the statue vetoes petty adoration.

'Didn't you know?' it says. 'This also exists quite naturally in the universe – this thing you call perfection. And men are dwarfed not because it exists, but because they're startled by it.'

Nothing can touch such work. Boys rub the sweat off their hands on to the pedestal. Dogs raise their legs against it. A madman who took a bar of iron and smashed the David to pieces – even he couldn't touch it.

That was my feeling today.

Yet most of the time I'm blind. I hurry across the Piazza, and the statue blurs.

So it is. But I doubt whether I'm alone in this, for when, eleven years ago, they brought this sculpture from the Office of Works – how men reacted: now I perceive a lesson in it.

The job was started at night. Masons knocked out stones from above the door to allow the colossus to pass. As to why it was done by night, I suppose the authorities hoped for quieter streets, but, if so, they were disappointed. Florentines love a spectacle, whatever the hour, and half the city had gathered, as great a crowd as any in daytime, so that the darkness merely added hindrance to turmoil. Students came from the taverns, priests from their prayers, the rich from their suppers, and all the tradesmen and craftsmen were out, tanners and bakers, tinsmiths and silversmiths sulking because 'the show was late' – as I knew, since I stood among them.

A great crowd. Determination hooped us together. We were fierce in our curiosity. We would view this giant. Those who claimed they'd already seen it provoked in those who hadn't an envy mixed with desire to judge the thing for themselves, and find fault with it if they could; while for their own part, those who'd seen it appeared to feel a kind of ownership, so that they thought it their duty to watch the statue begin its journey. And besides all this, there was the problem of how to move such a massive object along the streets; wonderful innovations were rumoured, and these also served to keep men there, impatient, muttering, packed together, while the hammers knocked and stones dropped from above the doorway.

A soft rain fell. Dust mingled with the flare of the torches. Round the entrance to the Office of Works, self-important officials came and went, dodging about beneath the scaffold; and the sight of all this apparently fruitless activity so exasperated the crowd that, after a while, people began to chant and some to jeer – but few gave up the vigil and went home to bed.

As for myself, I knew I must wait – till dawn, if necessary. I'd refused to go with Piero Sassoli and spy this David out while it was still in the Office of Works; I'd felt no wish to fawn on Buonarroti, and strain myself with a chatter of compliments. But also I'd had a dread of the statue. Whenever I'd heard men speak of it, the snow figure had gleamed in my mind, and I feared to see that memory surpassed. Yet in the end, predictably, when the David was to be set in a public place where I'd have no choice but to see it, I was drawn along with the rest, anxious to catch a private glimpse while I could – and a crowd affords a certain privacy.

So we jostled and waited.

At last, the final stones crashed to the ground, and an angry ragged gap had appeared above the doorway. Then the chanting stopped. Masons scrambled down from the scaffold. Movement increased in the building's torchlit interior – men scuttling like insects about a form that was huge and shadowy.

We, who stood outside, craned our necks. A murmuring rose. And then, silence.

Slowly they brought it out: a towering wooden frame, mounted on a platform. And in the frame, the shape that drew our eyes, suspended by ropes.

Protesting, this construction edged towards us. The frame creaked. The winches that drew it along squealed as if in agony.

And now the shape swayed. And now it seemed to tremble. And now it threatened to break its fetters and come toppling down.

The crowd was struck dumb. Ropes groaned. The shape jerked. We stared. Then someone shouted an ugly word, and everyone laughed. In response, several indignant, sweating officials came bustling forward, ordering us 'Back! Back!' – which was nonsense since the giant advanced at snail's pace, and was still a sprint from our part of the street. But it was, 'Back! Back!' And faces began to grin. Someone shouted, 'By our Lady, they'll never get it there! It's wobbling like a rotten tooth!' – and a howl of derision went up.

It came to that. A great howl of angry laughter. How could it have been otherwise? Nurtured on reports – and some of us on the knowledge – of how magnificent the sculpture was, and excited by the tales of rare ingenuity to be used to move the giant – how could we not have been disappointed? The David, swathed in sacking! Resembling nothing so much as a pillar of dirty salt! And roped in, carted along the street as though to a public whipping! And then – so feebly secured, and dragged along so painfully as to make a sport of all our hopes for some device that did away with labour, some miracle of easy transport. Here was the truth of the matter: it was knots and risk, ropes and haulage, sweat and red faces in the end – for a sackcloth David.

The air resounded with jibes. Everyone vied with his neighbours, and flung out his morsel of wit –

And yet this didn't last long. Voices soon became subdued. Despite themselves, once their shock had passed, people were impressed – by size, sheer size. Here, we saw, was a prodigious work, no matter how grossly misrepresented. In addition, the worry and strain in the faces of those officials and craftsmen who milled about the structure, or who stood on the platform with arms upraised like suppliants, endeavouring to steady the giant – all this touched the crowd, so that there grew a sense of concern for Buonarroti's offering, this new and precious Florentine burden, whatever it looked like; and although men continued to laugh, the derision was filtered out of it.

So it was all the more inexplicable that a group of youths should act as they did. They picked up fragments of stone from the rubble that lay round the Office of Works and, closing in behind, they hurled their missiles at the David. Most succeeded in striking it. Then the stones came pelting down on to the platform, where the men who were steadying the giant winced at the blows.

This incensed the crowd. It began to yell in earnest. Faces turned in a wave. Groups surged into the middle of the street. Curses took the place of laughter. Fists were shaken. A riot seemed imminent – but was averted by a thickset fellow who looked like a blacksmith. Stepping out from among his neighbours and seizing one of the youths by the arm, this self-appointed corrector struck such a blow across the mouth that the boy fell whimpering. Onlookers roared their approval, and the other transgressors fled, taking the one path open to them – past some shocked and baffled dignitaries into the Office of Works, where doubtless they were rounded up and given a drubbing.

Planks were erected round the David after that.

Four days it took to drag this statue to the Piazza. There, once it stood on open view to everyone, although men could – and did – most strenuously admire it, each in his own way waxing eloquent, I think that many of those who'd watched its progress through the streets, planked, roped and swaddled in sacking, could no longer show that ecstatic admiration which they'd expected to feel.

So it is. Cheated once in our expectations, when the moment finally comes we may have no reaction to give.

And so it is that first, because of dread, and afterwards, because it seemed a lesser thing than I'd feared – I quickly dismissed the David. Until today, I've ignored it. And today, the timing was none of my own. I'd made no resolve to stop and look. What I perceived, I hadn't sought.

This David surpasses the snow figure.

Yet can never replace it.

From the farm – a gift of pears, out of the store which Piero Sassoli lovingly keeps in his cellar. Filippo brought them, and he says the merchant's words were: 'Take them for Gismondo. I know how much he enjoys fruit.'

But these pears are hard and green. The three I had served with my supper tonight were unfit to eat – so I've made an experiment: one I've placed on the window ledge to receive full benefit of the sunlight, and one I've set behind the ledgers on this table, where little of the sun will reach it, but it receives the candlelight; and the third I've placed in my chest, where it may benefit from the warmth in the room, such as it is, but from no light at all.

By this I hope to demonstrate whether light and warmth are both required for the process of ripening, or whether warmth alone is sufficient; and if light is essential – must it come from the sun?

For green fruit – what other use?

I suppose the gift was well meant.

XLVI

SILENCE. No one sends for me.

This afternoon, I thought I saw her steward approach the gate, but the man walked past and, in any case, I mistook him.

A sort of malaise afflicts me. I'm restless, nervous. Anxiously I wait for news from the farm, but when it comes – a mumbled report by Filippo: how the merchant rests, how he sleeps long hours and lives on broth and herbs – I hardly know what to make of it; I frown at the man, and send him away in silence, while my mind swings round on a pivot, saying, 'But whatever else you looked for – that must come from a different quarter; and you're obliged to be patient.'

So. Patience.

The season shifts. Four golden evenings we've had in succession. Old men sit in the doorways, and talk of spring. Everyone shares their anticipation. Yesterday, I refrained from lighting a candle and tried to work with the window open – but it appears I've lost the skill; the sounds from the street distracted me. They circled round in the room like trapped starlings until in the end I felt I must lead them back to the air, by going out myself.

So I hurried my work. I've seldom rushed as I did last night. With so much trafficking to and from the farm, and the goods to be bought for the banquet, and no one here but myself to authorise anything – the household accounts need more care than ever; all the same, I shut the ledgers early – and walked to the Arno.

I stood on the Santa Trinità, breathed in the stench, and found it wholesome. This happens sometimes, although often the river sickens me just as a gutter stench does. And I peered down at the rubbish that floats against the bridge – sticks and rags, cabbage leaves and orange rinds – a mat of filth, from which now and then a scrap breaks loose, and swirls downstream. For some time I stood watching the process. There was a piece of yellow cloth caught on a branch. I saw it straining in the current – then pull free and spin away. This event was mildly pleasing. I waited for others. Night deepened; the Arno turned from grey to black and still I was peering down, when a small and shabby boat loaded with ox-hides passed directly beneath me.

A lamp hung at the stern. The two men at the oars were silent, but another who stood at the back shouted up as they passed, 'Well? Are you going to jump?' and before I could speak, he burst out laughing. His face shone yellowish in the lamplight and his broken teeth were clearly visible. His joke seemed to give him vast enjoyment. I was struck by the thought that he relished his miserable life on the river and pitied those mortals who spent their lives otherwise. He'd looked up at a man on the bridge, and the sight had set him laughing.

After that I felt absurd, and came away.

But not to the house. I wandered about, vaguely searching for something – and after a while I knew what it was. I wished myself in Rome. To be with the whores. To drink from a filthy cup. To see the brown girl, Angelica, and hear her speak of Africa. Soon the wish became desire. As I walked, I began to ache, and to sweat like a common labourer.

Could I find such a whore in Florence? This question, long neglected, now seemed urgent. To act the sinner here, where I've always kept above reproach – what was it but to heighten the risks, and with them my pleasure? Yes. But I hungered for more than my customary risks. I wanted to bury myself in this woman –

The very thought revolted me. I stopped – I was in a street behind the Ognissanti – my eyes had misted. My cheeks were wet. In fact, I was close to blubbering like a simpleton. So then I hurried, taking the shortest route, and all the while I could feel my strength ebbing away, so that by the time I reached this room, I was faint with exhaustion.

I flung myself on the bed and quickly sank into dreams, base and unhallowed – but was it in truth Angelica they delivered to me?

The whore in my sleep had the face of Madonna.

When I woke at dawn, I felt unclean.

Pardon, Madonna.

These clamourings of flesh – how could I think these desecrations?

Before I left for the warehouse, I took the opal from the chest and placed it in my purse. There it nestled among the coins, just as once in Rome, and throughout the day it served to reproach me. For who knows better than I the power of whores: their delight in sullying everything?

And tonight the opal rests beside me, smiling in the candle-light, and even now reproaching.

So may my thoughts be scoured clean.

XLVII

A letter today from the merchant. Such tremulous writing! It tempts one to think as Rigogli does – of priests and funerals. Over the months, Piero Sassoli's writing has changed, until now it resembles scratches in dust – such as one makes with a twig. It contradicts all thought of recovery.

In this, as in his previous letter, he makes no mention of health, nor any matter concerning trade. He sends no thanks for prayers and kindly wishes. All he writes is of his son. Our Gabby returns to Florence in two days' time.

XLVIII

WHAT entertainment for our golden boy! Rome might have kept him longer, but here's a richer pastime – he and I alone in the house together . . . the merchant ill! Oh, I expect to be baited. Only his schemes for the 'gentleman' and the coming banquet – only those may divert him, but I'd be a fool to depend on it.

Last night, cold and unable to sleep, I conjured his voice out of the darkness:

'No one lives for ever, Gissy, and once he's dead, what's to become of you and me? Or – to put it more succinctly – what's to become of you? Oh, but you'll have your plans. No one as gifted as you could fail to have plans. And means – I'm sure you have those. Well, and I hope so. My father – I grieve to think it – is decidedly extravagant, and much too trusting. I'll have to salvage what I can . . . trim the household . . . and you . . . A niche, you say? I promised you a niche? Why, so I did . . . and if I must . . . would you care for the stable? I've always thought that Bruno such an idle lout.'

These words spoken softly round my bed.

And nothing decided. Nothing. I wait for miracles. My life has narrowed to a line with fantastic hopes to the one side and, to the other, panic. I write as if I owned this table, as if the chair could never be taken from me, nor the pen snatched back. I shrink from change. Only my senses seem alert to welcome it, whether it's fair or evil, behaving in ways that are unfamiliar to me; and so I'm driven from my work by a few sounds at the window; then I weep in the street, and now – this business of the florins:

Girolamo Paccalli, who's borrowed from the merchant over many years, brought a payment to the warehouse. He set down a leather bag before Rigogli (he rarely shows the least regard for *me*), and declared it contained three hundred golden florins.

This threw Rigogli into a flutter. He appealed to me to do the counting, which I did, taking care not to hurry – the longer Paccalli was made to wait, the better it pleased me. I sat at the merchant's desk, because it was in the sunlight, and was busy stacking the coins – when all at once I was struck by astonishment at their beauty. Not florins, gold like any gold to be used for bartering: these seemed counters designed for some mystical ritual that could open a world beyond my understanding. They glinted with power, secrets. My heart beat faster. Each coin was cool and significant on my fingers; each felt different from the others – as though these were the first I'd held in my life; and I placed each on its stack only with great reluctance.

What was this but a sharpness of my senses?

A disturbing fact. Rigogli says that Paccalli pays as much as he can in case the merchant dies. He fears Gabriello would raise the interest. So these are the thoughts abroad in the markets.

Tonight, I've eaten the pear from the window ledge. Already a perfect yellow, and just ripe. Still firm, yet sweet. But the one on the table needs two more days at least; and the one in the chest both feels and looks as it did when I placed it there.

XLIX

GABRIELLO'S back. He has friends to supper. There are still three weeks to the turn of the year,* but he celebrates because, he says, his own new year is already upon him; the gift he brought from Rome has been well received by 'the gentleman', and everything goes according to plan – whatever the plan. Fortune pushes him up. Well, let him be merry. The wheel keeps turning!

As I write, there's a clatter of knives and spoons. I'm regaled by music and laughter. I sit in this room, and pretend that I've no desire to leave it. Maybe I have none. The house has become a cage where I'm grateful to crouch in the smallest corner, provided I'm left in peace; but it taxes my wits even to safeguard that – the simple right of an animal to curl away and be still; for the baiting has begun.

I've just escaped. A short while ago, Gabriello invited me to join his friends, and 'drink his father's health' – a request he knew I couldn't refuse, not without offending all the Sassoli, living and dead. And the message – to which he required an answer – he sent by Anna, so that the servants would know if I rejected this fine civility. Naturally, I went.

But tonight I resolved not to suffer my role for long. I used a trick I keep for rare occasions – or else he'd soon discover it. A cheap defence.

The fact is – and it's a precious fact – Gabriello lives in terror of illness. A sneeze, a modest shivering somewhere in his

*The first day of the Florentine year was March 25th, the Feast of the Annunciation

neighbourhood – and he recoils. The heavens in their mercy have granted this.

So, I entered the hall. And saw the usual company: Andreuccio, Francesco, Cristofano di Giunta and the others. Six or seven in all. No women. Everyone slumped at the table; and as I came forward, slowly their faces turned; each one smiled. And even the hired musician, whom I recognised as Berto di Giovanni, the same who plays with such tender feeling at many of Ser Romoli's suppers – even *he* immediately took his flute from his lips and, leaning against the wall, grinned at me.

Gabriello sat where he always sits when the merchant's absent – at the head of the table – and breaking off in the middle of some joke as I appeared, he mocked me with a show of politeness.

'Gissy!' he murmured. 'I'm very glad you've come. I knew you'd be sitting alone, and worrying. No use at all. The best we can do is pray – and drink my father's health. Fretting won't help. It might even shorten your own life – which God forbid! Here . . . a cup for Gissy!'

'Thank you.' There was nowhere to sit. I stood by the fireplace. Agnolo brought me the cup and I raised it, saying, 'May Piero Sassoli soon return to confound his enemies!' I drank.

No one said anything.

Then Gabriello's eyes grew smaller.

'What was that?' he asked, nudging Andreuccio who sat next to him. 'Did you hear a sort of creaking from the fireplace?'

'You mean that sound like a rotten plank beginning to split?' Andreuccio shrugged. 'Ancient timbers,' he said. 'I suppose this house is a venerable age? Parts need pulling down . . . '

But Gabriello couldn't enjoy these witticisms. He was looking at me, and his mouth had become like a tight string.

'Couldn't you find a braver voice?' he demanded. 'Is my father's health such a trifling matter? I realise that it may be so to many, but you, I thought, would be concerned . . . Of course, if I was wrong, excuse me . . . '

I coughed. I shivered. 'Nothing concerns me more, as you know very well.' The words came out in an excellent graveyard whisper.

Gabriello stared, and then he mimicked: 'Nothing concerns me more . . . For God's sake, Gissy, are you ill? You sound – '

'Lovesick!' squeaked a fool down the table – I think it might have been Agnolo – and our golden boy smiled again.

'Well,' he said, 'are you?'

I ignored the attack.

'Just a sore in my throat . . . I suppose it must be an ulcer. It seemed nothing this morning, but as the day's gone on I've found it painful . . .'

'The devil you have. A sore?' Now he became alarmed and, almost as much, he was annoyed. Fear and disbelief – I saw them warring together. Seizing his cup, he drank deeply, his eyes on my face, until suddenly he cried, 'And look! He's shivering like a rabbit! Get away, Gissy. Go to bed, with your damned sore!'

'I will.'

He laughed; but as I came near the table to set the cup down, although I was careful not to look at him, I could sense him shrinking from my arm as I stretched past. Then I made to leave. The whole assembly watched in silence. I felt its resentment on my back.

At the last moment –

'Yes, go to bed – and enjoy your dreams!' Andreuccio cried, drawing a snigger from everyone. And Gabriello rallied.

'Get well quickly!' he shouted. 'Or who'll look after my banquet? And you'll need your strength in the new year. I've several other banquets in mind!'

May the new year bring me nothing worse.

So I sit here, caged.

They watched me closely tonight. The penned-in creature. I believe they know something. Even the flute player. Gabriello – to heighten the mischief of summoning me – had told them something, his plans for my future once he sits at the head of the table every day. And whatever he plans, I'll be the last to learn of it. It's always so.

There! They laugh. A curse on them! Tonight, I feel that all their mirth centres on me. They wish me to hear them. I'm the very stuff of their jokes. They laugh the louder because they wish me to know it – and feel the treachery that creeps towards me. Gabriello's plans.

But why should my wretchedness gladden these people?

When did I ever stab any of these in the back, or spit in his face? It seems I'm favoured with many enemies for little effort.

And now these ink blots on the page, because I'm shivering. No mummer's antic, this, such as it was in the hall: the room feels cold. Fear. I've packed the room with fear. And why? Because some dolts laugh over their wine? How can I know they discuss me? The world affords them other interests – women and acquaintances, boasts and bets – yet they laugh, and at once I'm convinced they're plotting treacheries!

And what if they do?

Here I hide, shaking, as if there were nothing to sustain me, no inner resources, nor any possibilities beyond their plots. What if I'd stood my ground, and said, 'You laugh to think I have no future. It amuses you to look on me as friendless and an outcast, but although the Sassoli show such contempt for my services, it may sober you to learn of one who's placed me high in her estimation – '

And so direct their jests to her?

Never. Better any cheating trick than that! I've known other treacheries. Da Vinci – what was that but one? And now I think of it – the very birth of our golden boy. Yet I exist. I hold together. I've weathered many betrayals: the merchant's, and da Vinci's, Fra Girolamo's –

The burning of the Heretic.

Fra Girolamo. He, who showed me a God to believe in, One for whom I threw my lute from the window and sacrificed to the flames that silver cup which Monna Margherita had given me. Fra Girolamo, who taught me how to purchase redemption (for who could doubt that the price being paid, the goods would be delivered?). His enemies, the lovers of this world – and foremost amongst them, our Holy Father, Keeper of the Keys – they triumphed. But still more heinous, even before they burned him, he let them triumph, and what was that but treachery?

Yet my mind held.

I was twenty. Those who wished to see Fra Girolamo dead had plotted for months. Easter came; and a mob was never more cunningly set on a man – thanks to the Franciscans. Sour brothers in Christ. Ever jealous of the pious Dominicans – and encouraged by many who cared not a fig for piety – they issued a challenge: if Fra Girolamo had attained such a perfect state of grace, as he implied, let him ease the doubts of weaker mortals by some demonstration. If it was true that of all the holy men in Florence he stood closest to God, nay, closer than the Pope – let him prove it with a miracle! The cry went up –

And it was agreed. The Signoria agreed. Fra Girolamo agreed. An idea took shape: there would be a lane of fire: one of his most fervent disciples would walk between two walls of burning sticks, and emerge unscathed. A Franciscan, ready to die if he could only expose the spiritual pride of his rival, would keep the Dominican company. It would be a trial of saints. Proof by ordeal. A prospect that both shocked and delighted people. To those who hated Fra Girolamo, it seemed that the time was at hand when a fanatic's claims would vanish for ever, and the city could be rid of him. But to those who loved him, here was the time for the truth, when God would be seen to pluck down the mighty, revealing that His favour lay not with the Pontiff who schemed and sinned in Rome, but with this ugly man of virtue from Ferrara; and all his enemies, seeing what they saw, would surely believe and be saved – or perish.

A test like this, men said, must turn the gaze of heaven upon us; we'd be offering ourselves to God for judgment – but in all humility . . . although according to Piero Sassoli, others said that the whole idea was blasphemous, barbarous. I myself heard no such comment and, if I had, it wouldn't have troubled me. I was secure in my own conviction.

So, the day came. Guards sealed off the Piazza. Strangers were kept from entering the city. The walls of sticks had been built and soaked in oil. The Loggia dei Lanzi was crammed with those who hated and those who loved our Fra Girolamo – the authorised observers. But the guards kept the common crowd at a distance – 'a respectful distance' they called it.

Guards, crowds, and prayers.

I kept away. I hungered to go, jostle with the rest, feasting my eyes, but I chose to mortify this appetite. Who was I to witness a miracle? The implications terrified me. Heaven's intervention. God's statement here in Florence. And once the miracle had occurred, and Fra Girolamo's enemies were confounded, the last sceptics swept away – who could say what might not happen? Angelic hosts might visit us. Sinners might fall stricken in the streets. Of one thing I felt sure. There'd be no more half measures.

So I shut myself in this room, fell on my knees, and prayed – but kept the window open in order to hear the gasp, when it came, or the deep hush – I supposed it might be either – as the Franciscan turned to ash but the calm Dominican walked from the flames; and then, I supposed, a rhapsody of song, and all the bells in Florence ringing.

And I pictured to myself brilliant forms filling the air, and the bricks of every wall in Florence touched by a light that came not from the sun but from a source both spiritual and infinitely further away. Ardently I prayed: 'When Your new age dawns, Almighty, once this miracle unfolds, let me not be rejected from Your holy city . . . ' Noon passed, and still I prayed. And still through the window came the normal sounds of the street, only softer than usual, and, like a burr beneath them, the noise of the crowds that stood in the streets round the Piazza della Signoria.

'May I be acceptable, Lord.'

My knees ached. Time forgot to move forward. Then the sky darkened, for an instant lit up a sickish green, and darkened again. Thunder rumbled; rain streamed down the shutters – and finally, from the direction of the Piazza I heard shouts, but not the amazed and ecstatic sounds of my imaginings: these were angry. I forsook my prayers and hurried to the window. The rain was casting a grey veil over the street, drenching men as they came, first in groups, and then in a dense press, their shoulders rounded and, in spite of the downpour, walking slowly. All coming from the Piazza.

I ran downstairs and out of the house. I grabbed the arm of a sullen stranger.

'What happened?' I cried. 'Didn't they – ?'

But here I had no more words. My mind refused the questions. Had both Dominican and Franciscan died? Had the Franciscan triumphed? (How *could* he have triumphed?) Had Christ appeared to rebuke us all?

I stood before my stranger, speechless.

He jerked his sleeve away.

Nothing, he said. Only a tedious bickering. First, the Franciscans had objected to the Dominican carrying a crucifix into the flames, and then to his carrying the Host, and for every concession Fra Girolamo made, his spiteful challengers invented a new objection, prolonging the argument, until, at last – the lightning and the rain; which the Franciscans claimed to understand as a sign from heaven that the whole event was displeasing. And so, an end. Nothing done. No miracle – or sacrifice. Everyone packed off home.

Oh, it was cunning. Only a fool could think it wasn't devised. To send men away wrought to a fever; Fra Girolamo's adversaries, their hatred roused and trapped in their breasts. Skilfully done!

The next day – violent attack. The rabble, led by those who'd contrived it, set out to punish this maker of miracles who made none, and the God-fearing monks of San Marco found themselves in a state of siege – a misfortune they'd feared and provided for: they possessed a considerable arsenal. From the monastery walls, from the very pinnacle of their chapel, they hurled down bricks and lances on the yelping horde – while in his cell Fra Girolamo prayed.

I thought I understood. For the error of craving a miracle, I'd already reproached myself; and when on the following morning I heard the roar of this mob – and actually saw a part of it, rushing down the Via dei Servi – my thoughts fell into comfortable postures. God has ever commanded His Chosen to suffer. He always postpones the lustrous moment until the crowds disperse, and there's only the Fiend at one's elbow, offering a cup of despair. And Fra Girolamo, I realised, would be safe in this knowledge. Indeed, nothing that had happened could have surprised him, since he was far more familiar than I with the ways of heaven.

So I was lulled. Even the news, when it came, that he'd been forced from his cell by order of the Signoria and was to be examined – even that couldn't fluster me. I felt only a calm, made all the sweeter by contrition. Within the space of a day, I'd advanced from longing to see the Friar as the agent of some glorious sign that defied the laws of nature – to a pure acceptance of the fact that he must suffer. Every bone in his body must break. He must pay the price. Not until he'd reached the border of death would his God – and mine – deem it fit to intervene. I discovered it was obvious. The cleansing of such a mire as Florence must cost this much pain; and I relaxed deep in the understanding that it was right.

Until Piero Sassoli shattered everything.

He had friends among those who busied themselves examining the Dominicans; and there came an evening when he arrived home late, holding a toy, a pomander of silver fretwork –

'Here, Gismo!' he brandished it at me. 'For Bartolo Cattani! He has an embarrassing habit of giving me things whenever I go to supper. But he won't catch me empty-handed this time. Fill it with something suitable, will you? Fetch some herbs!'

I was soon employed at my task – a delicate one since the toy was all of a piece and couldn't be opened. I forget what herbs I used, but at first, as I sat there coaxing dried leaves through the fretwork, the merchant chose to stand over me, which made my fingers clumsier; perhaps aware of it, he began to pace about. Finally, in his impatience he flung out this information: 'Those poor men are to die! Unpleasant business. Why can't they simply lock them up?'

'Which men?' I asked, and I shook the foolishly designed pomander to settle the contents.

'Which?' Piero Sassoli stood still. 'Why, your Fra Girolamo! Your prophet and his moonstruck followers! You didn't think they'd go free, did you? Surely not!'

I went on with my task.

'They're holy men.'

'Oh, as to that, I wouldn't know. But they've confessed to crimes, heresies . . . hideous things. And now they've got to burn.'

'Confessed?' I gaped up.

'Careful with that!'

The pomander slipped in my hands. I tightened my grip. The merchant gazed at it sternly. I forced in more herbs. He was appeased.

'Naturally they've confessed. Anyone would, you know, the things they do . . . '

And with these words – either all he could, or all he cared to say – he snatched the pomander, and hurried off to his supper engagement.

Naturally they've confessed.

I remember Rigogli, too; how he shook his head and sighed,

and said it all went to show you could never be certain of anyone. That was the next day. By then the whole of Florence knew and talked of little else.

But the first night, it was silence, solitude, while I wrestled with this new-born wonder, this monster; Fra Girolamo had confessed. He was to burn. For the sake of ease, sinew and muscle, he'd said whatever they liked – the lovers of this world – so that now they could *do* whatever they liked.

I was gripped by a nauseous sweating. I fought to be blind, but the more I struggled to blank my thoughts, the more they dazzled me. A commonplace! Mere vanity! The Friar, whom I'd thought so versed in every type of peril – had failed to consider pain! His mind had belittled it – and what was that but stupidity, and lack of understanding? So this physical pain – most ordinary of all afflictions – had taken him by surprise. A thousand spiritual torments he could have overcome, but this – this, in his pride, he'd thought a trivial problem. The simple racking of flesh – especially of his own – he'd considered to be an occasion for contempt.

It was not. And in the terror of revelation, his arrogance had shown. He'd looked to God. Who'd have thought it? Fra Girolamo, trapped in a folly which any tortured spy or assassin would have quickly mocked and rejected: on the rack – he'd hoped to be spared. He'd thought he had special arrangements. God was close, so the spirit was surely more than the pain, which was nothing, nothing . . .

Except everything. His faith broke with his bones.

He was not, after all, a saint. Not even wise. He was just a man with a raucous voice – and delusions.

There was the fact. I bathed my face in cold water. I assured myself that I execrated Fra Girolamo – but in truth, the notion of this wretch, so abandoned and perplexed by his sudden plummeting into the pit of doubt and terror, oppressed me with a great weariness. So it was. In the middle of the night, I lay on my bed and slept the sleep of a child – velvet and dreamless. And in the morning, I noted that while I'd slept a curious warmth had crept across my mind, which I took to be Christian love for the tortured Friar. But perhaps it was only satisfaction.

Whatever it was, the burning scorched it out. Fra Girolamo and the others – I saw their shame, their fear. At least, I saw their lips moving very fast, so that although their words may have been prayers, none the less they were gibbering. They were hung from the scaffold in chains. Wax faces. Wax limbs. Candles for lighting. The wood was piled high and stacked with discretion to keep the smoke from a needlessly merciful role, suffocating the victims. And the people howled. Not just those sections of the people who may have taken part in the siege of San Marco – but honest tradesmen, sober merchants, and bankers. Their spiritual grooming of years gone in an instant.

How they hated this fool from Ferrara! How they despised him for all their wasted effort, their bitter steps towards Paradise. Let him die! Let him roast for the trick!

And I howled with them.

It was ridiculous. Also disgusting. The skin cracking open, limbs twitching, the fat oozing out, eyes melting in purple faces. Ever since, I've shrunk from a bonfire.

And in the end it came to ashes, smoke, and a fine black grease that clung to everyone's clothes. It came to chains, a few charred bones, and filthy jokes. Then a careful raking of all the dirt together, and away with it, into the Arno.

Away with it.

As I came from the crowd, I swore I'd never be tricked again.

After that, I thought of nothing.

Night came. I lay awake, staring into the shadows, numb with shock, as if I'd been scratched across both eyes; and vaguely I understood that I waited not for sleep, but for the day's abominable rituals to come stealing back, detail on detail, overwhelming my memory. It must happen, and I was passive.

Then eventually an image came – but it brought no fire: it wasn't a scaffold I saw, with naked men hanging in fetters; bones and flesh –

The darkness in the room shifted; and not behind my eyes, but rather, it seemed, in front of them, I saw an archway; and through it, a glimmer of light, and in the centre of that – the snow figure. The Grecian, as he'd appeared that time I'd seen him, in half-profile, straining with all his strength, aiming a spear over the courtyard wall, to soar above the roofs of Florence. Shining, and outside men's justifying – reaching beyond those confines which we build ourselves.

The whole night, I stared at him. He made no move. His arms never tired, the left stretched forward, the right reaching back, aiming the spear, its tip of ice towards the sky. And so he strained, rescuing me.

In part.

For part – all belief I'd held in Mother Church – had crumbled with the Heretic. Yet many other cherished beliefs might have crumbled; but thanks to this – the snow figure – there remained in me something

Fool.

What a fool.

'Something's bound to happen!' I said, and allowed the days to pass, the weeks to escape. Now they laugh at me. Everything. This room, a Sassoli room, laughs to see the poor fool blink. What was he doing? Scribbling, why, scribbling 'to clear his mind', he said, for the time when he'd be forced to act. And now when it comes, instead of being prepared – lo, he blinks, he blubbers.

Toad of a fool.

No. I say no to this. The Fiend take Creation.

All that's beautiful in this world – it's the gleam of a corpse.

All that's noble – it's sauce to a dish of carrion.

I've destroyed the mirror.

I refrained from hurling it to the floor and stamping on it, or smashing it with a candlestick. Gabriello might have been listening. So as to make no noise, I wrapped it in my hood, raised the foot of the bed and placed the mirror beneath. Then I let the bed drop. I lay down upon it, and wept.

Which is to say, the tears wept me. They usurped my will. They forced me to lie with my knees drawn into my belly. They forced me to open my mouth in a cry of silence, and stiffened my face. They marched down my cheeks like an army that had vanquished me.

But now I'm calm. Witness: I write with a steady hand.

The grey of dawn is at the window. I smile to see it. My mind peeps out and remarks, 'So now the things I've feared are puny things. Another dawn can bring no greater evil.'

Calm. Calm. The colourless day – face it.

As for the mirror – I've gathered up the fragments. I cut my finger on one, and its sharpness put me in mind of ice. And one is long and thin, like an icicle, deadly enough for stabbing with. I've wrapped them in my hood. I'll be rid of them today, and the frame as well. Mirrors I can do without.

'*Toad*' is it? Gabriello's word – how easily I accept it!

Well, and so I am: 'A toad, Gissy. Venomous – and hideous.'

Yes.

L

I write from habit. Every action has its price. My body screams to be still. The least movement – opening one of the ledgers – and I'm fatigued. I ache at tasks. As for reading figures – columns of figures – they press against my forehead as if they'd crush my skull. And if I'm obliged to speak in reply to a question from Rigogli, or if I have to talk with someone who calls on business, at first my voice refuses to come, and then it rises reluctantly, while my throat tightens, so that I want to clear a passage by shouting – or else to whisper. And I'm exhausted by a fitful impatience that would have me bang with my fist on the table – or do anything except the thing I have to do, which is to speak as if this world we live in were a place of decency, and mainly acceptable events.

But to do nothing – remedies nothing. Three evenings I've spent by the window. I've neglected household matters. I've sat with my purse at my belt – a meagre, lightweight token of a purse which I no longer care to open, although I sense this need to keep it with me – and I watch night come.

To frustrate me, it brings no true blackness. It spawns stars; and at the sight of those, I feel a sort of energy: I'd tear them down if I could. Then there's the moon; I have an urge to take up my pen and scratch signs – meaningless signs and numbers – on its surface, so that, for ever after, learned men would look at the moon and waste talents, years and calculations trying to read the wisdom there.

Lives lost on mindless scratches, counterfeits.

It would be fitting.

It's no more than already happens.

This is the fourth morning since Gabriello brought his victory to my door, bursting in as I wrote. And prompted by the Devil, how magnificently he timed it! For when he came, what was I writing but sentiments of hope, sweet words about the Grecian warrior? How, despite Fra Girolamo's treachery, and the loss of the God I thought he'd given me, there had remained in me something which refused to be broken. How my memory of the snow figure had held me up: a memory more vivid even than the burning of the Heretic –

Well. Time takes us all to school. The greater image is proved the greater lie.

LI

NEWS. News. It gathers like a storm. Today – from Piero Sassoli. He stays another week on the farm, but he writes that his health is vastly improved.

'Maestro Ruccelli has such strong hopes of my recovery that I expect to enjoy a full cup of wine at our celebration for Gabby.'

Our celebration for Gabby. That smacks of a certain knowingness. He knows I know. He implies that now I'm in on the secret.

It's all as I was told.

But thanks to this, the snow figure, there remained in me something –

And the door flew open. There stood Gabriello, drunk, lips curved, as beautiful as Lucifer, his bright hair dampened across his brow. And behind him, coming from the supper table – the laughter of his friends, the music of the flute player. Gabriello leaned against the door frame, so that at once this room became like the space inside a sorcerer's circle: he kept outside it, but the look on his face challenged me: 'Doesn't this boldness daunt you? Are you sure you're Master here?'

'Gissy!' he said. 'I thought I'd find you huddled up in bed. How's your throat? Have you taken your syrups and potions? Oh – but I see you're working!' He laughed. 'The wretched man can barely croak a civil greeting – and still he slaves, filching a soldo here, a soldo there . . . No. Don't start. I'm drunk. And drunkards shouldn't be crossed!'

I'd risen. The pen was still in my hand. These notes lay spread on the table, the ink still wet. I dared not gather them up. Had I done so, he'd have guessed immediately that here were more than lists and totals. In fact, so great was my terror in case by some fiendish means he knew already, and had come to seize my notes, that to prevent it I hurried towards him.

'What do you want? What gives you the right – ?'

'Oh, my dear, poor Gissy.'

He shook his head and softly closed his eyes to convey a kind of brotherly long-suffering. Then he opened his eyes again and murmured, 'But you've found your voice! That's wonderful. You must tell me what physic you use. To cure a sore within an hour . . . it's little short of miraculous . . . '

'Leave me alone.'

I tried to close the door – a mistake as, when he didn't move, I was obliged to abandon the attempt and stand there like a half-wit while he watched me almost fondly. He breathed a vapour of wine into my face. All at once, I began to curse.

'But I see you're feverish!' he said, smiling. 'I mustn't vex you. Don't you want to know why I've come? Of course you do . . . Well, on my way from Rome, I visited the farm. And my father and I . . . we talked. A long talk . . . '

'So? What of it?'

His eyebrows rose. 'Aren't you interested?'

'I trust his health improves . . . '

'And hope! And pray!' Again he laughed, tossing his hair. 'I feel for you, Gissy!' he added. 'Really I do! If he's spared for a few more years, I suppose you'll be rich. You've a lot to lose. And it's hard to know that soon you may have to turn honest . . . '

'Leave me alone. Go back to your friends! Why should I tolerate these insults?' – and this time I pushed the door hard, but his arm came up to stop it. And still he leaned against the door frame.

'In God's name, can't I jest? Listen. We had, as I say, a talk. And my father advised me – despite how churlish you've been, and you have been, you know, about my banquet – in short, he advised me to tell you . . . but you're not listening!'

'Certainly I'm listening! Say what you have to say, and go.'

Fear for these notes stifled all curiosity, so that I wasn't tormented by his words as I might have been if he'd started this speech at another time. I hadn't the patience to humour him with cringing and anticipating. And this he suddenly understood. He flushed. His features sharpened. He said coldly, 'Oh yes, I see I intrude. Some of us *know* when we intrude. Back to my friends? Gladly. I only came to do my duty. Filial duty . . . but that's nothing to you, I imagine . . . '

'What do you wish to tell me?'

'Oh, haven't I said?'

A display of surprise. Then he gazed at the ceiling, and again his eyes half closed while his smile altered, becoming delicate with inquiry – the kind of expression a philosopher might wear as he stabbed a mouse with a needle.

At last he said, 'I've been taken to task. I've been told you should know the reason for this banquet. Who it is I wish to impress. So . . . the fact is . . . it's the father of my bride. Yes, Gissy. I intend to marry. What do you say to that?'

Watching me as he spoke. And when he stopped, there occurred one of those evil mysteries that portend disaster: it seemed to me that he began to swell, upwards and outwards, filling the doorway, and yet even as he stood where he was, somehow he also encompassed me with his yellow hair and his red tunic. There was no escape.

I said, 'God send you many sons just like yourself.'

He was delighted.

'Why, that's noble! Thank you!' he cried. 'A blessing I hadn't hoped for! Not with the bride being who she is. Lucia da Fano.'

Or, the widow. Or, Madonna Lucia. Whatever he said – for already I was saying 'No.'

'Yes.'

'She's taken an oath . . . '

He laughed.

'Oh, very pious! She's also kept the most open house in Florence. She's tangled herself with so many lovers that – well – the lady's oath must go. She needs stronger proof of her virtue than that. Her reputation's somewhat impaired. Snared. Especially, you know . . . ' his voice dropped, 'especially since there are those who name her when they speak of murders . . . '

And all the time he observed me; and whatever he saw, it set him off into a spasm of soundless mirth while I stood helpless, and in my head I was saying, *None of this is true. He's drunk, and this is sport* . . . Thoughts that fell like pebbles into a dark pool, and were swallowed up.

'Besides,' he went on, 'believe it or not, she likes me . . . Though I admit it's the father I have to thank! Him and his sons. They convinced him he had to act, that she's mocked his authority long enough, and now the father storms about her house; he threatens to pack her off for a nun, or to move in himself and order her life. He even threatened to lock her up in a leper-house . . . '

'I don't believe it. None of it.'

'What? About the lepers? Oh, you should! He'd do it!' Gabriello smiled happily. 'The old fool hates her! She's transgressed. Wounded his dignity. A second marriage – that was the thing. A profitable match like the first one; and – sweet Lord, how she's fought him! Disobedience, Gissy. It's a monstrous thing in a child. And worse than that, the way she's lived – what worthy soul would have her? How the stories fly . . . '

'Stop!'

'Oh, the man cries stop!'

'I don't want to hear these stories . . . What are you saying?'

'Saying? Why, I'm saying the father's won. He's forced her into submission! He's placed his agents in her household. He's wooed her banker and bribed her factors. The woman's trapped. She's to marry the man he chooses. The father has his triumph, and now . . . ' Gabriello smirked ' . . . he means to exact his revenge. He's chosen a man he believes will torment her. A loose young fellow. A rake, whom he can depend upon to show her little respect . . . You understand? His malicious eyes discovered me, and he was enraptured. When he comes to this banquet, you'll see how completely he dotes on me. I'm the thorn to tear his too proud daughter . . . '

'She'll not have you!'

'Oh, my innocent Gissy!' Our golden boy shook his head and squealed with merriment. 'How little you know! Gissy, the lady adores me. She and I – we're *intimate*. She's often sworn that if she were forced to marry, of all her suitors I'd be the one. And why . . . You needn't squint like that! I suppose you think she swears the same to everyone? But listen, I know her. *And* her reasons! "I'd choose you, Gabriello, because I can see you lack reverence." Her very words. Passion and beauty, she says, are all she desires. One block of marble is more than enough in a lifetime – by that she means da Fano. As for the rest, I'm young. I care nothing for solemn business ventures, nor for godly trifles like fidelity . . . and all this pleases her. The contempt of it pleases her . . . It's true! Don't look like that! . . . Once, when we were walking in her loggia which is hung with splendid tapestries, she turned to me and asked, "Gabriello, if you wanted to buy a horse and found that your purse was empty – what would you do?" And when I replied, waving at the tapestries, "Sell these, for a start!" – she laughed. "Yes," she said. "If they force me to marry, you're my choice. I'd like to spit in the eye of the world." From her own lips I have it, Gissy. I promise you!'

Then, disgustingly, he laid his hand on his mouth and sneered, 'I've been there!' And after a while: 'So – won't you come to this banquet? Why be an outcast? I can't provide a glimpse of the lady – she's to play her part and keep away in horror – but have you no wish to meet her father? I know you've always nursed a tender feeling for her . . . '

I struck him. Only once. He fell back sprawling. And as he lay staring up at me, his eyes became as round as pan lids. Blood trickled out of his nose. But still he smiled faintly, and struggling to his feet, he panted, 'Very fine . . . A most handsome goodwill gesture!' – wiping his nose on his sleeve, spoiling the cloth – a thing that seemed to incense him more than my blow had done, for seeing the dark streak on the velvet, his smile vanished. His head jerked up. 'Toad!' he whined. 'You damned toad . . . '

And after that, in a tone of surprise he said it again.

'A toad, Gissy. That's what you are! Venomous and hideous. And just as small!'

I shut the door in his face.

LII

A pork jelly. A suckling pig. A peacock stuffed with spices. 'And Gissy,' he says, 'I've just been telling Bartola she must surpass herself. I want a pie that shows we Sassoli never skimp . . . So none of your usual miseries about the price of ginger and pepper!'

Only the best for our golden boy.

And, '*Would it pain you, Ser Cavalletti, were I to need your services in more than this?*'

– In such a fashion, no doubt! With feasts for Gabriello, and inventories of da Fano linen – the sheets and pillows she brings to her marriage; and lists of the wine she stores for her husband's pleasure. And – patience! I may serve in more than that! I may yet be counting the florins she spends on Gabriello's sons –

Such rare privileges!

Tonight, I've taken out the opal. At first I couldn't look at it. I laid it down, and set about totalling the cost of this list of spices which are required by Bartola. Gabriello's handiwork. 'On these she says you keep her short!' But as I wrote, I glanced up – as I knew I must – and saw only the thing I've seen for years: a gem like milk frozen, the lines barely breathed upon it, the face with its smile quickened by the candlelight – not Lucia da Fano, but so like her. And therefore more than like, since what is she but counterfeit? Why, here, after all, I have her. When I've reproached myself, 'You insult Madonna by treasuring this mere accident of a likeness,' – I've grievously wasted my conscience, for all the while I've treasured her very self: deceit, so worthless, yet so seeming precious, and partly deceit by accident, for what was I to her, ever? Unless our meeting in the Piazza was contrived. Did Gabriello encourage her to ridicule me?

Enough. Why inflict this torture? The plain fact suffices. A void. A fouled recess where I'd imagined riches.

Amen to that. And to everything as it is. Let her be what she is, do what she will.

But this deception has no end. The candle flickers, the opal glows, and her lips seem to move.

Madonna.

God confound her for eternity – for all except its last day!

And then, even then

LIII

EITHER I die like this, or I act.

LIV

FRA Bernardino twittered of mortal danger, and mingled with the horror in his eyes there was a craven plea: 'Leave me in peace. Don't bring me thoughts like this.'

I saw it. He made small attempt to hide it. Nevertheless, he presumed to offer comfort: 'I shall pray for you, my son! Never have I feared for a soul as I fear for yours. Keep constant watch. I shall cry to our Lord and His Blessed Saints . . . '

Twitterings.

'Is that all?' I asked.

He shrank back. 'What else did you look for, Gismondo?'

'Nothing,' I said. And then, because I could see he quaked inside his robe, as if he thought I might wring his little life out of him, I was angry. 'Twitterings,' I said, 'and mumblings. Exactly what you've given. That's all I looked for. By now I should know you've nothing else! But isn't it natural in a man to hope for more than he expects? Isn't the Church built on that folly? What else do you mean by "salvation"?'

At that, the friar spread his hands, abject, witless, while a certain pointing of his chin told me I'd offended him. Suddenly he piped, 'So, sir! This is how you value counsel! This is your respect for the Holy Church! I suggest you take yourself off, sir. Go and sample the Devil's help. Then we'll see . . . He's standing close behind you!'

'How strange!' I said. 'For I think I see him by your side.'

Fra Bernardino gasped. He crossed himself, and in another moment he scuttled away, calling back across his shoulder, 'You're lost, Gismondo! Satan has claimed you already!'

I let him go.

It was peaceful in the chapel. I felt in no hurry to leave. In his haste to escape, Fra Bernardino had left the side door open, and through it came the sound of birds in the cloister garden, and a thin shaft of evening sunlight. But the altar stood in shadow.

And the crucifix hung in shadow.

I studied Him. His limbs. I studied the rib-cage; drawing the deepest breath I could, I tried to imagine His agony – and failed. I found I required Him to suffer. No pain or torture I could envisage satisfied the requirement.

'Why shouldn't You suffer,' I thought, 'when every one of Your creatures is a thing of pain?'

I hated Him. As I gazed at this Christ, it seemed to me that no nail could be too blunt, nor driven in too slowly; no extremity of pain as the air was crushed in His chest, no torment of snapping sinews and gashed flesh – none of these could ever be enough, because none was more than any man might suffer, and this – this Lover, who writhes with such enticing elegance – doesn't He claim to be something greater than man?

'You deserve more,' I thought, 'and far more horrible.'

But there I became afraid. I trembled for my soul's safety. I tried to push myself towards compassion; and reaching up, where the rib-cage curves in an edge that looks as sharp as a blade – I placed my finger.

Yet this blade-edge couldn't cut. I shed no blood for Him.

As for His lips, waiting to be kissed, soliciting a blasphemy – that confusion of love by which He invites us into guilt and punishment and promises forgiveness – I found myself smiling, and despising them. Then I turned and walked away, quickly, with a new understanding. For it had occurred to me that if I refused to kiss this Christ, I contributed to His suffering. I left Him unappeased. I rejected the guilt He longed to offer, His punishments and forgiveness – the whole, smothering entanglement.

I chose freedom. While I walked through the chapel, there was a lightness in my step, and in my head a clarity. At last I'd assessed this artefact, this carved god.

A deceit, to be cast out. Little more than an opal.

But then I came to the door, the main entrance, and as I opened it, I looked back. Sunlight streamed in behind me. It rushed towards the altar, seeking out the crucifix. It bathed the head of the Christ. A torrent of light, white with dust. And either because it seemed not to flow towards Him but to radiate from Him, or else because I thought it had taken upon itself some duty which I'd rejected – this light affected me. Deep inside, pity leapt like a cornered animal.

I wanted none of it. I forced it down, and hurried out.

But from the altar to the door – for some fifteen paces – my mind had been as clear as crystal. And in it I'd seen a thing to do. Where such an action leads I didn't see – although I might have seen that, too, if I hadn't looked back.

In any case, tomorrow I'll do it.

LV

THE humblest I could find: a maggot-ridden establishment, with cracked shutters. I walked in boldly, and called for attention. I supposed I must make a show and be bold, or else be servile, and I felt in no mood to creep.

At once, a sickly stench greeted me, one so well remembered that it set me smiling, for that identical stench I've met in Rome. In da Vinci's rooms. Sulphur, glues and filth. How right that it should be here, also! I was still at work, suppressing any sign of my amusement or approval, when a thin mosquito of a man came from the inner room – the very worst sort of Florentine: starving, suspicious, and desperate in his good intentions.

As if he feared I might change my mind and leave, he half ran towards me.

The light in the shop was dim. As he came closer, his face appeared to float in the air, somewhere about the level of my neck; and I saw it was tinged a pallid blue from a lifetime spent inhaling fumes of noxious preparations. Then, looking down, I noticed his hands, twitching at his apron. They'd been stained bright orange by some substance he dealt with. But mostly I was aware of his eyes, which were those of someone who can't afford questions – neither to ask them nor to hear them.

And all this was satisfactory.

Only the coat he wore I thought too new for my liking. It was spattered with stains, but the cloth was of a reasonable quality, and noting this, I almost doubted him. But then my mind was eased by the sight of two small, swollen-headed children who came edging to the inner door: they were luminous with hunger. Both were dressed in rags. Their elbow joints had all but broken through their skin, and they stared at me exactly as though I carried a loaf of bread.

So then I knew; I'd come to the right place.

The mosquito's head bobbed nervously.

Toothache, I said. A remedy for toothache – and he grinned like a child, before hurrying off to fetch me some greenish dust in a paper. This he pressed into my hand, whispering, 'That's eighteen soldi, sir . . . but I promise you, it never fails. Most efficacious . . .'

I paid him in silence. It seemed wise to let him worry as much as he liked about my opinion of the price he asked. And next, I sniffed this dust, tasted it, and questioned him as to its contents. These he recited very eagerly, but without embellishments, so that I saw he still prided himself on knowing his trade. And this, too, was satisfactory.

I made my decision.

I pointed to my blemish.

'And now,' I said, 'another matter. You see this?'

At the far end of the shop, on a mean pretence of a workbench, burned a clay lamp, but the rows of flasks and boxes that stood between us and this humble object soaked up all the aid it gave to the twilight. So I made my way towards it. I raised it to my face, feeling the warmth of its flame on my left cheek.

'Ah!' The insect, who had followed close behind, now looked away. His fingers twitched. Then, looking again, 'Yes! Yes!' he whispered.

I set the lamp down.

'I've tried everything,' I said. 'All the salves of the famous physicians. As you see, nothing works. In fact, it's worse, if anything. So now I'm moved to desperate measures . . . ' I smiled, and he smiled back. 'Have you a substance,' I asked, 'which eats up flesh? Something I might apply over several days, to consume this blotch? And odourless? It must be odourless, and colourless. I can't sit at home and hide. I've business interests – '

'Well, yes, indeed . . . ' The insect nodded ecstatically. He rubbed his hands together, and began to speak in rapid spurts. 'Yes, sir! There are many compounds . . . all sorts of agents. But – odourless? And colourless . . . Well, white. It could be white. I can prepare an excellent ointment . . . '

'Liquid. I'd prefer a liquid.'

'Ah.' His smile wavered.

'And tasteless,' I added, without explanation. 'A very fierce consumer of flesh. To be rid of my blotch in, say, three days. But enough for several further applications, in case I grow another.'

'Ah.'

And now he was truly miserable. The hand rubbing had become hand wringing. His eyes flittered here and there, resting anywhere except on me. An unpleasant smell rose from his hands and forearms, as if, now that he'd begun to sweat, traces of some liquid which he'd recently handled were being released from his skin. He dithered wordlessly in front of me. I gave him the time it takes to count to ten – a sop for his scruples – then I remarked that his children looked in need of their supper. And he began to work.

Two florins it cost me. He might have asked for five and got them, but his need was too great: he feared to lose his customer. Besides, he'd evidently come to value himself at very little; when I said, 'I'll gladly pay two florins, but I've also a mind to give you something else' – he started in horror. Then his voice shot up: 'Something else?' and his fingers came fluttering for the coins. But playfully I drew my hand back – in the thoughtless way of a man who's enchanted by his own whim.

'Yes,' I said. 'You asked for two florins, and you shall have them. But I insist . . . *gratitude* insists . . . I'd rather not pay you at all than omit to show my appreciation . . . ' – feeling in my purse.

He watched. He blinked. He clutched at the phial – my phial – and smiled uncertainly.

'Well, sir . . . if it's your *wish* to pay more, how can I argue?'

'Indeed, how can you?'

Then I opened my hand again with the two florins on my palm, and beside them – the opal.

His face sagged. There was no surprise. His trade must have brought him many stranger incidents. He showed only dismay, crying out, 'But what could I do with that, sir? People would say I'd stolen it! And you – forgive me – you might come back and say I'd stolen it!'

That was neatly put. But before I'd entered the place, I'd examined my resolution, and found it steadfast. I meant nothing to trick me out of it. I grew cold.

'Take it,' I urged him, 'together with the florins. Or we can't conclude our business' – and hearing this threat, he stepped back, trembling, hugging my phial.

So I spoke more softly. 'There's no trap. What reason could I have?'

My desire to be rid of the stone was urgent: his ridiculous panic only made it the more so, and all the more I was determined that he should have it. He, and no other. I began to plead with him.

'You're a poor man – I can see that. Your children are obviously undernourished. I'm offering you a gift, and you may do with it as you please. Drop it into the nearest poor-box for the benefit of your soul. I suppose you're a man who cares for his soul? Or keep it as a dowry for one of your daughters. It's worth at least eight florins. You'd be mad to refuse it – and lose my custom. Or, I could argue it's a sin to refuse. When Providence sends us bounty, should we toss it into the gutter?'

Then, at last, a glimmer of courage: he shuffled forward, took both coins – and the opal, his fingers barely closing round it. One might have thought it burned. I took the phial. He looked at his new possession with a smile full of fright.

'The likeness of a lady,' I said, 'who lives in Rome.'

'Yes . . . '

'My countenance didn't please her. So why should I keep it? Yet I want to make no profit, but to give it away. And why not to you, who may rid me of this?' I touched the blemish.

'Yes . . . why not?'

He seemed cheered. Coins and opal vanished into some greasy hole in his apron. But just as I made to leave, his face darkened.

'If, by any chance . . . ' he began – and now it was I who felt alarm.

'What? Are you saying this liquid may not work?'

'Oh no! No! On the contrary . . . If by any chance it were swallowed by mistake . . . or applied by mistake to any part except that part you wish to remove . . . '

'Yes?'

He shook his head.

'There's nothing I could do, sir. You must understand. The damage is irreparable.'

And so I left. And despite his qualms, I left the man with an easier conscience than he deserved, for I could tell from the zeal with which he hurried me out that as soon as I'd gone, he'd bite hard on the sweetest explanation: I'm nothing but a lunatic lover.

Well, it suits me. As for the gem – charity or waste: whether it falls into the hands of a priest, or is grubbed about by that family of starvelings and traded at last for milk and vegetables – what's that to me? I've made a fair exchange.

Here stands the phial.

LVI

THESE four evenings – late at the warehouse; and while I work, Rigogli chattering incessantly.

'It's certain that he recovers? And he returns to us next week . . . after the banquet? Lord, how he'll make us jump! How he hates to be kept away! We'll all be answerable. The least error, mark my words . . . ' Then he titters with relief. I know his thinking. While the merchant keeps his own sick body out of its coffin, there's time yet for Rigogli.

And in his delight, he's more than willing to do as I do, and work far into the evening – 'So that Ser Sassoli, when he comes, may be spared excessive worries. All things in their place. Nothing unaccounted for . . . '

Tiresome fool! Every day I've been forced to work later than I did the day before. He yawns. He screws up his eyes – by candlelight he can see next to nothing – and still he sits, stubbornly.

But tonight I achieved my aim.

For the seventh time I was checking the details from a letter against my entries in the ledger, when he came to stand by my elbow, waiting, sniffing, afraid to break what he took to be concentration. I let him wait. Then, when I sensed he was growing restless, I glanced up.

'Rigogli?'

He looked sadly at my stack of papers.

'Have we much more tonight?' he quavered.

'A little more . . . ' and then, with impatience, 'but you look tired, Rigogli. Why don't you leave the key? My eyes are younger than yours. Take yourself home. I'll give the key back in the morning.'

He peered suspiciously over my arm.

'All these figures are already written . . . '

'Yes, but I wrote them in haste. Before Ser Sassoli reads the letters, I must be sure of my calculations . . . '

He yawned. He was peevish – but he surrendered the key.

And yet he did so with a mistrust even greater than I'd expected, for I saw a gleam in his eye which said plainly: 'I always knew it would come to this!'

To what? And how could he know?

Am I then so changed?

Oh, certainly! Here's venom on my table! I bring it out of the chest as soon as I enter the room. I need to see it. I'm soothed when I think of it – but none of this can be known to Rigogli. The truth is that he's never fully trusted me. No matter. Tomorrow, when he lifts the page to his nose, straining to spy an alteration – he'll not be able to find one. I made none tonight.

The wine for the banquet has come. Beautiful wine from Cyprus.

Gabriello acts strangely. First, he behaved as though I'd never struck him, and morning and night he followed me round the house, harassing me about the banquet: '. . . Cheeses, Gissy . . . and fish; I hold you responsible for the fish!' – smiling brightly all the while. But now he avoids me. He disappears from rooms as I enter. And today, when I came across him in the loggia, idling over a cup of wine, I saw that my presence startled him. There came a righteous twist to his lips – such as I neither thought nor wished ever to see on Gabriello – like that which Bartola wears when she sends out the maid to give a crust to a beggar, and I think he'd have got to his feet and walked away if I myself hadn't hurried past, apparently unaware of him.

LVII

SUCH help! Such mighty intervention!

Half-way through my supper tonight, I'm called downstairs, and who do I find in the hall but Fra Bernardino with a sweet and ghostly smile, and tears in his eyes?

He was distractedly watching the clock when he heard my foot on the stair – or else he sensed me – and at that he scurried about: he watched my descent. His hands were clasped in his sleeves. He had come, he said, to beg my forgiveness. These past few days had greatly troubled him.

'My son, I spoke in anger when you needed comfort. I failed you. Yes! It's so . . . And I wish you to know that I make amends . . . There's always hope, Gismondo. I call upon Christ to give you strength and forbearance . . . Four nights I've spent on my knees for your sake . . . '

Now there's a force to turn the drift of things. Fra Bernardino gives up his sleep for me!

The pear I'd placed in my chest – and had forgotten: it's covered with mould.

Tonight, for the second time, Rigogli surrendered his key. Indeed, he did it almost willingly. Just as I'd hoped, he searched through the ledgers this morning, and when he could find no alterations, it seemed to convince him that any tampering of mine would be so subtly done that his tired old eyes could never discover it. So – having risked a betrayal once, why not twice? It must pain him that his lumpish grandson – though he makes a perfect watchdog for the night, snoring on his trestle bed – hasn't the wit to note my movements: which papers I look at, which ledger I read; but all evening the idiot sits in his corner and hums, and peers out into the street, and stores up nothing. How that must vex Rigogli!

It's all nonsense. In the past, I might have done as I pleased at any time of the day, but with Piero Sassoli sick, this ancient minion glories in his 'responsibilities'. While he's fresh, he's tediously over-scrupulous, inquisitive; and as I work, he watches me – to see how far I flick back the pages; then there are always the questions: 'You're looking back a month, Gismondo? Is it to do with the cloth from England? Shall I have the letters fetched? Have you all the letters?' And in his estimation of where I work in the ledgers – the month, the week – until he tires, he's seldom wrong.

But I'm saved by his age. These evening hours have defeated him. I have the key.

And tonight, I made a small amendment. And tomorrow, there'll be another.

Also tomorrow – because he places little faith in Piero Sassoli's recovery – our debtor Paccalli brings another payment.

LVIII

IN the end, how easy!

Not the ease which comes with practice, nor from a natural aptitude, but the ease, as I imagine it, of walking in one's sleep on the edge of a precipice!

An adjustment in the cost of freight some fifteen days ago, another last month – and 120 florins of the sum received today are gone. Accounted for. They can't be missed. The ledgers say so. The correspondence says so. Even the banker's note will say so, for with the remainder of Paccalli's payment I banked other payments so that no one can quickly point a finger and say, 'Here! Look! There's a shift in the pattern!'

And besides, the final totals are all correct.

120 florins in my purse. Silent. As if there's no conceivable reason why they shouldn't be there. Overwhelmingly simple. No wonder Gabriello couldn't believe me innocent – if he truly didn't.

But as to that – it's all one.

LIX

A well-aimed blow!

'Do you require the key? Or have you finished your checkings, and your checkings of checkings?'

'I've finished,' I said. 'My main concern is now to see that the house . . . '

'Of course!' Rigogli nodded. 'Still, before you leave . . . about this German's payment . . . I know it was over a year ago . . . the brown ledger . . . but I can find no trace of it!'

And the paper he held came trembling over my desk.

His voice was sharp with accusation, so – placidly – I opened the ledger; I found the place, and pointed at the figures. The old man clucked.

'Such a vile script, Gismondo, I can never decipher it!' – and he shuffled away, muttering.

A rare performance!

Whether or not he ever finds my tamperings – he has his compensation. Thus I'm informed of everything: all his suspicions, all his opinions of me.

For this has nothing to do with chance: I lack the purity to think it.

As I turned the pages of this now completed ledger, which in recent months I've seldom used – pressed inside: a folded note, and written across it in my hand: *Lucia da Fano*.

I crushed it into a ball. And when I left, passing by the Hospital of Santa Maria Nuova, I flung it on to a cart that stood outside. Among the filthy rags and wrappings.

And so to face Rigogli as if this never happened, and protect myself to this extent – that I give no sign by which he gauges his revenge, the fullness of it!

– How can I doubt that none of this is chance?

LX

A lull. What can be done is done. We rest from our toils for the merchant's comfort. The whole house smells like a rose. His room – so scrubbed and rubbed that a humble beetle on the wall seems a calamitous thing. The linen on his bed – clean and sweet, and we warm it tonight, a good full day before his flesh must be bared to it. We have veal and mutton in the kitchen, according to the instructions he sent. We're in every way considerate.

No one exists to whom I can turn and ask, 'Where will these actions lead? If I do this or that – what next?'

God waits for our prayers. Is there no angel who doesn't wait?

LXI

HE'S back – and yet he isn't back. This man is thinner than Piero Sassoli, and quieter. He walks with more caution, he fusses less. He looks round for his physician and, when he doesn't find him, he sighs, and moves to the nearest chair.

Rested he may be, but the truth is undeniable: never has the merchant looked so ill. He has changed on his farm. He has been thinking.

Both of us – we've changed.

I was standing at the door to greet him, and I could tell he was pleased. He smiled; he took my hand; 'Gismo!' he muttered.

'Not overworked, I hope? It's good to see your solemn face. Are you well?' He was extremely warm and solicitous. And as he entered the house, he leaned heavily on my arm, saying, 'I couldn't have taken a rest, you know, not without you.' After that he was silent. He concentrated on his breathing; I could think of nothing to say. Then, in the hall he wished to sit down, and once he was seated he asked, 'Where's Gabby? Is he out?'

'Yes,' I said, seeing no reason to soften the fact.

The merchant nodded – as much as to signify, 'So. So . . . That's just as I expected.' I stood dumbly. He sat dumbly. Then – 'I've done a deal of thinking,' he said. 'There was nothing else to do. Nothing but walk, and sit, and think. Gismo . . . you and I must have a talk . . . '

'Oh?'

'Not now!' Suddenly he looked agitated. In my surprise I'd spoken sharply, and I saw that he thought I desired this talk immediately. 'Not now,' he repeated. 'Let's get this banquet over, first! I'll need all my strength for that! From now on, Gismo, it's one thing at a time . . . I couldn't . . . ' he laughed and, becoming short of breath, he made rasping sounds as he panted. Both of us were obliged to wait. 'I couldn't let Gabby down! After all, he's my son. But once we've had the banquet, when things settle a little, then you and I . . . ' he broke off, stared at me, and all at once he sputtered, 'Do you know, I might have died without Ruccelli? I was very low on the farm. Very low, and I'm still not sure whether I'll see another birthday . . . But you're not to go about saying that!'

'I understand. As to our talk . . . '

'Later. Later. Help me up.' He clung to my wrist. 'I'm tired. I'll go to bed. Have them send me some boiled milk, and – Gismo, God bless you,' he said pitifully.

A talk.

'As to our talk,' I'd meant to ask, 'does it concern myself?'

It must do, surely. Not just plans for trade and future transactions, but for myself, Gismondo Cavalletti. Plans that wouldn't have come amiss some twelve or fourteen years ago. I can't doubt the nature of this talk. Nevertheless I longed to hear him say, 'Yes. We must make some provision for you!' – or at least to hear him give some hint of it. But there was none.

'Later. When things settle a little . . . '

A talk.

So he's done some thinking on his farm. Oh, I see how it is. It would hardly do to die in debt. He must go to God with fair accounts. Somehow I must be recompensed. What will he do? Pay off old Rigogli and think to set me in his place? Make me steward of the farm? ('Gismo should be good at that, being peasant stock himself!') Or infinitely worst of everything – entrust me to his loving son? ('Gabby and his wife, they'll need a decent person round the place – ').

Clinging hard to my wrist.

What would we do without you, Gismo?

To be scarcely more than her own servant: that same strutting peacock who spoke so loftily when he stopped me in the Piazza, straining himself with condescension. Or maybe not a finger's breadth above his station, but he in the da Fano house, and I in this: and everywhere – in the rooms, the garden – some token of her preferences corrupting the very sunlight.

And I, to creep about in such an atmosphere, frequently summoned to bow and whisper household matters, while she smiles, and half invites my eye to watch for mysteries, secrets of her person – which for Gabriello are as open as a split fig!

Would the merchant's 'talk' amount to this: the promise of such a placement? ('Surely Gismo would relish that. To work in close proximity to the lady!')

Could even Piero Sassoli think so foul a gift proof of good intentions?

I've no faith in this 'talk'.

LXII

HE looks so child-like. There's a questioning in his eyes; the skin of his face is peculiarly smooth. These past few weeks, his years have gone spinning backwards, and in his voice I hear an infant's desire to please – not me, but everyone. A desire to smooth all truths into a paste that's easily digested.

Piero Sassoli.

And whatever's essential, if it can't be smoothed, the policy is to avoid it. Not one word has he said about this likely betrothal and what it means to me, although he can't help but know – yet he prattles continuously about the banquet. He seeks to set his mark on every arrangement.

Tonight, on the other hand, seeing me less than jubilant when I went to talk to him about the wine, he apparently felt the need to offer me something, for he spoke out brightly. 'Gismo, I'd forgotten! Before he left for Venice, Maestro Ruccelli asked to be remembered to you!' And this he offered with every sign of eagerness, as if he and I must both believe it remarkable that anyone should wish to show me a courtesy; as if I must be overwhelmed by the distinction, so that all my tribulations are diminished.

The first guests arrive tomorrow.

LXIII

HIS sister has come. Loud and bustling, much as Piero Sassoli himself has always been until recently, but lacking his smiles. With her have come her husband, her daughters, and her daughters' husbands; also a sickly-looking boy. We house this tribe as we can.

The child – a son of Piero Sassoli's eldest niece – was to have slept in here with me, but at the suggestion he crimsoned and blubbered so much that he sleeps instead with Gabriello. For this escape I can thank my blotch.

And regarding that –

Now, when I have no mirror, I would have one. Not that I used it often, but that I knew I could if I wished, and finding myself without this freedom – here's a strange conviction: if I could only study my face, I feel that my mind would clear again, and I'd see the action I have to take – just as I saw it in the chapel, when I turned my back on the crucifix.

It's unaccountable. Something is certainly necessary, for now I've come this far – the opal spent, and in its place a phial of poison; these florins in my purse – my thoughts have become confused. I pine for a mirror, and having none, all clarity of purpose seems to elude me. What then? Must I go back – back to the Christ on His cross, and despise Him afresh, and experience whatever it was I felt as I turned from Him –

And risk another encounter with wretched Fra Bernardino, squeaking about remorse and charity?

Never. Impossible. The thought of the man and the place – both sicken me. I came away for good.

Yet – this confusion.

Tonight, and one more evening: then, seated together, politely festive, both fathers and our glorious lover! And I learn today that one of her brothers will also come, while she – the queen of hypocrites – chastely protects her widowhood, shrinking from sight, as though these schemes revolted her, praying in her house, the image of outraged piety – but inwardly burning to hear her chosen husband named: none other than Gabriello. And so she waits the feast out – while I, the conscientious attendant, go from guest to guest, inquiring whether the wine agrees with their palate?

No. The world will fold like a mat first, and be burned on a rubbish heap.

LXIV

HE sits in his room. From a chair by the window he peers out into the garden. Everything is 'excellent'. So he disposed of yesterday and the day before. Today has been no different.

There, this afternoon I visited him.

He greeted me, smiling timorously.

'Gismo! Everything under control? At the warehouse?'

'Yes.'

'Excellent. But haven't you come home rather early?'

'There are preparations for tomorrow . . . '

'Oh, quite! Quite! Nothing wrong, I hope?'

'On the contrary,' I said. 'What could go wrong? Ser Romoli's cooks will come at dawn. The musicians by noon. The pastries are baked. The sweetmeat Gabriello so much desires is even now being made by Bartola . . . '

'Excellent . . . So all goes smoothly downstairs? I can hear them rushing about, but to tell you the truth, I haven't the strength to face them!' – and there he laughed, a sound that bore the same relation to his old laugh as the mew of a cat bears to the bark of a dog.

'And the table?' he asked.

'The cups and plates are already set out. Flowers will be brought at dawn, and the main device . . . '

'Yes?'

'I've obtained a net of finest cotton. Rose-coloured, as you wanted. And scarlet poles to hang it from. Bruno and Filippo are arranging it. Tomorrow morning we'll fill it with blossom. And we've devised a cord, by means of which at the end of the banquet it can be loosed, so that the blossom falls . . . '

'Excellent . . . and linen? I've heard this fellow's a tyrant for napkins . . . '

'There'll be enough. I've bought an extra dozen. I presumed you'd wish to be sure.'

'Oh, certainly . . . And *you*,' said Piero Sassoli, without warning. 'How do *you* fare, Gismo?'

'I beg your pardon?'

Now, now, I hoped, some sympathy. Apology. But he only smiled.

'I'm well,' I said.

'Good. That's right. You mustn't overtire yourself.' And he looked relieved, even exonerated. On the window ledge, his right hand moved once, then was still. It resembled a crab – a creature that at any moment might scuttle away from his wrist – for in all the bulk of his body there seemed to be no other hope of movement. But he soon disproved this fantasy, turning his head to the window, squinting out; then quickly he drew his eyes back, and whispered, 'Where's my sister? Gismo, I beg you, keep her from me! She comes in here like a pack of hounds, roaring and yelping. In all these years, I'd forgotten. Where is she now?'

'In the kitchen. She insists on supervising everything. Her daughters are with her. Their husbands are riding with Gabriello . . . '

'Well, keep her from me! Tell her I'm asleep . . . And that cripple she married – there! Look! He's out there, sniffing at my bushes! Keep *him* from me! He exhausts me with his pains and ailments . . . Any news of my cousin yet?'

'A message came – did no one tell you? He's to arrive in the morning.'

'Ah, I remember. And my brother-in-law? Why isn't he here?'

'Didn't he write to say he'd be late? Just before sunset?'

'Yes, so he did . . . Excellent. He may sleep with me . . . But tomorrow, you must give up your bed for my cousin, Gismo. He's old and proud. A bed he must have.'

'Naturally.'

'And he'll bring two servants. He never travels without two servants. That's two more to sleep in the stable.'

'Yes.'

'Good. So it's all arranged . . . ' Piero Sassoli sighed and, as he did so, he looked at me most particularly. 'You remember Monna Margherita,' he said, 'don't you?'

'Of course I do!'

At this he nodded. My answer apparently gave him new information, and his expression grew earnest.

'I'm glad,' he said. 'She was very fond of her Gismo . . . But don't let me keep you. I know how busy you are!'

I went out again, and banked his 120 florins.

Who could rob such a child?

And in any case – such a paltry theft! To snatch a few coins! My life – the account made straight by 120 florins? To think so is an insult.

But something I must do. Events have shaped into goads. The merchant dies by degrees. Our golden boy governs the house. He has Madonna. My life – such as it was – collapses.

And where's my resolve? My plan – where is it, Gismondo? So diligent with notes and secret appraisals, 'clearing the mist' – and now: do you 'see plainly'?

I must go downstairs. I must brave the jibes of Gabriello ('Gissy refuses to sit with us tomorrow because he knows the fish is rotten!'). I must laugh at his little pleasantries, and ask if the guests have all they require for the night – blankets, candles, spice burners. Pretend there's nothing to life but objects we lift and set down where we desire them. Pretend it's only to place one foot in front of the other, and take in breath after breath, and tread about in the wilderness, until we meet with some destination that finds us at last.

They sleep. They snore. They roll in their sheets and dream.

Even Gabriello has given up prowling, cup in hand, and gone to his room.

It's late.

Late. So little time. Here on the ledgers stands the phial.

I've taken out the stopper. Odourless. Colourless.

I was right, at least, about the florins. Only a life can pay for a life. I could creep down tonight to the kitchen and add this venom to the jug of wine that stands on the table – the morning wine, which he never fails to have brought to him, no matter how much he's revelled the previous evening. Bartola always sleeps soundly – but of the maid I'm unsure. And there's another – a girl who came with Piero Sassoli's sister – and since this house is strange to her, she may be wakeful. So I risk detection. Trapped, a wretch with a phial; the women staring! This is more than a risk; it's half-way to a certainty, and there's no wisdom in it.

So – when?

The proper occasion. When the servants are fully occupied, fetching and carrying. Once the guests are assembled, when I break the seals on the Cypriot jars, and I myself who sought and bought that elixir of Cyprus, taste it, before it goes to the table. There's my opportunity!

And so Gabby, raising his cup to the man he claims for a second father, and crying out fulsomely, 'Here's to your health, sir!' – on these words, swallows the acid drop.

It's a nice justice.

And so this venom flows into every cup. Merchant, sister, nieces – all destroyed, as it were incidentally, just to be sure of our archangel!

And I – slip out of Florence. A nobody, without resources – but what of that? Once it's done – Piero Sassoli has friends: they'd be honour-bound to hunt me down, a task of no great difficulty: with a blotch like mine, I could hardly excel at disguises. But none of this matters, for why should I wish to escape? Having extinguished so many lives to fill my need, why should I baulk at the loss of one more, even my own, once the need is satisfied? Surely this is a commonplace of vengeance, to consume in a single act all one's store of future – which is a dark load of uncertain worth, in any case.

In fact, this begs the question: if it's escape I'd have – why be so wasteful? Here's the phial: I've only to drink it off, and suffer a foretaste of hell – to be found in the morning by Anna or the potboy, whoever they send to see what keeps me from my civilities.

– And I'd have become a minor inconvenience! Everyone crowding to the door. Piero Sassoli's sister saying, 'He might have chosen some other day! Brother, you mustn't vex yourself. The man was mad. Anyone could see it. It's a wonder you kept him so long!'

Then, in the evening, they'd sit in their places and feast, and forget – unless it was noted, after their tongues had quickened, that despite his ungracious departure, Gismondo Cavalletti had obliged: 'At least he saw we had excellent fish before he went!'

Laughter. A guest in every place. There'd be no gap.

And so they defeat me utterly; and Gabriello can preen himself to the end of his days. He, and Madonna.

It's a poor comfort, that I should be dead while they thrive.

But if I use this venom at the banquet – what if Gabriello isn't the first to raise his cup, but Piero Sassoli, or someone else? And whoever drinks, immediately he shrivels, writhing – a spectacle to prevent the others from drinking?

Such a blunder costs me dearly. By poisoning the banquet wine, I hazard everything, and still can't be safe in my mind that I have him: Gabriello.

Better to go now, while he sleeps and –

And rather than take his life, pour the liquid on his cheek. Slowly. For as long as it takes. Until he wakes up howling to find his beauty ruined. I could even lend a candle ready lighted at his elbow.

Let him scream at himself in his mirror. Let him watch his flesh dissolve, the bone showing white. First, a scorching, and bewilderment; then the dawning of a truth to make him frantic: his fine looks turned to blisters. And better, even better – what enchantment for Lucia da Fano's father! A freak with half a face to serve his daughter! While she – now here's the finest jest – Madonna shrinks in earnest.

Why, this is perfect. Everything fits together, and yet I never thought of it. It comes of itself, grows of itself.

– Bringing an end to everything. For the boy in the room must wake and see me; and Gabriello must see me, unless I tiptoe out, and forgo the kernel of my pleasure – watching his antics. And why forgo it? To what purpose? Anyone could guess whose work this is. Stay, then, and relish. And so – an end for Gismondo. But more than that. A sweet fulfilment.

As for the merchant, hurrying in with a sheet pulled round his fat-laden body to see why our Gabby shrieks – what of him?

The death-blow, surely. His son, with all his brilliance eaten up. His worthy Gismo, standing with phial in hand – how could this tableau not destroy him, when the slightest alarm could 'rub him out like a taper'? So Ruccelli said.

Piero Sassoli, naked in his linen. A death with no understanding.

But for Gabriello – all I could desire. Living his years behind a mask. Ducking about in the streets, avoiding his former acquaintance. His nights spent grabbing at his wife. My pale Madonna – in the embrace of wreckage.

Perfect. And I never saw it.

Sleep, bright lover.

I've opened the door. The toothed clock in the hall – I can hear it. To be sure, when I go, that I meet with no restless spouse of a niece, who ambles about in search of wine – I'll wait a while. Sleep, Gabriello. Sleep, Piero Sassoli, and all the Sassoli. We draw to a tidy conclusion.

Is there another?

'You and I must have a talk, once things settle a little' – is that a choice? To wait for a 'settling', which might never come before the merchant shuffles into his coffin? To have faith in sick-room promises, and busy myself, tamely attend at the banquet, go in when I'm called for, and daintily sip at the cup they offer while I'm inspected ('So this is the oaf who'll keep the accounts! Appropriate looks – for a eunuch!'). And later on, shall I help Piero Sassoli to bed, and have him burp in my face, 'Thank God that's done with! Well, that's Gabby satisfied . . . Now, let me rest . . . And some day, Gismo, you and I must talk . . . Goodnight, dear fellow, and as you go, will you shut the door?'

Was that ever a choice? This 'talk' if it happened – could he offer enough?

A month ago he might have done. But he offers nothing in time.

'Before he left for Venice, Maestro Ruccelli asked to be remembered to you' – even that he was tardy delivering. He stored it for use when he needed some pleasant remark. Late. Always late. And shall I hold my hand for this 'talk'?

What else have I done for twenty years?

No. There's no alternative. Or if there is – it's not to wait, but to leave tonight. To walk out simply. For the especial 'contempt of it'. Disdain to touch a single Sassoli head. Spurn the logical end of things, and leave the venom on the table. Walk away. Shed them all – Madonna, the merchant, Gabriello – And afterwards? Shall I travel in the East, like Ruccelli? Seek out Angelica's Africa? And starve?

I've fourteen florins, and some soldi.

But have I no skills?

I could be, at worst, a sort of dismal scrivener – and live.

As for malicious rumours – there are places other than Tuscany.

'*Agents of healing*,' Ruccelli said. '*During my travels, I learned a lesson. The agents of healing are everywhere . . .*'

How cruelly life entices us! And never more so than when we approach a point that must sever us from all that's familiar. This candlelight – a solitary drudge of a flame – there's an argumentative beauty in it. 'Be as wretched as you like,' it says, 'and still the world is full of loveliness. Any life is richer than death.'

It's cruelty brought to the last refinement.

What's a daub of acid on a cheek compared to this? What's a father's grief, or a twenty-year humiliation compared to this – the voice in a single flame that cries out, 'Life, at any price!'?

Pity me, God.

The clock ticks. It drags me towards the point. Decide. Decide.

That great clock in Pavia – the one Ruccelli spoke of – with a dial for the Primum Mobile, and one for the moon and each of the planets. Such a work of complications. A dial for the day with its twenty-four hours. Wings, inscribed with times of sunrise and sunset. A circlet marked with feast days and length of days; a series of chains for the solar cycle or lunar cycle, or else for something which I've forgotten. An intricate, yet harmonious construction. But the physician said that it broke down once, after a hundred years or so, and all the world had to be scoured before they discovered a man who could set it going again. An unlettered person. A humble craftsman. After the learned and famous had tried and failed; when the mathematicians and engineers had confessed they were baffled, this simpleton came, and set it going.

'It took no more', said Ruccelli, 'than that rare form of patience, which observes a design as a whole – however incomprehensible – and refrains from tinkering with parts.' Then he added, suddenly smiling, 'But who's to say that next time so gifted a man will be found?'

AKÉ

Wole Soyinka

'What if V. S. Naipaul was a happy man? . . . What if Vladimir Nabokov had grown up in a small town in Western Nigeria and decided that politics were not unworthy of him? . . . *Aké* locates the lost child in all of us, underneath language, inside sound and smell, wide-eyed, brave and flummoxed. What Waugh made fun of and Proust felt bad about, Mr Soyinka celebrates . . . Brilliant' John Leonard,
The Sunday Times

'A superb act of remembrance . . . dazzling reading . . . *Aké* has an enchanting effect . . . Soyinka's memoir makes everything seem wondrous'
Village Voice

'Enchanting' *The Observer*